**Also available from Therese Beharrie
and Carina Press**

*A Wedding One Christmas
One Last Chance*

**Also available from Therese Beharrie
and Harlequin**

*The Tycoon's Reluctant Cinderella
A Marriage Worth Saving
The Millionaire's Redemption
United by Their Royal Baby
Falling for His Convenient Queen
Tempted by the Billionaire Next Door
Her Festive Flirtation
Surprise Baby, Second Chance
Second Chance with Her Billionaire
From Heiress to Mom
Island Fling with the Tycoon
Her Twin Baby Secret
Marrying His Runaway Heiress*

While Sophia and Parker's story is filled with romance and happiness, they also deal with some serious issues. Content warning for dementia, an absentee parent (father) and the death of a parent (father). Your mental health is important to me, so if at any point you feel it might be in danger, it's okay to put down this book and prioritize yourself.

ONE DAY
TO FALL

———

THERESE BEHARRIE

carina
press

carina
press®

Recycling programs
for this product may
not exist in your area.

ISBN-13: 978-1-335-28499-0

One Day to Fall

First published in 2019. This edition published in 2020.

Carina Press
22 Adelaide St. West, 40th Floor
Toronto, Ontario M5H 4E3, Canada
www.CarinaPress.com

Printed in U.S.A.

ONE DAY TO FALL

Chapter One

She won't care if I'm not here.

The words were on the tip of Sophia Roux's tongue. She glanced over at her mother, who was sitting at her side. Charlene Roux worried her thumbnail, staring off into the distance. Sophia's sister, Zoey, was on Sophia's other side. Zoey alternated between pacing the small space of the hospital waiting room and annoying Sophia. The latter was currently happening. It was part of why Sophia was plotting her escape.

'Babies don't care who's there when they're born,' Sophia whispered to Zoey. She ignored that Zoey was tapping her thigh with a finger. 'Besides, the baby hasn't even arrived yet. Let me get back to my life.'

Slyly, she looked over at her mother. Charlene wasn't paying any attention. Sophia wouldn't be punished for trying to escape.

'Angie would stay if it were your baby,' Zoey replied, all logic despite the thigh-tapping, which was gradually increasing in speed. 'She'd probably be in the room with you.'

'Hell, no,' Sophia said with a shudder. 'One, I'd have to want a baby for that to happen. Two, even if I did,

I can't imagine wanting to see people after I pushed a human being out my vagina.'

'Sophia!'

Oh, damn. Her mother had heard *that*.

Zoey snickered. The three people who were sitting in the row in front of them looked scandalised. Sophia wondered if her mother's reaction was because Charlene was offended, or because those people had heard her.

She hadn't meant to raise her voice, but surely she hadn't said something scandalous? They were in a hospital, for heaven's sake. She could have sworn she'd used the scientific term for where babies generally came out of in church.

Because it wasn't like God had created vaginas or anything.

'I'm sorry,' Sophia said. She was speaking to her mother, but she eyed the people still looking at her. 'I meant after I negotiated the terms of my baby's release with the stork who only delivers to hospital rooms where my partner and I are present.'

'Sophia,' her mother said again, her tone disapproving, if reserved. 'Can't you try to support your sister instead of…' Charlene lifted her hand, dropped it.

Sophia purposefully unclenched her jaw.

'I'm here, aren't I? Supporting Angie.' *Even though Angie didn't support us when we needed her. But let's forget about that, shall we?* She pulled herself back to the present. 'All I'm saying is that Angie's baby will have done the equivalent of an intergalactic move. Would you want to entertain guests after that?'

Zoey laughed. Her mother did not.

Not that it surprised her. Charlene had always disapproved of Sophia's sense of humour—amongst other things. Though the sense of humour issue was likely because Sophia hadn't inherited it from her father or mother. She wished she could say it was a combination of their genes, but that wouldn't be true either.

Her mother had no sense of humour.

Miraculously, Sophia didn't snort out loud at her little joke. Instead, she simply sat, her conversation with Zoey ended by the Vagina Saga. Time ticked by slowly. As it did, Sophia felt her soul die.

She'd already been there for ninety minutes. Angie had been in labour for longer, but Ezra, Angie's husband, had told them it was pointless coming to the hospital since it was still early. The only reason the two of them had gone to the hospital was because Angie had tested positive for some bacteria and needed to be put on antibiotics so it wouldn't be passed to her baby.

This did nothing to change Sophia's mind about not wanting a child.

In any case, Charlene had decided not to take Ezra's advice. She'd wanted to come to the hospital immediately. She'd demanded Sophia and Zoey go, too. Sophia had wanted to say something about it, but then she'd seen Charlene's expression. Her mother was terrified.

To be fair, terror *was* the state Charlene lived in since her husband's death. Sophia sympathised. It was scary to build an entire life around someone, then have to live it when they were no longer there. But she wouldn't coddle her mother. She wasn't Angie, who soaked up everyone's emotions as if she were a wet sponge, cleaning up their messes in the process. Nor was she Zoey, who would do whatever she wanted to regardless of the people around her. Yes, Sophia felt for her mother; she also needed Charlene to get her act together.

But after five years of dealing with her mother's terror, Sophia knew when to pick her battles. This was not one of them. Today's terror came from a mother's fear for her child. So Sophia bit her tongue, woke Zoey up, and now they were in the waiting room...

Waiting.

She'd sent Ezra a message as soon as they got there, but there'd been no reply. He'd either turned off his phone or put it on silent. Or he simply wasn't interested in checking it.

When Angie had introduced him almost two years ago, Sophia had realised he was different to the men she knew. He watched Angie with an intensity that made her think he was trying to anticipate Angie's next move. He paid attention to Angie even when she wasn't paying attention to him. Sophia could only imagine what would happen when Angie actually needed his support.

But it had been ninety minutes. Almost two hours now, she saw, checking the clock on the blue wall of the waiting room. The bubble of anxiety around her mother was growing larger and larger. Charlene needed an update, and Sophia needed to get out of there before she got trapped in the bubble. Not because she would feel the anxiety, but because she nearly always popped the bubble. Her mother didn't need that today.

She stood.

'Where are you going?' Zoey asked. Charlene's gaze rose with her. It was curiously blank.

'I thought I'd try to find some news,' Sophia told Zoey.

'I'll come with you.'

'No,' she said immediately. Zoey's eyes widened. 'Sorry, Zo, it'll be easier if I do this myself.'

'Okay.'

Zoey's voice was breathy. It was the tone she used when she was hurt but didn't want to show it. Sophia softened.

'Can I bring back something for you?' she asked, wanting to make it better. 'Chips? Chocolate?' When Zoey didn't look up, Sophia lowered her voice. 'Both?'

There was a long pause before Zoey looked at her. 'Lightly salted chips. Fruit and nut chocolate. And something to drink.'

'Of course,' Sophia said with a smile. She turned to her mother. 'And you, Mom?'

'A water, please.'

Sophia nodded, her smile disappearing as she walked away from her family. She felt hollow and full at the same time. The hollowness was because these events made her remember her father. Nothing much had fazed him. Generally, that attitude had spilled over to her mother. Charlene wouldn't be the mess she currently was if Daniel Roux had been there.

Sophia didn't engage with that hollowness. It was simply there. An observation. A consequence of death.

The fullness was more dangerous anyway. Emotions that swelled into the hollowness. Resentment, betrayal. A cesspool of negativity that Sophia fed each time something like this happened.

When she felt out of her depths with taking care of her mother. Or when Zoey needed someone who could nudge her in the right direction. Whenever she thought that Angie would be better equipped to deal with the remaining members of her family. When they thought so, too.

But after their father's death, Angie had run. All Zoey and their mother had left was Sophia. They'd often made it clear they didn't think it was enough. When Angie had finally come back, Sophia could see why. Angie was exactly who they needed her to be, even if she had come back changed.

Sophia hadn't changed though. And the differences between her and her older sister were sharp and aggravating. It didn't matter that Sophia had picked up the slack when Angie couldn't. It only mattered that she was there when *Angie* needed her. Because families were there for one another.

Except their family had conditions.

If only Sophia adhered to those conditions, too.

'What are you alluding to, Dr Craven?'

'We suspect your mother has dementia,' Dr Craven said, obliging Parker Jones's request and cutting the bull. Parker wasn't sure if that was a good thing now that he'd heard the words come out of his mother's doctor's mouth. 'There's no one test I can administer to give you certainty, but the testing we have done up to this point has made me fairly confident. The behaviours you've described over the past few years are also good indicators.'

An unreasonable wave of guilt washed over him. They were making this diagnosis based on information he'd provided. Behaviours he'd questioned his mother on and she'd brushed off. Now those behaviours were part of how they knew she was sick.

He felt sick.

'The good news is that it's in the early stages. Your mother still has good years ahead of her. It will require some adjustment, but there's no reason why things can't be normal for the foreseeable future.'

How is that good news? he wanted to ask. He didn't. Instead he looked through the small window in the door of the room where his mother lay. She was alone. His father had stepped in and paid so she could have privacy.

Parker blew out a breath. 'Can I see her?'

'She's sleeping.' There was the briefest of pauses. 'I'm more than happy to answer your questions, Mr Jones.'

'That won't be necessary,' he replied woodenly. He held out a hand. 'I appreciate you caring for my mother.'

When Dr Craven had shaken his hand, Parker walked away, leaving the confused doctor behind. Parker knew what the man was thinking. Someone who'd just been told his mother might have dementia shouldn't walk away. He should have questions. He should ask those questions so he knew what to do next.

Parker was well aware of what he should have done. It was why he'd walked away.

Not his best moment, he could admit. But there was too much going on in his head for him to think logically. He hadn't been able to since he'd got the call from his neighbour telling him his mother had been hit by a car. Fortunately the car hadn't been going fast, and Penny Jones's injuries were minimal—a broken arm, a cracked rib, some bruising. The real problem was the police report an officer had conveyed to him shortly after the incident.

A car hadn't bumped into Penny; she'd walked in front of it.

He gritted his teeth, quickened his steps down the white hallway of the hospital. Though he wasn't in any of the wards, the smell of sterility that attempted to mask illness churned his stomach. The walls were tall, the windows high, not allowing him a necessary glimpse of the outside world. He needed to prove to himself that he wasn't trapped. Not by the terrible building he was in, or by his mother's possible illness.

Or perhaps he needed to be around people, he thought, his legs still moving despite the fact that he didn't know where he was going. If he made his way down to the cafeteria, he'd be exposed to the busyness that was always there, regardless of the time. Busyness meant noise, which meant people, and energy. Surely that would distract him. Pull him out of his own head.

Instead, he lost his breath.

He didn't know what had happened until it was too late. He was already falling, propelled by a force that couldn't only have been a person since his breath was knocked out so completely. He was on the floor when he saw it wasn't someone with machinery or the like. It *was* only a person. She looked tiny, sprawled on the floor across from him, though her expression made him think she had little to no awareness of this fact.

He got to his feet, held out a hand to help her to hers. But she was already up, gathering the snacks he only now realised had scattered at their collision. He lowered, reaching for a water bottle, but she snatched it away from him before he could get a grip on it. When she was standing again, she glowered at him. He frowned. Neither of them said anything for a moment.

'You're not going to apologise?' she asked in a prim voice.

'Are you?'

'Why would I apologise?'

'You walked into me.'

'*You* walked into me.'

'Really?' he asked lightly, though annoyance had stretched its wicked arms and gripped his tongue. 'How do you know that?'

'You weren't paying attention.'

'The fact that you can say that tells me you *were* paying attention, which means you knowingly walked into me. Your fault.'

Her mouth opened, as if she wanted to say something, but no words came out. It drew his attention to her lips. Plump, with an intricate network of creases imprinted into their fullness that he'd never seen before. They were neither pink nor red, those lips, but fell somewhere in between, or formed a fascinating combination of the two.

'Hey,' she said sharply. 'My eyes are up here.'

He lifted his gaze. 'I was trying to figure out what you'd say next. Nothing good, I imagined.'

Colour spread on her cheeks, making him notice the dark spots on the brown skin for the first time.

'This is what I get for speaking to a man I don't know,' she muttered, rolling her eyes. 'Listen,' she continued more loudly, 'I don't care that you're a jackass who knocks people over with their tank-like body and then refuses to apologise. I—'

'Why not?' he asked.

'Why not what?'

'Why don't you care?'

'I can handle it.'

He smirked. The colour on her skin grew deeper.

'Continue,' he said, folding his arms. Her eyes dipped to his biceps. Then she met his eyes and he swore the look she gave him could set the world on fire.

'I don't need your permission to continue.'

He waved a hand.

'Out of curiosity—are you just an annoying person?' she asked. 'Or are you saving this side of your personality for me?'

He only smiled, because that seemed to annoy her more than anything and for some perverse reason, he enjoyed seeing the way her colour changed when she was annoyed.

'Of all the days I could meet an inconsiderate—'

'Unfair,' he interrupted. 'I'm not inconsiderate.'

'Considerate people apologise.'

'We've already established that you were the one responsible for this. Usually the person responsible for the action apologises to the victim.'

Her entire face tightened. 'Victim?' She barked out a laugh. 'Get out of my way. I have enough of those in my life.'

The abrupt change in her demeanour had him giving her space before his brain could catch up with what had happened. When it did, the anger that had taken a back seat to his amusement flared.

'Now you're being rude, too. *You're* the annoying person in this equation.'

She whirled around. 'Hey, buddy, you don't get to

call me rude when you're being rude yourself. When you're purposefully going out of your way to get a reaction from me.'

Now he opened his mouth. Shut it. Because she was right, and he would *not* tell her that. He wouldn't lie either.

He clenched his jaw, hating that she'd put him in a predicament where he couldn't have the upper hand. Her eyes dipped to his mouth, and she smirked.

'It isn't so fun when you're on the other side, is it?'

She walked away.

Chapter Two

Sophia was still bristling when she returned to the waiting room. She might have won whatever weird, petulant argument she'd got into with that strange man, but the fact that she'd had an argument at all annoyed her.

It didn't help that she'd had a frustrating time trying to find out which room Ezra and Angie were in. She'd been bounced between counters as if she were at a shop and not a hospital. Eventually, when she got the information, she was told visitors were only allowed during visiting hours. It was five in the morning. Visiting hours weren't until the afternoon.

After that, she shouldn't have been surprised the vending machine had stolen all of her cash. Security had been no help. Apparently, vending machines were used at 'own risk'. She'd eventually found a small shop in the cafeteria to buy Zoey and her mother's things at. They'd only been selling coffee at that point, but she'd begged and begged and had somehow convinced the clerk to sneak her the chips and chocolate.

Of course bumping into a *giant* and having an argument with him had annoyed her then. He could have killed her if he wanted to, yet he'd refused to accept responsibility for the attempted homicide. He was grumpy, too, which she would have been fine with if he hadn't purposefully taunted her. That self-satisfied expression on his handsome face hadn't helped.

Handsome face? Wait, when did that happen? She didn't think he was handsome...did she? Okay, sure, objectively, he had an okay face. But handsome implied she liked it, and she wouldn't like someone who was purposefully contrary. She didn't care how muscular his giant body was.

'Why are you shaking your head?' Zoey asked, taking her chips from Sophia's hands though it was at the bottom of the pile she carried. Sophia corrected to make sure the rest of her haul didn't drop and glared at Zoey.

'Because I knew you were going to do something stupid like that,' she said. 'I was trying to warn you.'

'Alas,' Zoey said cheerfully. Sophia bit back a sigh.

'You might as well help me with this now.'

Zoey tilted her head, opening the bag before slowly bringing one chip to her lips. 'First apologise for being snappy.'

'What is it with people wanting me to apologise for something they did wrong?'

'People?' Zoey repeated. 'Who else wanted you to apologise?'

'No one,' she brushed off impatiently, feeling her cheeks go red. 'Nothing. Are you going to help me?'

'Why are you blushing?'

'Zoey,' Sophia growled.

Zoey set the chips aside and helped Sophia organise the items on the small table between the chairs. When

Sophia sat down, she noticed for the first time that her mother wasn't there.

'Where's Mom?'

'Oh, she's in with Angie. Ezra came to get her fifteen minutes ago.'

Sophia spent the next seconds staring at her sister.

'What?' Zoey asked, her mouth full of chips.

'Why didn't you tell me?'

'Why would I tell you?' There was a beat during which Sophia glared at Zoey. 'Oh, because you wanted to speak with him?'

'Zo, the entire reason I left was because I went to look for him so I could bring back some news for Mom.'

'Oh. Oh, right.'

She had the grace to look sheepish.

'Did neither of you think to tell me?'

'Well, to be fair, I think Mom's a bit distracted now.'

'Not that she would have thought to tell me anyway,' Sophia said with a shake of her head. 'I'm tired of the selfishness.'

'Hey,' Zoey said with a frown. She finished her chips and began folding the empty packet into squares. 'I think this reaction is overdramatic.'

Everything inside Sophia stilled. 'Did you just call me overdramatic?'

'Yes. Because that's what you're being. Right now, too, in fact.'

Sophia stood again. She was not in the mood to be patronised by her baby sister. She wasn't in the mood to witness her mother be overly concerned about Angie either. How had she given so much of her time and effort to two people who weren't the slightest bit considerate of her? Who didn't even seem to *know* her?

'Where are you going?'

'Somewhere I can be overdramatic in peace,' Sophia announced, and gave her sister the middle finger as she walked away.

Parker called his boss as soon as he'd recovered from his interaction with that woman.

'Marcus,' he said when he heard the man's voice. 'I'm free for a shift this morning.'

'Are you sure?' Marcus's voice was cool, professional, the tone of a man who'd already conquered his morning even though it was only five am.

'I am,' Parker confirmed.

'What about your mother?'

Parker's spine straightened. 'She's fine. Minimal injuries, considering.'

'And how much sleep are you working on?'

He wanted to tell his boss he'd never felt more alert in his life. There was no way he'd sleep, so he might as well make productive use of the time. He was a freelance journalist when he wasn't driving people around. Since the latter job would result in a stable income with flexible hours, he appreciated the work. His mother's illness would no doubt add to the bills. Because he refused to accept the help his father offered—on principle—he needed the money.

'I'm fine.'

'Give me an estimate. How many hours? Four? Five?'

'I'm fine.'

'Parker, I'm not giving you a shift to drive people around when you haven't slept. Which I'm assuming is why you don't want to tell me,' Marcus added, his voice sounding almost bored. 'You won't be driving until you've had a couple of hours of sleep. Talk to me then.' There was a pause. 'I'm sorry about your mother.'

The phone clicked off.

Parker locked his jaw, his hand curling around the device. It took concentration for him to let go; more to not throw his phone against the hospital reception wall.

He couldn't talk to his mother since she was sleeping. There was no chance *he* would be able to sleep, and now he couldn't even distract himself with work.

He stood in the reception area for a moment, then walked out into the parking area. He'd been lucky to get a parking space close to the entrance, and hadn't had to use the fact that he drove a car service vehicle to do so. The job had few benefits, especially considering he drove his own car—it had a higher hourly rate and the signage had been covered by the company—but being able to park for his customers' convenience was one of them.

He clicked to open the car, started it, and pulled onto the road. He'd rolled forward metres when he heard a hand slam on the bonnet and his back door open. He would have been more alarmed had he not recognised the voice, or heard the words, 'The Company's Garden, please.'

Parker's gaze lifted to the rear-view mirror, and he almost laughed when he realised why the voice was familiar. Her eyes met his at the same time.

'Oh, no,' she said with a groan.

'Oh, yes,' he replied mildly. 'It's your punishment for getting into a car without knowing who's driving it.'

'This is a taxi.'

'Car service.'

'You have your rates printed on the back of your car. What kind of car service does that?'

'We want to appeal to more than our elite clientele.'

'How do your elite clientele feel about that?'

His lips curved. 'They aren't always thrilled. But we have a good reputation.'

It was an understatement. Marcus Carlton was a South African millionaire who the business industry had nicknamed Midas. Parker had no doubt that Marcus knew about this nickname—had likely been the one to start it—but even Parker couldn't deny the implication was true. Everything Marcus touched did turn to gold. He had an eye for which businesses to invest in, and his desire to help unemployed communities in rural areas meant a range of people liked him.

It also meant people forgave Marcus for his bad-tem-peredness. It hid a soft heart, Parker had been told, and it paid a more than decent salary into Parker's pocket every month. The people he drove around ranged from the richest of the rich to middle class. Granted, the richest of the rich rarely had him drive to their fancy events, but he didn't care. As long as they thought they needed to tip him and did so generously in case he told his boss he'd been slighted, he'd drive them from the kitchens only their staff used to their lavish backyards.

'I don't care about your reputation. Although,' she said thoughtfully, 'maybe I should, considering the company hires people like you.'

A hoot came from the car behind them before he could give a less than pleasant reply.

'You need to get out,' Parker told her calmly, lifting a hand to apologise before putting on his hazards. It didn't help considering the road out the hospital was one way and he was blocking the entirety of it. 'Fast.'

'Why?'

'I'm not working. Even if I was, I'm not sure I'd agree to take you anywhere. Considering what kind of person you are.'

She narrowed her eyes. Another hoot sounded. She shifted forward.

'Okay, look. I need to get out of here now. If my sister realises I've left the hospital—' She broke off on an exhale. 'I will pay you double your damn rate if you take me to the Company's Garden.' There was a second before she said, 'You have to decide before there's another hoot.'

He thought about it for a second.

'Fine.'

A chorus of hoots pierced the air.

This is a bad idea.

I know.

Well, then, as long as you know.

The conversation Sophia was mentally having with herself had her reaching discreetly into her handbag and taking out her phone. She switched it onto silent, then messaged Zoey.

I took a car service to the Gardens and now I'm freaking out in case the driver kills me.

She sent it. Bit her lip.

This is the only reason I'm telling you. Otherwise I wouldn't have let you know and have you freak out on me.

She pressed send just as she got an incoming message. *Messages.* For the life of her, Sophia would never understand why Zoey couldn't say what she needed to say in a single message. Almost as soon as she thought it, she realised the hypocrisy considering she'd sent two messages herself. But that was different.

YOU TOOK A CAR SERVICE TO WHERE??????

THE DRIVER'S A CREEP?!

MAKE AN EXCUSE. COME BACK!!!

I AM NOT FREAKING OUT.

Sophia almost snorted at the last one, but managed to catch it in time. She didn't want Mr Tall and Intimidating to pay attention to her. He hadn't said a word since he'd agreed to drive her, and she preferred it that way. At least until she managed to tell Zoey who to look for if her remains were found floating in a river somewhere.

Sure, she typed. Totally sounds like you're not freaking out. If anything happens to me, look for a tall guy, brown skin a little darker than ours, big build, really broad chest, terrible personality.

There was a longer pause between this message and Zoey's next one.

One, it sounds like you're describing a date not a possible serial killer. Two, how do you know what his personality's like?

One, no one said anything about a serial killer. It had crossed her mind though. Two, we bumped into one another in the hospital earlier. He's an asshole.

Because you're such a ray of sunshine.

Sophia glowered at her phone. Listen, if you don't care that some guy might kill me, just say so. Sophia added some emojis. Don't be passive aggressive.

I'm sorry I can't be aggressive aggressive like you.

Another message came through.

Send me a picture.

Sophia's gaze immediately shot up to the driver's, checking whether he was looking at her. As if somehow, he could see what her sister had asked. He was still facing forward, concentrating on the road as they made their way toward the city centre. She let out a little breath of relief.

How am I supposed to take a picture of him? I'm sitting on the back seat. He's driving.

Side profile.

She considered it for a second. On the one hand, she didn't get a serial killer vibe from this guy. Jackass vibe? Yes. Asshole vibe? Absolutely. Were those different things to her mind? In this case. But he didn't seem like a serial killer. On the other hand, most serial killers became serial killers because they didn't have a serial killer vibe. In fact, according to the numerous horror movies and documentaries she'd watched, they were charming, good looking, trustworthy. Until they locked up their victim in a shed and cut off their fingers one by one.

Oh, no, she was going to have to take this picture. While she still had her fingers. Or if she wanted to keep them.

She slunk down, lowered her phone to beneath her chin, and tried to find a good angle. Turned out, Mr Annoying had a lot of them. His cheekbones were surprisingly defined, his nose not sharp, but not round either. He had a scar on his chin, visible even beneath the stubble of hair. It added to how his jaw jutted out in that pronounced way she'd only seen movie stars have.

Hmm. Maybe he *was* handsome.

She took the picture, and closed her eyes when the *click* sounded. When she opened her eyes, he still wasn't looking at her. Her breath of relief was deeper this time. She looked at her phone, but the picture was blurry, and she clenched her jaw.

She spent the next five minutes trying to find where she could switch off her camera's sound. When she got another text from Zoey, she sighed and slunk back down.

'You know, you could just ask.'

She immediately slid her phone into her handbag and looked out the window.

'Not sure what you're talking about.'

'Personally,' he said, as if she hadn't replied, 'I think

my right side is better, but I suppose the left would do.'
He glanced back at her, a light gleaming in his eyes,
then looked forward.

She frowned. Had his eyes always been that colour?
A deep brown that contrasted the lighter brown of his
skin?

And had he always looked so young? There wasn't
a line on his face; nothing giving away that he was her
age or older. She was only twenty-six, but there were
lines on her face. Perhaps the gods had seen into her
soul and identified her as the raggedy old bitch she was.

'I still don't know what you're talking about,' she
said, when she realised she'd only been amusing herself. 'I was…checking my make-up.'

'Another lie.'

'You don't know that.'

'There's nothing out of place on your face. Your
make-up is perfect.'

She stared at him, then dropped her head when she
caught his eyes in the rear-view mirror.

'What?' he asked.

She shook her head. She would not say what she
wanted to say, which was that she wasn't wearing any
make-up at all. Instead, she busied herself by reaching
for her phone again, sending the blurred photo to Zoey,
telling her sister it was the best she could do.

As the time ticked by, the air in the car tightened. It
was strange to have tension with a stranger. It wasn't
even the *we're in a small space and aren't talking* kind
of tension, but a more layered one, filled with emotion.
Annoyance, for the most part, because the longer the

silence extended, the more she was sure he was doing it to annoy her.

She was also annoyed at herself. She'd long ago put her phone away, ignoring Zoey's messages, not having the energy to deal with them anymore. She'd told her sister where she was, and Zoey's messages had veered into the territory of why she'd left. She was still figuring it out herself, and grappling with the fact that she'd decided to figure it out while Angie was in labour. Feelings were so damn annoying.

Overwhelmed, she looked out the window to see the tall buildings in central Cape Town rise into the sky and the sun light the blue with a brilliant yellow. She watched the people looking for public transport to get to work, even though it was six in the morning on a weekend.

Those people were the fabric of cities like Cape Town. They were the people who made sure the rest of society could do their shopping for the week or relax at a restaurant for breakfast. They worked their butts off to make sure their own families could eat and survive in what was sometimes a cruel world.

Usually, Sophia loved to appreciate those people. She loved watching the routines and tried to suss out characters. She supposed she could blame it on her choice of career in Human Resources. A strange one, both she and her family had thought at first.

Though her family might still believe it, Sophia didn't. Her personality was perfect for Human Resources. She cared about whipping people into shape. In her job, she could do so without being emotionally attached. If only she could say the same for her own family.

She didn't indulge the thought, or her penchant for people-watching. She couldn't when her eyes somehow kept slipping back to him. It was involuntary, which made it worse. She'd catch herself looking at him, and would then turn her head so she wouldn't. Minutes later she'd feel her eyes move again. It wasn't that he was pretty; it was that he was upset.

The muscles in his jaw were swollen with tension. They rippled every few minutes, telling her he was clenching his teeth. His left eyebrow would quirk ever so often, and his lips would move, as if he were speaking with someone. No, not speaking, arguing. It was fascinating to watch, though she didn't like that she thought so.

Deliberately, she looked away, and forced herself not to turn back. It took more willpower than a stranger deserved. Each time she felt her head turn, she'd resist, and wonder what compulsion he'd created inside her. By the time they'd found a parking space, she was afraid she might have damaged her neck. She felt strange, too: alert, aware. It irritated her.

She took the money out of her purse and thrust it to him. He took it, but before she could move her hand away, his fingers closed over hers.

'Do you want me to wait?'

'No.'

'How will you get back?'

'I don't know if I'm going back.' It sounded more morbid than she'd intended. 'To the hospital, I mean.'

'I got it.'

There was a pause. It gave her time to feel the heat pulsing through her body, its source the point of contact where her and the driver's hands touched. She pulled her hand away, but realised she'd taken the money with it. Clenching her jaw, she offered it to him again. He didn't reach for it.

'What happens when you're done?'

'I'll figure it out.'

'How?' he asked, his tone reasonable. 'I appear to be the only car service in the vicinity.' She refused to look around and give him what he wanted. 'It would be simpler if I waited for you.'

'Hey, man, I don't need you to wait for me. I'm a grown woman. I can do whatever I want.'

'I'm not disputing that.'

'Great. So take the money and let's call it a day.'

He didn't move.

'What?' she said sharply. 'What could possibly be keeping you here?'

'Your safety.'

She rolled her eyes. 'Don't worry, I can handle myself.'

Again, he didn't move. She bit down on her teeth, the alertness, the awareness exaggerating everything she was feeling.

'You understand that this is a job, right? You're not responsible for what happens after I leave the car.'

'You're upset because I'm concerned for your safety.'

It wasn't a question, so she didn't answer.

'You know,' he said after a moment. 'You're the first person who's been offended because I'm concerned about them.'

He angled his body more fully toward her. Since she'd moved to the middle seat to pay him and was still leaning forward, it put his face a short distance from hers. It helped her see his other side profile was as good as the one that had been facing her. More so, if she considered his scar a sign of imperfection. She didn't. Which made things worse.

'I don't need anyone to be concerned about me,' she said stiffly, refusing to shift back on principle. 'I told you I can take care of myself. I do.'

It was why it didn't matter that Angie had left after their father had died. Or that her family hadn't appreciated Sophia's efforts when she'd stepped into Angie's shoes. She had done what needed to be done. She had taken care of herself and her family. Did the how of it really matter?

Yes.

No, she corrected that voice in her head. She didn't believe in coddling her mother or sister; she certainly didn't believe in coddling herself. Not even mentally.

'No one is saying you can't take care of yourself,' he said, emotion she didn't recognise deepening his voice. 'But for heaven's sake, stop being so stubborn about it. Just accept that someone wants to help.'

Chapter Three

It occurred to him too late that he was overreacting. Or that somehow, this strange woman's face had turned into his mother's and he was saying words he'd said too often in the last year.

'I'm sorry,' he said stiffly.

She narrowed her eyes. 'Finally, the apology I deserve.' There was a beat. 'I do not accept.' She popped the money into the cup holder and got out the car.

He stared after her, then swore under his breath. Grabbing some change, he paid the car guard. Waited impatiently as the woman printed his slip. He put it on the dashboard and ran after his passenger through the Garden's entrance.

His feet faltered. The path he was walking on was shaded by massive trees on either side, planted in the middle of large areas of grass. Early morning sunlight trickled through the gaps in the trees, giving the pathway a mystical feel. Right ahead of him was an impressive stone fountain, the sound of the water trickling over its sides echoing in the morning stillness. The only other sounds were the music of the birds chirping. It was a symphony only nature could compose, and he was in awe of its beauty.

It wasn't the first time he'd been there, but the last time he'd been too young to appreciate it. His father had brought him on his birthday, so he must have been ten or eleven. Before he'd become disillusioned by his father's presence in his life. In any case, Wade Jones had bought Parker a packet of nuts to feed the squirrels, and any memory he had of the place revolved around that.

He could still feel the joy he'd had in that moment, though when he remembered his father's expression now, he recognised the caution there. He'd never felt his father's reservations around him as a kid. Granted, Parker didn't know Wade. Back then, he'd only spoken to his father on the phone on his birthday. Wade reappeared in Parker's life when Parker was nine, taking him out on his birthday, his mother a vigilant companion.

He hadn't wanted to do anything other than spend the day with the dad he somehow idolised despite his absence. That had stayed true at ten and eleven. Then twelve had come and his father hadn't pitched up for their birthday date. He'd been disappointed, and old enough to realise his father *was* a disappointment. That had ended his contact with Wade until six years ago. Now, Parker felt like he saw his father every week. Not that that had translated into a relationship.

He pulled himself from the past and jogged forward, trying to find his passenger. He couldn't see her, so he took another path to his left, looking out for the baggy white top she was wearing.

The fact that he remembered that would have disturbed him more if he weren't distracted by his search. More people had joined the path, more than he expected to see at a park this early in the morning on the weekend. He gritted his teeth, tried to manoeuvre his way through them, relieved when he finally saw her.

She was standing still, toward the front of a crowd of people he hadn't noticed because his eyes had rested on her. He walked forward, trying to get to her. She didn't notice him. Her eyes were looking ahead. He only allowed himself to follow her gaze—everyone else's, too—when he stopped beside her. And then his breath caught.

They were in front of a large pond. The water was green and murky like with most ponds, and he would have never imagined it as a backdrop to beauty.

But four people stood at four different spots in front of the pond, the crowd stretching out behind them. Next to them were large crates of flowers. He had no names for those flowers, but they were beautiful; bright colours on pads of green leaves. They were pushed into the water at steady intervals, turning the murkiness into something breathtaking. Blues and pinks and yellows filled the pond, until there was nothing of the dark green water left. There was only colour and the smell of spring, and a feeling in his chest that Parker had no words to describe.

Perhaps this was a metaphor of some kind. His life looked pretty damn murky at the moment. Maybe the universe was telling him the flowers would come. That someday he would look at it all and see beauty.

But a voice in his head scoffed at that. He accepted. He couldn't see how things could become beautiful.

His mother was facing a life-threatening disease. And if things went on as normal as Dr Craven had said it would, weathering the disease wouldn't be easy.

Penny Jones was stubborn. She'd refused to visit doctors when he'd first suspected something was wrong. When he'd begged her to. Even without Dr Craven's words, Parker knew his mother would be stubborn about it now. He'd have to care more about her health than she did. How was he supposed to find the beauty in that?

Still, the picture in front of him enthralled him. And hope flared, as unreasonable as it was.

'You know,' she said conversationally from beside him, 'you following me here makes you the exact kind of person you wanted to protect me against.'

He looked at her. He hadn't even realised she'd noticed he was beside her.

'If you hadn't run off and we'd finished our conversation, I wouldn't have had to.'

'If I hadn't run off, you wouldn't be standing here, watching this, with that dopey look on your face.'

He inclined his head. 'My face is never dopey.'

She rolled her eyes. 'Stubborn and full of yourself. What a winning combination. Your parents must be proud.'

He waited for the insult to flare his particular sensitivity about his parents.

It didn't.

'They are,' he told her. 'How do your parents feel about your inability to accept concern?'

She turned to face him, her lips curving into a cat-like smile. 'How do you think I learnt it?'

* * *

She'd been lucky to witness the Spring Ceremony. A colleague had mentioned it to her the day before at an obligatory water-cooler interaction. She'd had no intention of going—she knew what spring looked like: bright green leaves and clogged sinuses. But it had been the first thing to pop into her head when she'd been running from her family, so here she was.

She hadn't counted on being able to witness the expression on this man's face, too. Which, while dopey, was endearing.

She'd cut off her own tongue before she admitted it out loud though.

'I'm confused. Are you saying your parents don't allow people to be concerned about them, so you followed their example? Or did they teach you not to accept concern because they were too concerned about you? Or not concerned at all?'

Why was she finding the frown on his face adorable?

'I'm saying I didn't develop the skill as a child.' She said it lightly, because it was true and, really, what would she get from being emotional? 'My parents had a strange approach to parenting.'

'How so?'

'They let us do a lot of it by ourselves.'

'Ah.'

She turned back to the pond, wondering why she was telling a stranger this. Perhaps having his name would help—although she fully knew she was grasping at straws. Having his name might make things more familiar between them, but only a smidgen. Not at all enough to be sharing her life story with him.

It was too late to worry about that now though. She'd already told him about her parents; she might as well embrace the situation. And ignore the fact that it didn't feel as uncomfortable as it should have.

'You know, I should probably know the name of my stalker so I can send it to my sister in case something happens.'

'It would be a lot easier to stalk you if I didn't give you my name.'

She shrugged. 'I guess you're right.'

She didn't push him, mostly because she didn't care enough to push him. They had a weird dynamic, stranger or not. Life story or not. It wouldn't change if she knew his name. Besides, he'd figure out soon enough that she wasn't in the mental space to start a friendship. Or whatever the hell it was that was happening between them.

'I like it,' he said softly.

She followed his gaze to the pond. She could only see the flowers now, bright and bold, the perfect symbol of spring. Their beauty sharply contrasted the heavy greens of the trees that surrounded the pond. The sun was still rising in the sky, its rays highlighting the kaleidoscope of colour even more.

It soothed the ripples of hurt that she was still feeling about that morning. She couldn't place her finger on exactly what had caused it, perhaps because the causes were myriad and complicated. Regardless, she accepted the soothing without question.

'Me, too,' she said.

She spent a few more seconds appreciating it, then she turned and began walking. She wasn't surprised when she heard his steps behind her. Or when he spoke up from beside her.

'Will you stop running away from me if I give you my name?'

'I can't promise that.'

'I guess I'll take the chance,' he said dryly. 'It's Parker.'

'Sophia.'

'Hmm.'

'Hmm what?'

'Nothing.'

She rolled her eyes, but didn't take his bait. Instead, she took the path that led to the restaurant and joined the line to get inside.

'I didn't realise the restaurant was so popular.'

'It's a good restaurant,' Sophia answered. 'But it's busy today because of the Spring Celebration. Usually the Garden only opens at seven, but they made an exception for today. The restaurant followed suit. And they're taking advantage of it.'

She waved a hand at the blackboard advertising a number of Spring Celebration breakfasts. Parker didn't reply, but he waited in line with her. They were two people from the front when he spoke again.

'I have no idea why I'm here.'

She turned. 'What?'

'I don't know what I'm doing here,' he repeated. 'I'm standing in line with a stranger whose constant state is being annoyed at me when I should be at the hospital with my mother. Or at home trying to get some sleep so I can be with my mother when she needs me.'

She opened her mouth, but he barrelled on.

'I could have killed you.'

'*Excuse me?*'

'I haven't slept in over twenty-four hours,' he informed her. 'I shouldn't be driving.'

'Oh. Oh,' she said again. 'And you wonder why my constant state is being annoyed at you. How did your boss let you take a shift today?'

'He didn't. I asked but he said no.'

'Oh,' she said for the third time while her mind processed. 'This casual thing you're going for here when you could have actually killed me is not endearing, by the way.'

'My mother might have dementia.'

She looked at him. His expression was one she'd never seen before. He looked confused, as though he hadn't expected to confess that. But there was more, too. A pain she remembered seeing on her family members' faces throughout her father's illness. A helplessness. The lines of Parker's face held guilt as well. She didn't understand it; but then, she didn't think Parker did either.

'Oh.'

'They think her erratic behaviour over the last year points to it. Yesterday she walked in front of a car, so now they're confident enough to tell me to start thinking about the future with someone like that.'

She narrowed her eyes. 'Are you having a panic attack?'

'What?' Parker asked, looking at her. His eyes were wild, his chest moving up and down in quick intervals. 'I'm not having a panic attack.'

She studied him, unconvinced.

'Don't look at me like that.'

'I'm going to be completely honest: I don't know what my face is telling you right now. There's a lot of stuff happening in my brain.'

'Exactly.'

'What? That makes no sense.'

'Table for two?'

They both turned. The waitress was looking at them with a tight expression on her face, as if she'd heard their conversation and was trying not to add her two cents. Sophia tilted her head, before turning to Parker.

'Will this be a table for one or two?'

'No.'

She didn't bother telling him his answer made no sense again.

'For one, please,' Sophia said.

'No, for two,' Parker said with a shake of his head.

Sophia didn't reply, just nodded her head at the woman. They were led to a square table outside of the main restaurant. Tall trees with green leaves surrounded them, plants and other greenery a few metres behind them. The restaurant felt as though it was in the middle of nature, which Sophia assumed was the point. Even the main restaurant had been designed that way, with sleek wooden panelling between long glass walls.

'You're a mess,' Sophia told Parker when they were alone. She perused the menu as she said it. She figured the statement wouldn't be welcome and she didn't want to look at him and feel bad for telling the truth.

'You don't seem like a Sophia,' he said in return.

She lowered her menu. 'How do Sophias seem?'

'Sweet. Kind. They sing songs to cheer people up.

They are polite enough not to point out when people need a moment.'

She ran her tongue over the top row of her teeth. He'd summed up the battle she'd fought her entire life in a few sentences. She was impressed. Not at all bothered by it. Just…impressed.

Right.

'You're describing a cartoon character, not a human being,' she said. 'Except maybe for that last thing. That was unnecessary. Probably.' She thought about it. 'Actually, I think you *are* referring to a cartoon character. There's a princess named Sophia, isn't there?'

'No.'

'Do you really know that? Or are you denying it because I said it?'

'No.'

She lifted a brow and his lips curved.

'The latter.'

'Thanks,' she replied dryly. Then, because her conscience had woken up while she'd been too distracted to toss it some sleeping pills, she said, 'I'm sorry about your mother.'

He opened his hands as if to say 'what can you do'. The gesture had more of an effect than his ranting earlier. Reminded her, once again, of what had happened when her father got sick. She could have easily made that same gesture seven years ago when her father had first been diagnosed with his brain tumour. It signified a feeling of helplessness that could easily overwhelm him if he allowed it to. If he did, that feeling would sear itself into his brain, waiting to be triggered by the slightest vulnerability.

She knew because she'd witnessed it happen to her mother. And to her sisters, to different extents. It hadn't happened to her because she hadn't allowed it to. After her father's diagnosis, she'd told herself to grieve and function at the same time. She'd had no choice but to. Necessity had tested her strength, and she'd passed. She continued to pass after her father's death, too.

Things had changed now though. Before Angie had come home, maybe, but definitely after. Sophia didn't know how to define herself and her strength in the new-ness of it. She hated the uncertainty that came with that. The negativity it stirred inside her. It only gave her family more reasons to point out what they perceived as her failings. And she only failed because Angie was the standard.

Sophia didn't come close to the standard. She wasn't sure anyone did, at least not in her family's eyes.

She clenched her jaw, but got a moment to recover from the unexpected tension when a waiter came to take their order.

'Black coffee,' she told him.

'Hot or cold milk?'

She frowned, but bit back the sarcastic reply. 'Neither. Black coffee.'

She waited until Parker had placed his order—a cappuccino—before opening her mouth to ask him what she wanted to. Except he spoke before she could.

'Well done. That must have taken a lot of strength.'

'What do you mean?'

'You didn't call that guy an idiot for asking about milk when you said you wanted it black.'

'I want to say thank you, but I feel like you're being sneaky about judging my behaviour.'

He gave her a smile that had an insidious heat creeping into her belly. There was no sign of the man who'd started panicking in the line.

'Why do you feel your behaviour needs to be judged?'

'I don't,' she said flatly. 'But I've had people—men in particular—tell me I should be kinder. Sweeter.' She kept her eyes on his. 'Sing songs to cheer people up. Be polite enough not to point out when people need a moment.'

He winced. 'Touché.' There was a long pause before he added, 'I'm sorry for saying that.'

'Don't be,' she told him. 'I'm not entirely kind or sweet. Hell would freeze over before I sang a song to cheer someone up, and I could probably be politer.' She straightened in her chair. 'You should apologise for making a general judgement about a name—a female one, since I'm sure you don't go around telling men they don't look like their name counterparts—and then assigning a moral judgement to that name.'

He stared at her. She sighed.

'You think I'm a bad person because I'm not all the things you accused me of before,' she elaborated.

'Not at all.'

'None of what I told you sounds familiar then?'

'No.'

'Do you have sisters, Parker?'

'No.'

'Brothers?'

'No.' He frowned. 'Why does that matter?'

'It doesn't. Not to this conversation at least. But it tells me you're an only child, and you're going to be facing your mother's illness by yourself.' She leaned forward. 'You can't let feeling helpless make you helpless. Got it?'

Chapter Four

He gathered his thoughts as the waiter set down their coffee and took their breakfast order. It was a challenge. His thoughts had galloped out onto the fields somewhere between the moment he'd left the hospital and now. Some of them were grazing on the pasture of his mother's illness; others, in this frustratingly complex woman sitting across from him. Emotions joined them, making the entire thing tough to sort through.

She was right. He was a mess.

When the waiter left, Sophia sat back in her chair, looking at him. It was unnerving, the way those light brown eyes took him in. He felt as if he were being sized up; he wasn't sure he'd make the cut. He'd never experienced it before. Though it didn't surprise him that it was Sophia who made him feel that way.

'Are you done?' she asked casually, bringing her cup to her lips.

'With what?'

'Freaking out about what I told you.'

'Are you psychic?'

She laughed, a deep, throaty sound that he hadn't expected. It suited her perfectly.

'I wouldn't be here with you if I were a psychic, Parker. I'd be out playing the lottery before going home to my creepy mansion and feeding my black cats.'

'That was…detailed, for someone who just came up with it. You're obviously a witch.'

'Psychic or a witch?' she said, her cheek lifting in a half-smile. 'They're not interchangeable.'

'In your case, they would be.'

She laughed again. 'I like that I don't know whether that's a compliment or an insult.'

'You like it?'

'I'd like it more if you told me.'

The tension between them turned seductive. He leaned back, wondering whether he should entertain it.

'A little of both,' he answered carefully. 'Though I don't think either of those things are worthy of an insult.'

'And yet you still managed to insult mc with them.'

'It's a talent.'

'I think so, too.'

Silence stretched.

'You're avoiding my question,' she said.

'I am.'

'That's fair.' She traced an invisible pattern onto the table. It made him notice her nails. Short, no polish. For no reason whatsoever he found it endearing. 'Can't avoid what you're going back to though.'

'Is there a reason you're pushing this?' he asked lightly. The emotions he felt rumbling inside him weren't as harmless as the tone.

'Yes.' Her eyes didn't leave his. 'I know what it's like to have a sick parent. You can try to avoid it if you like, but the sooner you accept it, the easier it is to deal with. For the both of you.'

'Just because one of your parents is sick doesn't mean you get to tell people how to process things.'

'You're probably right. But my dad isn't sick. He *was*. He died five years ago.'

The anger fizzled immediately, replaced by an acute embarrassment that he'd been so insensitive. The embarrassment meant he had no idea what to say, so he didn't say anything, not for the longest time. His brain couldn't accept what she'd implied either. That at some point during his mother's journey, Penny would die.

His fingers curled into fists, and he lowered his hands to his knees beneath the table so she wouldn't see his panic.

'Did he have dementia?' he asked, before he could help himself.

'No,' she said. The bravado had faded. She sat perfectly still, though she looked at him with a steady expression. 'He had a brain tumour.'

'How long?'

'Two years.'

'He was only sick for two years?'

'They don't have the same illness,' Sophia said softly. 'Two years for a brain tumour the size my father had was good.' She cleared her throat. 'It was good enough.'

He didn't know how to comfort her. She wasn't crying, so he couldn't offer her a tissue. She wasn't hysterical, so he couldn't try to calm her down.

She was upset though. He was helpless to do anything about it. It was exactly like the time he'd come home and found his mother muddling up a recipe she'd made hundreds of times before. Penny had refused his help, and had grown more and more panicked as she threw in ingredients that had no business being in a curry.

The meal had been unsalvageable. Later that night, she'd come into his room and kissed his forehead. She didn't say a word about it.

'I'm sorry,' he said eventually. He took a gulp of coffee, almost hissing when the heat of it burned his mouth. Then he took another gulp, hoping it would burn away that lump in his throat.

'Thank you,' she said. 'My point, however, is that facing it gives you an ability to deal with it. It's not the brave choice. It's a smart one. I guarantee your mom will thank you for it.'

'You make it sound so easy,' Parker said, leaning back in his chair. 'Did you find it easy?'

'Hell, no,' she said with a laugh. 'But it was necessary.'

'You said you had a sister. And you made it sound like the fact that I didn't have any siblings was going to make things worse.'

'Is there a point to that statement?' she asked when he didn't continue.

'Are you saying your sister stepped in and helped?'

For the first time, Sophia didn't give him a straight answer. She slid back in her chair, her lips curving into something that wasn't a smile.

'Fine, I'll stop pushing you.'

He mentally debated his reply, wondering if he would give her what she wanted and change the direction of their conversation. Since it would make things easier for the both of them, he did.

'Answer me and you can push as much as you like.'

'You're a weird guy, Parker,' she told him.

'Part of the charm.'

'Not sure I'd call it charm.'

'Maybe not you...'

'Who then? Other strange women you drive around, almost kill, then stalk?'

'I'm happy to say you're the only one I've ever done this to.'

'What makes me so lucky?'

'I don't know,' he replied honestly. 'You're annoying and way too smart. You don't follow normal social cues, and I can't wrap my brain around why your snarkiness is appealing.'

He'd said too much, but the way her eyes widened made it worth it. He felt his mouth curving. Felt it because he didn't know when the last time was that he'd smiled like that. His mother's actions had taken a toll on him over the last year. He was worried about her memory for longer than he could admit out loud. Had had a very inactive social life because of it. He went to work, came home, and made sure his mom didn't do something to hurt herself.

But now he was smiling—full out grinning—and the muscles in his face thanked him. They felt like a cat in the sun, stretching, purring. Except the sun was Sophia in this case, him the cat, which was a problem because likening Sophia to the sun—a sarcastic, blunt sun—would get him nowhere, like most interest in relationships. They were distractions, relationships. Or disappointments. He needed neither when he was facing the biggest challenge of his life.

And yet he couldn't stop himself.

'I... I mean, I think... You shouldn't...'

'What's going on?' he asked. 'You sound like someone who's struggling for something to say. In the ninety minutes I've known you, you've not once been at a loss for words.'

Those full, unique lips of hers turned white from the force of pressing them together.

'Still nothing, huh?' He leaned forward. 'What happens when I tell you I like your eyes then? They're a light in your face, and there are little specks, right in the corner, that flicker gold when you're annoyed. So all the time,' he added with a grin.

'Then there's the curves of your very impressive cheekbones. Your freckles. The skin around your eyes crinkles when you smile, which is hardly ever, but the lines of them are faint even when you're not smiling.'

Getting into it now, he allowed himself to enjoy her features. Didn't realise until that moment that he'd been keeping himself from doing it.

'Your face is the perfect shape for that haircut. Not everyone can pull off short hair, let alone with curls, but you do it. But my favourite thing about you are your lips.'

Her tongue darted out and licked them. His entire body responded, tightening, telling his brain that this joke he'd decided to play wasn't funny. Except now he was looking at her lips, at those fascinating creases, thinking about how soft they looked. Closer to them now, he saw that their colour was natural, and it sent another wave of desire through him.

'Why?'

He blinked at the sound of her voice. 'What?'

'Why are my lips your favourite?'

His gaze lifted. Her cheeks had taken on a pink hue, and her eyes were bright, as if desire had got to her, too. He let out a long, shaky breath when their waiter interrupted with their food. Looked at the full-house breakfast he had on his plate, barely remembering he'd ordered it.

When the waiter left, silence extended between them. Whatever spell had been on them had broken, but he couldn't think of anything to say that wasn't about that or the other thing they had in common. Sick parents. He picked up his utensils and cut through the bacon. His knife screeched against his plate. Clenching his teeth, he forced himself to speak, and said the first thing that popped into his head.

'Why were you at the hospital?'

He sensed the slight hesitation before she answered him. 'My sister's in labour.'

'Oh. Congratulations.'

She gave him a funny look. 'What do you mean?'

'You're an aunt.'

'I'm going to be an aunt, and it's really not something to congratulate me on. I didn't do anything.'

He rolled his eyes. 'It's a thing people do, Sophia.' She was already frowning, but his words deepened it. He sighed. 'Please don't tell me you're upset because I told you it's something people do. It's not a criticism. I meant—'

'No,' she interrupted. 'It's not that. It's… I think that's the first time you said my name. Properly, I mean. As in, in conversation.' She shook her head quickly, as if she couldn't believe what she was saying.

'Did I pronounce it wrong?'

She still had a funny expression on her face. 'No. No, it's not that.'

'Then what?'

She shook her head again. Again, it didn't feel like it was directed at him.

'It's a silly thing people do.' She was focusing on buttering a slice of toast, deliberately avoiding his eyes, he thought. 'Anyone besides the parent shouldn't be congratulated on the birth of a child. It had absolutely nothing to do with them.' She paused. 'I'm being generous to the father here, too. At that stage, they've really only offered the sperm.'

He stilled. 'Humour me?' he asked. She frowned again, but gave a small nod. 'Do you mention sperm during breakfast all the time, or do you reserve it for strangers?'

Her gaze met his, and she grinned. His breath stumbled on its way out his lips.

'It's funny you should say that. Today is the second time I've shocked strangers with talks of reproductive… I want to say organs, but sperm isn't an organ. Despite what some people believe of its importance,' she added, giving him a look.

'I didn't say anything.'

'I was anticipating it.'

'You anticipated wrong,' he told her. 'I don't think sperm is important.'

Her eyebrows rose. Suddenly, he was blushing.
Damn it.

'I mean, I do think it's important, but in a reproductive sense. Not for, you know…' Her eyebrows rose higher; his cheeks grew warmer. 'The thing is, when you don't want children, that importance doesn't really matter, does it?'

'You don't want kids?'

'No.' He frowned. 'Are you asking so you can judge me? Should I remind you about what you told me about judging people?'

'No. I don't care what you think about your sperm. Or what you do with it.' There was a pause. 'It's just that I don't want kids either, and almost every person I've told that to has looked at me as if I'm a traitor to those who do.'

'It's probably their own built-in prejudices. You're a woman, so they expect you to want babies. Hopefully none of those people is still in the picture.'

She'd stopped eating, and was watching him. The longer she did it, the stronger the urge became to squirm in his chair. But he wasn't a child being told off by his mother. He was a grown man who could stare back if he wanted to.

Right now…he simply didn't want to.

'What?' he asked, when he could still feel her eyes on him.

'That was a pretty woke thing to say.'

'Why do you sound shocked? Men can be woke, too.'

'Oh, I immediately regret saying something nice about you.'

He let that one slide with a smile, and they slid into

a surprisingly easy silence as well. Surprising, because there was still a… He wouldn't call it tension, but an awareness, sizzling between them. It wasn't uncomfortable, nor was it particularly welcoming. Still, he entertained the thought of what would happen if it *were* welcoming. If his world weren't about to change, would he be excited by the awareness? Would he want it?

There was nothing in his dating history that pointed to that. Which didn't stop him from teasing her when they were done eating.

'I can't believe you were messaging your sister while she's in labour. Let alone sending her my picture.'

'I don't have a picture of you,' she refuted. Lied. 'And of course I wasn't messaging my sister while she's in labour. I have two.'

'So you sent the other one my picture.'

She only gave him a look.

'No brothers?' he asked, smiling again. He could almost forget what he was running from. Could almost fool himself into thinking he was running toward something more hopeful.

'No brothers, thankfully. I can only imagine how exhausting that would be.'

She narrowed her eyes, obviously referring to his behaviour as exhibit A.

'Not fair.'

'Satisfying though.'

She popped the last piece of food in her mouth and chewed.

She wasn't sure why she felt comfortable around him. Annoyed? Sure. He was annoying. He said things to annoy her. He did things to annoy her. But there was nothing about their relationship or how they'd come to meet that should make her *comfortable*.

It was a puzzle she was still trying to figure out when the bill came.

'I've got this,' he said, taking out his wallet.

She set her hand over his when he reached for the bill, tilting her head. 'Why? Why do you have this?'

His eyebrows knitted together. 'Because it's a nice thing to do?'

'I guess. But why would you want to do something nice? You barely know me, for one. For two, this isn't a date. We're literally two strangers sharing a meal. We could have been sitting at two different tables. We should each pay for ourselves.'

As she spoke, his face twisted into what could have been a comical expression if it hadn't been aimed at her.

'Do you have to make a big deal out of everything?' he asked, his voice serious. 'I get it. You're independent. You don't need my help or concern or money. But I'm not offering you a date or a relationship. I'm trying to do something nice. Accepting it won't rob you of any of that.'

She blinked. Her mind played around with replies, trying to find one that felt right. Except nothing did. Which told her the problem was deeper than merely wanting to do things for herself.

Slowly, she lifted her hand from his and gave a quick nod. She sat back, watching him go through the motions of paying. When he was done, they walked back through the trees in silence. It felt awkward, and she knew she was the cause of it. Usually, she wouldn't care about that. But now she felt responsible for trying to make things better.

Her mind played around with that, too. It came up with answers she didn't like.

'Look,' she said as they stopped at the fountain that stood in the middle of the park. 'I'm used to taking care of myself. Not only myself, but my family, too. Being in the opposite role is…weird.'

It shouldn't have been, she thought suddenly. Her entire life had been Angie taking care of her and Zoey. Their dad had, too, but he'd left a lot of the emotional heavy lifting to Angie. It had been part of what had made Sophia so mad when Angie had left. Because then, Sophia had been the only person who could lift the weight. Her mother wasn't made for emotional responsibility, and Zoey… Well, Zoey took after their mother. So Sophia had stepped up after Angie had left.

But Angie had only been away for three years. Sophia only had to take full responsibility for herself and her family for three years. The years that came before those were full of Angie's help.

Why couldn't she accept help now then? What had happened in those three years that had superseded the twenty-odd before them?

'I get it,' he said after a moment. He was frowning. 'The same thing happened with me and my mom. We were alone for the most part, and I got used to that.'

'What changed?'

'My dad came back into the picture.' Parker's jaw clenched. 'They got divorced when I was two. After that, I only heard from him on birthdays. Only saw him again when I was nine. Again, only on birthdays. At twelve, I'd figured some things out and I didn't want to see him again. I didn't.' He fell silent. 'When I turned twenty he came back for good.'

'He reconciled with your mom?'

'Not quite.'

Parker didn't offer any more information and she didn't push. She didn't say anything supportive either because she was hardly an expert on relationships with fathers. Before Daniel Roux had got sick, she would have described their relationship as…strained. They hadn't fought much, but they'd never confided in one another either. She'd seen him have that bond with her sisters, but never her.

The ache in her heart had faded somewhat after his death. Perhaps because there wasn't anything she could do about it at this point.

'Thank you,' she said suddenly, gesturing back to the restaurant with a thumb over her shoulder. 'I appreciate you taking care of the bill.'

'Sure.'

Before she could say anything else, she heard a rattling sound. Turning, she saw a family walking toward them. A man with short, dirty blond hair pushed a stroller that was almost as wide as the pathway. A double stroller, Sophia realised, looking into it and seeing two little boys. Another man, older based on the hair greying at his temples, walked behind the stroller carrying a little girl who looked old enough to walk, but clung stubbornly to her father's neck.

She and Parker parted, getting a tired smile of thanks in return, and when they reclaimed their spot on the pathway, both stared after the family.

'Did you see how exhausted they looked?' Sophia asked after a moment.

'Like they haven't slept in years.'

'Twins plus a third child?' Sophia shuddered.

'And all three of them look like they enjoy making their parents lose sleep.'

'Terrors.'

'So unnecessary.'

They looked at each other.

'This is why you shouldn't have children.'

'Me, personally?' Parker asked, a grin claiming his lips.

She hadn't noticed before, but there was a small dimple pressed into his cheek, right next to his mouth. She'd been distracted by the scar, but now that she'd noticed the dimple, she didn't even care about the scar.

It took a moment to realise the reason she'd noticed the dimple was because she was essentially standing beneath him. It must have happened when they'd come back together after letting that family past. She'd been so distracted by the horror of it that she'd overcorrected.

Her head tilted back. Had she realised how tall he was? Or how broad his shoulders were? They blocked her view of the grass that stretched out behind him. A tall tree shaded them, too, blocking the sky from their view, making it feel as though they were the only people in the park. Birds chirped; running water sounded from the fountain. There were people chattering somewhere, but Sophia barely heard them. It was as if nature had amplified its symphony, adding a stillness, a sacredness that cocooned the two of them.

How silly, she thought, as nerves sparked in her stomach. Then their eyes met, and a tree rustled, and she didn't think it was silly anymore.

His teasing smile had disappeared behind a screen of blankness. She was sure it was a sign she should step back, away from him. She imagined he used that expression to set boundaries, for himself as much as for others. But his body hadn't got the memo. It leaned in toward her, shadowing her as the trees did. It angled, cutting them off from the rest of the world even more.

Curiosity sparked inside her. It eclipsed the thoughts lingering at the back of her mind. Thoughts of her responsibilities; of how today, of all days, was a bad time to be overwhelmed by emotions relating to those responsibilities. Her family would wonder where she was. They might need her. But for once, Sophia was thinking of what *she* needed: to be curious about Parker. To give in to that curiosity.

It was the kind of curiosity that usually got her into trouble. It threw caution to the wind for the sake of its satisfaction. And it was ignoring that she'd had reservations about her attraction to this man barely an hour ago.

But now… She felt different. The curiosity was a strong persuader. It was reckless, too. Similar to the recklessness that had told her to leave the hospital that morning. It didn't care about emotions or consequences. It convinced her she didn't need to either.

Why the hell not?

She tilted her head, looked straight into his eyes. 'What would you say if I told you I wanted to kiss you?'

Chapter Five

Parker didn't do things without thinking them through. A lifetime of responsibility had taught him that. He'd learnt the skill after witnessing it with his mother, had practised it as soon as he could, and was now a master. It was a curse at times, but it was also a blessing. It kept him out of trouble. Kept him from making careless spur-of-the-moment decisions. Like following strange women into parks. Having breakfast with them. Being attracted to them. Entertaining the idea of kissing them.

Clearly meeting Sophia had taken that skill and tossed it aside. Or perhaps it was receiving the life-changing news about his mother's health. Either way, he couldn't bring himself to regret it.

'I'd say yes.'

'Are you sure?' she said, though her eyes had already dipped to his lips and his body was responding. 'I'm a complete stranger.'

'That's why I'm saying yes.' He waited till her eyes met his. 'Are *you* sure?'

She smiled. It had his blood rushing out of his head long before she stood on her toes and pressed her lips to his. His stomach dropped to his toes, his heart clung to his chest bone, and for a solid minute, he thought he might die. Before he could scoff at his thoughts, she pressed into the kiss, stunning the breath out his body.

It was extraordinary that the mere touch of their lips had made him feel that way. It had barely started and he already felt changed. He stood no chance then, when she tentatively opened her mouth, tasting him, allowing him to taste her.

There was nothing distinct about it, only the fresh mint from the sweet she'd eaten after their breakfast. But he felt as if he were dining at the most exquisite restaurant. When she opened her mouth wider and their tongues met, he felt as if the chef had designed a distinctive dish for him alone. He was happy to award the meal the highest possible honour.

The kiss itself was slow, exploratory. He let her lead because he liked the idea of it. The feel of it. Not that he generally enjoyed the passenger seat; it was because it was with her that it was so appealing. Her hands rested on the base of his waist, just above his hips, her fingers digging into his skin. If he were clay and she were moulding him, he'd have no problem with the dents she'd leave there with her grip. The pressure sent shocks of need to his groin. His own hands moved then, mirroring hers, sinking into her flesh. He groaned.

Dully, he remembered they were in a public place. So the fact that he was still moving his hands down, over her waist, was entirely inappropriate. But he couldn't help himself. She was curvaceous, fuller than any of the women he'd dated before. He didn't think he preferred a single body type, but as he'd never touched one like

Sophia's, perhaps he had. He'd certainly have one now, leaving this embrace.

Hers.

The swelling of her hips were like handles. He wasn't sure why society derided them so much; they were perfectly placed, designed for the best purpose. They allowed him to pull her in closer. He could even lift her up if he wanted to. And he wanted to. Desperately. But there was still a part of his brain working, and it reminded him they were in public. It meant he couldn't give in to the desire to slide his hands further down so he could cup her butt. To discover how the roundness of it felt. Was it firm? Soft? He couldn't think of a problem with either, apart from the fact that he wouldn't know. A travesty if there ever was one.

She pulled away from him, lowering to her feet so abruptly that it sent a vibration through them. Their gazes locked, and Parker fully expected her to look away, to hide the emotion on her face. She didn't. She kept looking at him, sucking in her bottom lip, allowing him to see her confusion.

'Oh,' she said softly. She tried to pull away. He loosened his arms, giving her some space, but he didn't drop his arms.

'No.'

'No?' she asked, confused. Then her expression cleared and her voice got sharper. '*No?*'

'You can't move or you'll give those kids behind you a glimpse at how they got here.' He clenched his jaw. 'Not sure you want to have a talk about sexual reproduction with children today.'

'No,' she said again, though she'd stilled and her

voice had thawed. 'I'm not in the mood for a biology lesson right now.'

His lips curved. 'There are times when you *are* in the mood for it?'

'Sure. In fact, most days.'

'How? Why?'

'I'm an honest person. That means I'm in the mood to talk about pretty much anything, including biology, any time, with anyone. Simple.'

'So you not being in the mood to talk about it now means you're not feeling honest?' he asked. 'You won't tell me how you felt about that kiss?'

'No.'

He nodded.

'But not because I'm not in the mood,' she continued. 'I don't know how I felt about the kiss. Which I think you could probably use as an answer, too.'

He smiled. 'I think so.'

She rolled her eyes. 'Don't look so pleased with yourself. I've been speechless after plenty of kisses before.'

His smile disappeared. 'Really?'

'No,' she said immediately. 'But keep acting like a cat who ate the cream and I'll try to find someone who'll turn the answer into yes. Now,' she continued before he could reply. 'Do you have yourself under control?'

He angled his head in confirmation, allowing her to walk ahead so she wouldn't see his smile. But as she passed him, he couldn't resist saying, 'I wouldn't say you taste like cream, but I did enjoy it.'

She snorted, but didn't reply. That's how he knew she liked his answer.

* * *

When they stopped in front of his car, Parker gave her a look and shoved his hands into his pockets. She sighed.

'Has anyone told you how dramatic you are?'

His mouth curved, and of course, after tasting it, she found the movement incredibly sexy. Okay, fine, she'd found it sexy before, too, but it was worse now. She didn't care for it. It made her want to stare. She knew staring would make Parker get that cocky look on his face again. Which reminded her of what had been pressed into her moments ago, and how he'd asked her to stand in front of him after.

Oh, no, that kiss had broken her brain.

And your body, an inner voice helpfully offered. A shiver went through her, emphasising the words, and she had to consciously tell herself to behave.

'You could solve this quite simply. Just tell me whether you want me to drive you somewhere.'

'No,' she said with a decisive shake of her head. 'I don't want that. I should probably call another car.'

'What?' he asked, panic crawling onto his face. 'I'm right here.'

'Yeah, but with what happened inside there…'

'You can't be serious.'

'You're right, I'm not. But it's cute that you were worried.' She walked forward with a satisfied grin. It grew when colour spread over his cheeks. 'It's not embarrassing that I find you cute, Parker. Besides, isn't this what you wanted? Me, accepting your concern?'

He glowered. She smiled sweetly. Held out her hand.

'What now?' he asked tightly. 'You want more of my pride?'

'It's one of the deadly sins for a reason. It wouldn't be this easy to take away. No,' she said after a beat. 'I want your keys.'

'Why?'

'You haven't slept in twenty-four hours. I'll drive you home so you can get there safely and then get a car from your place.'

'You're going to drive a rental car to my house and then call a rental car?'

'I'm trying to help, jerk,' she said with a frown. 'Get in the damn car and let me take you home.'

He opened his mouth to argue, but she stared him down, using the same look she'd practised on Zoey as a kid. It had worked about fifty per cent of the time. She liked to believe that was because Zo wasn't easily intimidated. Her baby sister also knew how lovable she was, and relied on that when she wanted something. It had been cute at ten; less so now that Zoey was a grown woman. She couldn't count on being lovable to bail her out of bad situations.

Fortunately, her intimidation techniques were more effective with Parker. After a relatively short stare-down, he handed over his keys with a sigh. Sophia smiled. Wider when she got into the car and felt the displeasure radiating from him.

'Oh, this is nice,' she said, running her hands over the steering wheel before moving to the gearbox. In all honesty, she had no idea whether Parker's car was nice. She just knew, deep in her gut, that saying so would annoy him.

'It's the same as any other car.'

'Even this?' she asked, peering closely at a dial on

her side of the steering wheel. It was the lights, she thought, recognising the symbols. But she drew back. 'That doesn't look familiar.'

'It's the lights,' he said, flatly. 'Have you driven a car before?'

She hid her smile, pushing the key into the ignition. He gave her curt directions as they drove. Refused to engage with any of the other questions she peppered him with. It made her happy to mess with him. By the time they reached his house, she wasn't even trying to hide her smile.

To be fair, he didn't seem to notice. His brush-off grunts had got deeper and deeper as they drove, his body slumping further into the car seat. Even in that state he managed to maintain his miserableness, which Sophia gave him credit for. When she stopped in front of his house, his eyes were half-closed, though he'd given her a thumbs-up when she'd asked if this was his place.

'Thanks for driving me.'

His eyes closed fully.

'Parker, you have to go inside the house.'

'No. Fine here,' he mumbled.

Sophia watched him for a moment, then looked around the neighbourhood. It looked okay. There was a park down the street, with some trees and a swing and see-saw. It seemed to be in a decent condition, but it was oddly empty for a weekend morning, which felt wrong. Gates enclosed most of the residential properties, ranging from large sizes to smaller ones. None of it really told her whether it would be safe for Parker to sleep in the car or not.

Her gut told her no, probably because she didn't

know a world where sleeping in a car was a choice. Besides, what if someone busted through the window in concern? She'd seen it happen with dogs. The jury was still out on whether Parker was better than a dog, but he needed air, too. She probably shouldn't leave him here.

She poked him in the stomach. Felt a surprising amount of resistance as she did. She hadn't been able to run her hands over his body during their kiss. She regretted the missed opportunity, especially since she thought that resistance meant abs.

He didn't move though, so she poked him again. Harder this time.

'Huh? What?' he asked, opening his eyes.

'We're here.' He stared at her blankly. She sighed. 'At your house, Parker.'

He turned his head toward the reddish-maroon house with its neat garden. Slid down into his chair. 'K.'

'Parker,' she said again when he closed his eyes. 'You have to go inside.'

'I's fine,' he mumbled. 'Go.'

She stared at him, mentally going through her options. When she realised what she had to do, she sighed again. Harsher, louder. He didn't budge. She pulled the keys from the ignition, holding them up and spotting some extra keys she hoped were to his house. Moments later she was opening his car door, reaching in and unfastening his seatbelt. As she moved out, he stopped her, his grip surprisingly strong for someone who was half-asleep.

When she looked in his eyes though, they were sharp.

'You're pretty.'

Her skin heated.

'Come on, let's get you inside.'

'Did you hear me?' he asked, though he allowed her to angle his body.

Ignoring him, she helped him out the car. He carried most of his own weight but lifted an arm around her shoulders. She shut his door, locked the car, and took the short grey pathway to his house. It was one of few that didn't have a fence enclosing the property. The front door was secured by a sturdy black gate.

At some point during their journey, he'd started walking entirely by himself, but his arm was still around her. It made them look like a couple, which irritated her. She couldn't figure out why. Who would see them and think that? And why did it matter if they did? She had no answers, but something inside her refused to back down. It made her angry, which irritated her even more. Confused her more. The emotions weighed so much that her hands shook, and she struggled to open the damn gate.

'Is this because I called you pretty?' Parker asked softly after her fourth try.

'No,' she said through clenched teeth. She almost cried out in triumph when the gate opened; instead she held her breath as she tried the door. It opened easily, and she resisted another victorious cry.

'Come on. Inside.'

He obeyed wordlessly. When he passed her, Sophia thought about locking the gate behind him and throwing the key into the house.

She had no responsibility toward this man. In fact, she'd probably taken *too* much responsibility for him since she'd already driven him home. But she could hardly let him die on the road. Considering his current state, that outcome seemed dangerously close to being a certainty. He should be safe inside his own house though.

Except that she would worry about whether she'd abandoned him. The guilt would kill her. Heaven knew she didn't have the energy for that.

Because you've been battling with the same thing since Angie came back? Or because you abandoned your own family at the hospital today?

That's different, she told the inner voice. When it asked how, she only shook her head, refusing to indulge the personification of her conscience. She walked determinedly into his house, before locking up and turning.

The front door opened into a living room. It had shaggy beige carpets, thick red curtains, and a TV in the middle of an oak cabinet. The curtains had been drawn, the windows closed, making the room dark and stuffy. As her eyes adjusted, she saw pictures on the cabinet shelves beside the TV. They were of Parker at various ages. There was one of him with a woman—tall, lean, with his exact features except for her mouth, which was wider—at a graduation. They looked ridiculously happy, and Sophia felt a pang of sympathy. Not because Parker would lose these memories as the dementia progressed, but because his mother would.

A groan distracted her from the thought, and she turned. Parker had stretched out his body on a couch that was too small for it. She assumed the groan had come from the satisfaction of getting his body horizontal. That satisfaction wouldn't last. If he stayed there, fell asleep there, he would pay for it the moment he woke up.

She let out a little breath. If she woke him up, she might have to endure another round of unwanted compliments. She should leave him there. He was an adult. He'd made this decision.

Guilt nudged her again.

'What do you have to feel guilty for?' she grumbled under her breath. 'You know him less than a day. Hell, you know him less than two hours. How *can* you feel guilty?'

There was no answer, only another nudge. With a sigh she walked toward Parker. She knelt, placed a hand firmly on his shoulder, and squeezed.

His eyes opened immediately. Then his face twisted.

'Hey,' he said, straightening. Frowned. 'Stop pinching me.'

She released his arm. 'I wasn't pinching you. I was waking you up.'

'You couldn't have done it gentler?'

'Oh, I'm sorry,' she said. She softened her voice, injecting in that sickly sweetness that turned some people into suckers. 'Should I have whispered it into your ear?' She dropped her voice. 'Wake up, little Parker. Time for bed.'

His expression darkened. 'Did you call *me* dramatic?'

'You are,' she told him, standing. 'But you told me I'm pretty, so I'll let it slide and say you're not a drama queen at all.'

'I didn't… I wouldn't… When did I call you pretty?'

'You don't think I am?'

'No… I mean, you are. I'm just saying that…' He released a breath. 'When did I call you pretty?'

'When I helped you out the car,' she replied with a smile. 'You were offended when I didn't accept the compliment.'

'Why wouldn't you accept the compliment?'

'Because you were obviously too sleepy to realise you'd given it. Proven by this very conversation,' she added. 'Besides, I'm not here for compliments. I woke you up because you fell asleep in the car and then on the couch. Your body should thank me for it.' Her eyes widened. 'Because I stopped it from getting stiff, I mean.' Now she closed her eyes with a little sigh. 'Just tell me where your bedroom is and I'll help you to it.'

Her face had already been burning; with that last sentence, she thought she'd combust. But she opened her eyes, kept her gaze on him, refusing to let embarrassment allow him to win. His expression was amused. Content, too, as if sparring with her was a habit that gave him pleasure.

The thought had her blinking, looking away. Which was probably good, considering how things were going between them. They'd been sparring before their kiss. She could only imagine what would happen now that they were alone. With no one watching to keep them in check, one lingering look could spark into something Sophia wasn't sure she wanted. Especially since she was still recovering from that kiss.

'You should get some sleep.'

'No.'

'You're obviously exhausted, Parker,' she said, exasperated now. 'You need sleep.'

'I'm not disagreeing with you. But I don't want to go to sleep and wake up to find you gone.'

Her head almost reared back in surprise. She managed to stop it.

'That's exactly what's going to happen.'

'I know.'

'I shouldn't even be here.' She was trying to wrap her head around it. And why his words affected her. 'I wanted to help.'

'Thank you.'

She waved a hand. Waved the thanks away. 'I don't owe you anything else.'

'I'm not saying you do.'

'Okay.'

She'd needed him to know though.

'I should probably…go to bed then.'

Parker stood. He wasn't giving any signs of it, but Sophia felt the defeat. She wasn't sure what had defeated him. Surely not her, the stranger in his home? No, she thought. It couldn't be her. It was probably because his mother had been diagnosed with an illness and he still hadn't faced it.

Not your problem, a voice told her. It was right. Totally right. But she'd never felt so torn before. She met Parker's eyes.

'Go to bed. I'll make you some tea.'

Chapter Six

He woke up feeling groggier than before he'd gone to sleep. He'd known that was a possibility considering how tired he was, but he hadn't been able to keep his eyes open. Not in the car when Sophia had been driving, or in the vague moments as he'd stumbled to the couch. Even the conversation he'd had with Sophia after felt like a dream.

He lifted his arm, rested it on his forehead. She was probably gone by now. Let herself out after she'd made his tea. He hadn't even drunk it, he thought, looking over at the still-full mug on his desk. He remembered her coming into his room, telling him about it, and leaving. If he tried, he could still smell her perfume. Something floral and light, which matched her name, but not her. He smiled when he heard her voice in his head warning him about prejudices.

It made him think that it wasn't only his sleepy conversation that seemed like a dream, but Sophia herself. She wasn't the kind of person he'd conjure up if he had a choice though. He'd probably have gone with someone a little less prickly, less sarcastic, less honest. Which spoke wonders about him as a person.

Pondering it, he got up and took a shower. The water was cool, not because he needed it—though he did—but because he hadn't put the geyser on when he'd got home. He and his mother lived economically, trying to save where they could, and manually putting the geyser on and off had seemed like a good idea. It usually was, too. Unless someone forgot to turn it on.

He dried himself off, slipped on the underwear he'd taken to the bathroom, and opened the door. Jumped at the shriek.

'Parker!'

'*Sophia?*'

'Parker!' she said again, sharply, holding out a hand and blocking what he imagined was her line of vision to his penis. 'Put on some clothes.'

'Why are you still here?'

'I got distracted cleaning up. Please,' she said, shutting her eyes, 'for goodness' sake, put on some pants.'

Amused now that his heart had returned to its usual pace, Parker leaned against the wall.

'I'm pretty comfortable the way I am, actually. You're not?'

'I'm—' She broke off, opening her eyes though her hand was still in front of her. 'Are you trying to get me to look at your...?'

'Depends on what "my"—' he paused, letting the silence stretch '—is.' He grinned.

'Oh, you're insufferable.'

Deliberately, she lowered her hand. The action, however, was defeated by how stiffly she held herself up. How she didn't drop her gaze even a fraction of a centimetre from his eyes.

'Did you sleep well?' she asked politely.

His smile grew. 'Not particularly.'

'I'm sorry to hear that.'

'Yeah, well, I knew it would happen.' He lifted a hand, ran it through his hair. Her eyes flickered up and, very carefully, went back to his face. 'I think I'm in that zone of being too tired to sleep well unless I have an entire day.' He frowned. 'How long was I sleeping?'

'Just over an hour. I'm surprised, actually. I expected you to be out for at least a couple.'

He studied her. 'You would have liked that, wouldn't you?'

'What? Why?'

'I wouldn't have caught you in the house then.'

'If I didn't want that to happen, I would have left as soon as I brought up your tea,' she said coolly, though it was undermined by her blush. 'I knew this was a possibility.'

'Finding me without clothes on?'

She clucked her tongue in answer. His smile widened.

'Why does it make you so uncomfortable?' he asked, enjoying it. 'Have you never seen a man in his underwear before?'

She narrowed her eyes. 'You don't want to play this game with me, Parker.'

'What game?'

There was a beat before she stepped toward him. It closed the distance between them by a fraction; it changed the air with a snap.

'You know exactly what game you're playing.' She took another step forward. Her gaze never left his face.

'You think teasing me about not wanting to look at your body is fun.' Another step. His breath turned shallow. 'You think making me uncomfortable is going to annoy me.' Another step. She was almost in front of him. 'Except you don't know me, Parker.' She stopped a breath away from his body. 'You don't know that I win every—' her voice dropped to a whisper '—single—' she brought her lips to his ears '—game—' a finger trailed down his torso '—I—' the finger hooked into his underwear '—play.'

She pulled back, but only leaned far enough away to look into his eyes.

'It's okay,' she whispered with a smile. 'You probably haven't seen a woman do *that* before, have you?'

Abruptly, she turned. But not before snapping the elastic of his underwear.

'Come find me when you have some clothes on,' she called over her shoulder, and disappeared down the hallway.

He stared after her for longer than he would ever admit. His body was still recovering from that onslaught; his mind still trying to comprehend it. Logically, he knew she was putting him in his place. But his body had interpreted the interaction as an act of seduction. Which both he and Sophia knew, considering his state of undress.

Bemused, he went to his room and threw on some clothes. He took a moment before he went downstairs though. Inhaled and exhaled deeply. Tried not to think of how turned on he'd been at her teasing. How his body was still pulsing from it; how his mind was still replaying her words.

You probably haven't seen a woman do that before, have you?

He hadn't. Damn.

When he was as recovered as he could be, he found her in the kitchen, drinking from a mug. He didn't spend much time thinking about how his house looked. He'd grown up there, hadn't moved out because he'd been worried about his mother. Before, it had been to leave her alone in general; now, it was because he was worried about her health. Usually, he didn't care about the aesthetics of the house. His primary concern was functionality. Except for at that moment.

Seeing Sophia sitting at the old kitchen table with its crack through the middle felt strange. Made him notice the antique-like oak cabinets that ran in an L-shape above the once-white counters. Had him thinking about the two plates on the stove that she would never know didn't work, but he wished he'd fixed.

He took in the patterned backsplash along the walls that matched the floor. It was better suited to the eighties than modern times. Then he stopped. Frowned.

'It's clean.'

'Yeah, I cleaned. I told you.'

'I know, but… It's *really* clean.'

She rolled her eyes. 'I clean well.'

'Obviously.'

There'd been stacks of dishes he hadn't got to, dirty pots and messy counters. His mother hated the untidiness, but things hadn't been usual in the last week. She'd lost her job at the grocery store because she'd been, they claimed, unreliable. Parker had gone over there and found out for himself. He'd shouted and said things he probably shouldn't have. Had left steaming. Not because he was upset she'd lost her job, but because the reasons they'd given were valid. His mother *had* become unreliable recently. Hence the dishes.

The unexpected emotion of it had him pulling out his own chair and folding his body into it.

'Do you want some tea?' she asked after a moment.

'Why do you keep offering me tea?'

She looked at him as if he'd asked her why they needed air to breathe.

'It's tea,' she said. 'It solves everything.'

'I don't have anything to solve.'

She snorted, but lifted her hands in surrender when he opened his mouth. 'Do you want some?'

He nodded, letting her do it. He should have brought down the cup he hadn't drank earlier, he thought as he watched her. But then he got distracted watching her. There was no hesitation in her movements. Which was strange, since this wasn't her house, yet she seemed to know where everything was.

'You must have spent a long time cleaning this up,' he said with a frown. 'How did you have time to clean anything else?'

'Oh, I didn't,' she said over her shoulder, getting the milk from the fridge. She set it on the counter with the mug she'd prepared and leaned forward, waiting for the kettle to boil. 'I thought it was weird that I was in your house for an hour and I only cleaned your kitchen, so I purposefully made my earlier statement vague.'

'So, to clarify, you don't think it's weird that you're in my house at all?'

Her face turned pink, and her phone pinged. They both looked at it.

'You're not going to check that?' he asked when she didn't move.

'I probably should.'

She stayed perfectly still.

'Should I?'

'Would you?' she asked, genuinely. Then she did a quick series of blinks and shook her head. 'No, I should do it.'

She picked up her phone, biting her lip as she read the message. Her body sagged against the counter and she put the phone against her chest.

'Everything okay?'

'Yeah. Yes,' she said again, turning when the kettle clicked off. 'My sister's still in labour.'

'Is your other sister the one who messaged?'

'Zoey,' she said with a quick nod his way. 'She's been keeping me updated.'

'She isn't annoyed you've been away for the last three hours?'

'Oh, she definitely is. But after my father...'

She trailed off, finished the tea. When she set it in front of him, he thanked her. She nodded. Lifted her own mug and leaned against the counter again.

'The thing with my dad put communication into perspective for us,' she continued. Her voice sounded detached. 'We all wanted to make sure the family didn't fall apart while he was sick. Plus, there were practical things like doctor's appointments and school pickups... Anyway, no matter how we feel, we don't play around with letting the other know we're safe.'

'Does she know where you are right now?'

'She knows I'm safe.'

'But not that you're here?'

'She doesn't have to.'

He nodded, took a small sip of the heated liquid.

'At least you've sent her a picture of me if anything happens to you.'

Her face relaxed into a smile. There'd been no resistance or reluctance in it, making him think she needed it. He acknowledged that some kind of instinct had inspired it, before smiling back, feeling himself relax, too.

'I haven't taken your picture,' she told him stubbornly. 'You're way too self-involved. You should look into that.'

'It's because of the steroids. It's forced my brain to only think in terms of appearance.'

'You're on *steroids*?'

'Yeah. Do you think my body is like this because I spend hours and hours in the gym?'

She opened her mouth, but her gaze slipped down, over his body. She hadn't done it when he was basically naked in front of her, but a stupid comment about steroids had got her to.

Her eyes met his again, narrowed. 'That would explain—' her voice lowered '—you know…' She pointed down.

He frowned. 'I don't know.'

'Well, during our…conversation, upstairs, I realised… um… Some parts of your body don't quite fit with the other parts.'

His frown deepened. 'I hardly feel like this is a fair conversation to have.'

She pursed her lips, then grinned at him. 'I'm sorry, I can't. I really wanted to keep this going, but your face is making me want to crack up so I won't keep going.'

He stared. Shook his head. 'Oh, you're really funny.'

'You started it.'

'All because you won't admit you've taken pictures of me.'

'I have—' She broke off with a sigh. 'I can't make you believe me when it's clear you don't want to.'

'So we have that in common then,' he said. 'Why are you avoiding your family?'

'What?' The teasing vanished from her face. 'I didn't say that.'

'No, but you are proving my point by not answering.'

'Parker—'

'You didn't have to say it,' he interrupted gently. 'You're here, not there. You're nervous about checking your phone. If communication is important to your family, you know there's an expectation that they know where you are. It all kind of speaks for itself.'

'I'm not avoiding them,' she said stubbornly. 'And they know I'm safe. Why does the rest matter?'

'You know the answer to that better than I do, but you literally cleaned my kitchen so you wouldn't have to go back.'

'It was dirty.'

'Why are you running, Sophia?'

'I'm not,' she said on an exhale. 'I have…feelings. I'm giving myself time to deal with them.'

'Why?'

He knew he was pushing, but it felt urgent to find out. Maybe because it gave him something other than his own family to think about. Maybe because she seemed vulnerable, and it was so outside of his experience of her that it compelled him to know more.

She sighed, then came to sit with him at the table.

'Our family is…complicated.'

'What family isn't?'

Her lips curved.

'Mine is unconventional, too.' She traced a finger over the edge of the crack on the table. 'Angie, my sister who's in labour, did a lot of the emotional heavy lifting when we were growing up. She isn't much older than I am, but she got the job because she was born first.' She paused. 'Or maybe she's the best person for the job.' Her jaw clenched. Released. 'I don't even know anymore.'

He gave her a moment. 'Did things change when your dad got sick?' He shrugged when her head whipped to him. 'You said you all helped. I assume that means you did some of the heavy lifting, too.'

Her expression was thoughtful, her eyes sweeping over his face.

'I guess I did.' She tilted her head, lowered her gaze. 'But Angie was there, and she eclipses things.'

'You, too?' he asked. She nodded. 'Impossible.'

She quirked a brow, but gave him a small smile.

'Things changed when my dad died.' She pursed her lips. 'My mom took his death really hard. Their relationship…' She trailed off. 'Zoey took it hard, too,' she continued a beat later. 'And Angie left to work as a teacher in Korea weeks after my dad's funeral. She left them in the midst of that chaos.'

'What about you?'

She blinked, as if she hadn't considered the question before. 'I helped my family through it.'

'No, I mean how did you feel about your father's death?'

She blinked again. Parker wondered who these people in her life were. Surely they must have asked her this? Surely she couldn't be surprised at a question about *her* grief?

'My father and I…weren't close,' she said slowly. 'I'm not saying I wasn't upset when he died or that I don't miss him now. But it was…different for me. It wasn't a person I'd lost. It was a…figure. A role. My *father*. It wasn't Daniel Roux, the man.' She paused. 'I struggled with both of them though, so I'm not sure that distinction helps.'

Her eyes lifted but she looked down quickly, her cheeks looking as if red dye had been spilled over them.

'I get it,' he said, not wanting her to feel embarrassed.

'You do?'

'Yeah. I didn't know my father growing up. He was a man who called me on my birthday. Came to see me for three years, then disappeared for the next seven, like I told you.' He played with the handle of his tea mug. 'The awe I felt for him when I was a kid was almost mystical. Like…for a unicorn.'

'You're comparing your father to a unicorn?'

He laughed. 'Yeah. I mean, I barely saw him growing him. He was as real to me as a unicorn.'

'What changed?'

'I did,' he admitted softly, thinking back to that birthday his father had missed. How his mother had scrambled to make up for it. He'd never forgotten it. 'I realised he was real and he wasn't magical. He was a human being who'd dumped his responsibilities.' Deliberately, he loosened his grip on the mug. 'He moved back when I was twenty.' He frowned. 'Which doesn't change that he wasn't there when I wanted him to be. Even if he visits every week.'

'You're saying that we both don't appreciate who our fathers are. Or were.'

'I'm saying that if my dad died, I'd probably be as nonchalant about it as you.'

Her expression changed. Went from being fairly open to shut as tight as the Queen's palace. 'Is that what you got from what I told you?'

'I...er...'

'Nonchalant,' she repeated under her breath. Shook her head. When she looked at him again, one emotion had slipped under the palace gates: disgust.

'Hey, I'm not judging you,' he said defensively. 'I get it.'

'You equated not being devastated by death to nonchalance. So, no, Parker. I don't think you do.'

Her phone beeped again before he could reply. She reached for the phone immediately.

I know you're avoiding us, but I could really do with proper food.

A second message came through as she finished reading it.

I'm obviously talking about takeaways.

Obviously, she wrote back, though she didn't really feel like teasing Zoey. She was still trying to figure out whether she was doing something wrong by not keeping Zoey up to date with her every move. Surely letting her sister know she was safe was enough? And if it wasn't, surely that was okay for now? She was going through stuff. She could put up some boundaries while she did, couldn't she? Zoey had done it after their father had died. For *three months*. Sophia could take a day to figure her own stuff out.

Except she needed—appreciated—the updates Zoey was giving her about how Angie's labour was progressing.

It was all confusing. Not in the least the fact that Parker had hurt her. Surprisingly. She wasn't sure if it was because he'd articulated what she thought her family believed as well, or because she wanted him to get it. How, she didn't know. Her feelings about her father were complicated. Death didn't change that. And sometimes, even she didn't understand it.

But there was a tiny hole in her heart that ached every time she thought about him. She missed him. On days like today, when her mother floated in her bubble. Or when things were tense in the family, like between her and Zoey now. He'd make a joke and it would instantly lighten things up. Not getting along didn't mean she was blasé about his death. Seeing him as a human with his flaws and recognising the mistakes he'd made didn't mean she didn't care he wasn't around anymore.

She shouldn't have to explain that to some guy she'd just met. But she wanted to. She wanted him to see that she wasn't a terrible human being for not having the traditional feelings about death. About her father's death. Or to understand that what she was feeling was still a form of grief. That grief didn't look one way.

She breathed through the emotions. Ignored her concern at how badly she wanted Parker to understand. She glanced at her phone when she got another message. Sighed as she weighed her options.

'I'm calling a taxi,' she said eventually. It was time to release herself from whatever the hell was happening between them. Today wasn't the day to indulge in romantic feelings, regardless of how compelling or vague they were. She had to get back to the hospital. To her life, and the less compelling feelings she had to deal with regarding her family.

'Where do you need to go?'

'To get food for Zoey. Then I have to go back to being a decent daughter and sister and return to the hospital.'

'I'll take you.'

'No, you won't,' she said, taking her and Parker's mugs to the sink. She washed them, dried them. 'You had an hour's sleep in the last twenty-four hours.'

'I feel fine.'

She eyed him warily. He did look pretty awake. And if he was anything like her, he wouldn't be able to sleep again for a while.

She shook her head. 'No. I think it's time for us to say goodbye.'

'Look, if this is about what I said—'

'It's not,' she interrupted. 'I think we could both be more productive if we weren't together.'

'I thought being together helped us to *not* be productive,' he said. She didn't answer. He sighed. 'I don't have anything to do today in any case.'

She narrowed her eyes. 'Your journalism degree is up on the wall inside. Did you stop writing to drive cars?'

'I write freelance and drive cars for the stable income. Both pay the bills.'

'Okay, then. What about your mom?'

'They won't let me see her until visiting hours.' He looked meaningfully at the clock. It was still a while. 'Besides,' he continued, point proven, 'that actually works in favour of me driving you because I have to stop at the hospital anyway.' He stood, leaned forward, braced on the counter. It highlighted the muscles of his arms. Delightfully so. 'Let me do this for you, Sophia.'

She lifted her brows, her heart still fluttering from those arms. 'No.'

'You're refusing help again?'

'I'm refusing you. You're too eager. I don't do needy men.'

'You don't…do them?'

She rolled her eyes. 'You know that's not what I meant.'

'You should be clearer. I don't *do* ambiguous women.'

'You're exhausting.'

She picked up her handbag and grabbed his house keys.

'Wait, where are you going?'

'I'm leaving. If you're ready by the time I get outside your house, you can drive me. If not, I'm calling a taxi.'

His chair scraped further back as she walked to his front door. She took a perverse pleasure in the sound of him trying to get ready. His steps thudded against the stairs. There was a small noise that sounded as if something had fallen, and then a louder one when something definitely fell. She thought it might have been him. She smiled.

She made no effort to slow down her movements. She opened the door, the gate, and left both open. Locking one of them would be mean.

Her feet stopped. She turned and locked the gate.

Laughing lightly, she walked down the pathway, pulled out her phone, and opened the car service app. She was accepting when Parker skidded to a halt next to her. He took the phone and cancelled.

'That,' he said, panting, 'wasn't nice of you.'

'What wasn't?'

'Locking—' *pant, pant, pant* '—the gate.'

She smiled. 'I'm not nice, Parker. Run while you can.'

'I shouldn't have used that term,' he said, ignoring the suggestion. His breathing was steadier. 'It isn't a suitable description for people. People are…more complicated.'

She studied him, feeling respect grow inside her. It was this part of him that made him so interesting. That was responsible for her disappointment when he'd made that comment about her response to her father's death. A man who understood that people were complicated should understand their emotions were, too.

Maybe that interaction had been a good thing then. If he kept being this…intriguing, it might have led her down a path she couldn't afford to go down. It was more than the fact that the timing was wrong. It was that Parker had baggage. She was familiar with the weight of it because she carried her own. She also knew what the weight meant. It would become heavier, and might drag him down as it had with her mother. Or it would make him stronger. At this point, she couldn't tell. But she couldn't take a chance. The feelings that had caused her to leave the hospital were proof that her baggage wasn't going anywhere anytime soon. She couldn't afford to add his baggage into that, too.

It occupied her mind as she told Parker where to go to get Zoey's food. They drove in silence for the first few minutes. Then he cleared his throat. She rolled her eyes. She was looking out the window as she did, so he likely hadn't seen it. Unfortunately.

'I upset you. Earlier.'

She didn't bother lying. 'Yes.'

'I didn't mean to.'

'Are you going soft on me, Parker?' she asked. 'We haven't really argued in the last hour. And you literally ran to take me on what are basically errands.' She waited a beat. 'I have to tell you, it's starting to get weird.'

'You're deflecting,' he replied. Accurately. Damn it. 'I'm sorry for upsetting you.'

She waved a hand, but she still didn't look at him. Didn't say anything either. The gesture was meant to give him her answer.

But then he took it. He took her hand. Rested it on her thigh as if it were normal. As if they hadn't just met. As if him touching her wasn't strange and unfamiliar and…and comforting.

The warmth of it seeped into her body. It wasn't like their kiss, where that heat had burnt and raged and demanded more. This heat soothed, like a hot water bottle on a cold night. Like a massage after a stressful day.

She looked down at their linked hands, the surprise of it mingling with the warmth and creating a tumble of anxiety in her belly. It didn't look strange, their hands linked. It *looked* normal. It *felt* normal.

She looked at him. He was looking straight ahead.

'This is weird.'

'What is?'

Her hand tightened on his in answer.

'It's called support.'

'I don't need support.'

'Fine. It's an apology.'

'You've already apologised.'

He sighed, but the sound lacked the irritation it usually contained. 'It is what it is, Sophia. Accept it.'

'I don't like it,' she said stubbornly.

'Do you want me to let go?'

Her grip tightened again, without permission. He didn't comment any further. Furiously, she looked down at her hand. At the traitor. It was her right hand, her dominant hand, so indulging fantasies of cutting it off wasn't practical.

If she was being honest though, her hand was being more courageous than the rest of her. It faced the truth. Embraced it. Holding his hand *did* feel like support. It did feel like an apology. She felt better for it, and she didn't like it.

She didn't like it at all.

Chapter Seven

It was an experience watching Sophia order food for her sister. Apparently, she'd been sent a list, so she read from her phone. As she finished, her phone beeped again. Her face twisted and she added to her order. It happened twice before Sophia put the phone in her bag and turned to him.

'Do you want anything?'

'I'm good.'

'And that's it,' she told the guy behind the counter. 'Praise the heavens.'

'Don't worry, I've seen worse.'

The guy smiled. Interest flared on his face as his eyes swept over her; the smile turned predatory. Something inside of Parker awoke, stood up slowly, prepared for attack. An animal, he thought dimly, protecting what was his. The thought paralysed him, and he made no move as the man asked Sophia for her number.

She blinked. 'Why would I give you my number?'

The self-assured smile slipped away. 'I thought... I'm sorry.'

'Good,' she said with a frown. 'I accept the apology.'

She paid and they walked to the nearest open table to

wait for their food. Her frown was still in place as they sat, but it deepened when she looked at him.

'Why are your fists clenched?'

'They're not,' he said, looking down to see that they were. He unfurled them.

'Is everything okay?'

'Fine.'

'Parker.'

'Sophia,' he replied with a calm he didn't feel.

It confused him, this feeling of possessiveness. Sophia wasn't his. He had no right to be upset by someone hitting on her. He'd had no right to hold her hand in the car either, or to want to comfort her.

They were things he'd add to an ever-growing list that had alarms ringing in his head. Distractions. Disappointments. That's what his parents' marriage had taught him about relationships. He didn't usually have to remind himself of those teachings when he was interested in someone. He'd go on dates, but he rarely felt anything that could persuade him to turn those dates into more. He'd certainly never felt the magnitude of what he felt about Sophia now, though he couldn't describe what those feelings were. The only reason he could come up with for feeling them was that he was still trying to process his mother's diagnosis. Things were complicated. He *wanted* the distraction, even if it was only for today.

It rang true enough that he didn't question it. The flimsy town of lies would topple over at the vaguest inquisition anyway.

'Hey, are you upset because that guy asked for my

number?' she asked suddenly, her expression brightening.

'No.'

'I was offended on your behalf,' she said after a moment. 'I was standing there with you. If things had been reversed, I'd be annoyed.'

'You know what's funny?' he drawled. 'If I told you I was annoyed, you'd probably tell me I have no right to be. We were just standing next to one another. And even if that implied we were in a relationship, I'm sure you'd have told me that being in a relationship didn't mean ownership or possession of, and that I was out of line.' Their eyes locked. 'Am I wrong?'

There were a couple of seconds where she blinked a lot, then she shook her head slowly.

'No, probably not.' She tilted her head, made a sound of dissatisfaction.

'What?'

'Nothing. Well, not nothing,' she corrected herself. 'I'm trying to figure out how I feel about how well you know me. Also, that you called me out.'

He let her figure it out, collecting her food when their order number was called. The guy studiously avoided his gaze, though Parker wasn't sure what had inspired it. The fact that Sophia had denied the man's advances, or the glower Parker had given him despite his passionate speech to Sophia.

He was well aware he was a hypocrite.

As they made their way to the car, Sophia said, 'You've made good points. And…' there was a short moment of hesitation '…you're probably right. I would have been mad at any of the things you outlined.'

'Probably?' he asked, amused.

She made a face. 'Take the victory, okay?' They got into the car, and drove in silence for a couple minutes. 'It might make no sense, but I think it's cute that you were jealous in there.'

'I wasn't—' He broke off when he realised the first part of what she'd said. 'Cute?'

'Take the victory.'

He smiled.

Almost no time later they arrived at the hospital. Parker eased his car into a parking space. When he switched it off, neither of them spoke.

'Well,' she said eventually. 'I guess this is it.'

'Yeah.'

Neither of them moved.

'Are you staying here because you don't want to go inside and face your family?' he asked.

'Are you staying here because you don't want to go inside and face your mother?' she countered.

'Yeah,' he said again. 'I don't know what to tell her if she's awake.'

'Won't the doctors have broken the news to her?'

'Probably.' His hands tightened on the steering wheel. 'That's not what I'm talking about though.'

'No,' she agreed softly. 'I guess the best thing I could tell you is to be honest. Tell her how you feel. Listen to how she feels.' She paused. 'There is no solution for this, Parker.' Her voice went even softer. 'There's no right answer. Take my advice, don't. You know your mother best. Trust that. Trust yourself.'

'Easy for you to say.' But he reached out and grabbed her hand. She squeezed. 'Now, what about your stuff?'

'What about my stuff?'

'I don't know,' he said in surprise. 'I don't actually know the real reason you've been avoiding your family.' He went through his memories, looking for something that stood out. 'Is it because you have to take care of them? Could be,' he thought out loud, 'since the only reason you're returning is to bring your sister food.'

'The reason I'm returning is because my other sister's in labour and I can't run away from that forever.' Her tone was amused. 'Not that I won't try occasionally.' She angled toward him. 'You were an excellent source of distraction. Thank you.'

'Ditto.'

There was a shift in the air, a softening of it. It made no sense, but Parker accepted it.

'I would say it's a pleasure to have met you, Parker, but that would be a lie.'

She grinned, then leaned over and pressed a chaste kiss to his lips. By the time his mind had caught up with what had happened, she was out of the car, walking to the hospital entrance.

A lethargy entered his legs, a combination of desire and resistance. He wanted to run after her, to stop her from walking out of his life. For leaving him alone to deal with whatever he would face the moment he walked into that hospital. But he knew that wasn't possible. It wasn't logical either. He had to face this alone. Just as his mother had taught him throughout his life.

They'd always been a team. A unit. They hadn't had anyone else to lean on, so they had to lean on one another. Things had got rough. His mother had tried to shield him from it, but Penny was too honest for her own good sometimes. When she was stressed about bills, he could see it, and he'd ask what was wrong. She'd tell him, but he never worried. He knew his mother would take care of them. They lived lean, but they'd never been in any real trouble.

Still, it hadn't been the childhood his mother had wanted for him. She'd told him so a million times; now, he'd tell her he wouldn't change it for the world. It had taught him how to be scrappy and independent. He had a work ethic second to none, so that even though he had a job as a journalist, he drove for a car rental business because they needed the extra cash. Most importantly, he had love that he knew was rare. His relationship with his mother was the most important thing in his life, and now he would lose her.

He would lose her.

Hands closed over his heart, squeezing so tight he felt the blood drain from the life-giving organ. When he thought there was nothing left, he got out the car, and went to face his mother.

While he still had her.

'It's not that you left,' Zoey said, her words muffled. She was still chewing. 'It's that you left without warning. And you left me alone.' She swallowed. 'I had to explain to Mom where you were.'

'You knew where I was. Kind of,' Sophia said with a grimace. 'What did you tell her?'

'Bathroom.'

Sophia paused as she reached for a chip on Zoey's plate. She had her own, but Zoey didn't like it when Sophia stole hers. So she kept doing it.

'She thinks I was in the bathroom for the last four hours?'

Zoey swatted Sophia's hand. 'To be fair, she hasn't really been paying attention.'

Sophia made a sound that was somewhere between a grunt and a groan. The motivation for it was as confusing. Was she upset her mother hadn't noticed she was gone? Or was it simply that she wasn't surprised by the information?

Zoey frowned. 'You're acting weird today.'

'It's been a weird day.'

Sophia let her mind wander to the kiss she'd shared with Parker in the car. How, even though it was a closed mouth, barely-there kiss, her stomach had fluttered and her body had prickled. There were also the emotions that had overwhelmed her regarding her family, but the kiss was easier—surprisingly—to think about.

'Why hasn't Mom noticed?' Sophia asked, shaking her head. 'She's been nagging me about being here basically since we found out Angie's pregnant.'

'She's been with Angie a lot.'

'Ah.'

'Labour's hard.'

'Hmm.'

'You're being selfish.'

Sophia's eyebrows rose. 'You're eating the food I paid way too much money for and you're calling *me* selfish?'

'It's not about that and you know it,' Zoey said seriously.

Zoey was never serious. She was the goof in the family, which Sophia had always attributed to the fact that she was the youngest. She could afford to be the goof. The responsibility buck would stop with her last, and since her sisters took responsibility seriously, she'd never have it.

Sophia sat back, studying Zoey. Her dark brown, almost black eyes were steady, and the long twists she wore her hair in more often than not framed her pretty face. It was too much of an effort to style it that way, Sophia thought. Since her own hair was short, she didn't think that would come as a surprise to anyone.

'Why don't you tell me what this is about?'

'I try not to get between you and Ange,' Zoey said with a little sigh, 'but things have been a bit ridiculous since she got back. Especially if Mom spending time in Angie's room while she's in labour upsets you.'

Sophia rolled her eyes. 'It doesn't upset me.'

'So the sarcastic little remarks are just for the sake of it?'

'My default setting is sarcasm.'

'Yeah, but it's become mean since Angie's been home. Remember when you told her you're glad she's home so you won't have to deal with Mom crying anymore?' Zoey's face twisted. 'You didn't have to tell her about Mom crying. You know she already feels bad about leaving.'

Sophia gritted her teeth. Then forced herself to relax her jaw. 'It was the truth. And if she felt bad about leaving, she would have come back a lot sooner than after three years.'

'You didn't mind that she was away,' Zoey said. 'Why are you making her feel bad about it?'

'Of course I minded.'

'Really? Why are you so mad that she's back then?'

She rolled her eyes. 'You don't get it, Zo.'

'I get more than you give me credit for.' Zoey spoke primly now. 'When Angie left, you could finally take care of the family like you always wanted to. You didn't have to deal with Angie's opinions or pretend to agree with them like you usually did. You could tell me and Mom what to do like Dad used to.'

'Hold on a second,' Sophia said, lifting a hand. 'You think I *wanted* to take care of you?'

Zoey opened her mouth, but it was too late. The annoyance and frustration that had been growing inside Sophia for much longer than that day—but especially that day—came spilling out.

'You seriously think I wanted to take care of you and Mom? You, who never takes responsibility for anything. And of Mom who… Well, Moms.' She lifted a hand, as if it explained it all.

Zoey's eyes were wide. If Sophia looked hard enough, she knew she'd see hurt there. So she didn't.

'I've never wanted to take care of this family. But Dad raised me to. He *told* me to. So, while I know you and Mom prefer Angie's maternal and caring nature to my *meanness*, I didn't have a choice.'

She pushed to her feet.

'I know I'm not as…intuitive, or whatever, as Angie is. I used to leave the emotional stuff to her because I know I'm not maternal and caring. I know I'm hard. I know that. And I'm pissed at Angie because she left you guys with hard and *mean* when you both needed maternal and caring. Not because I'm jealous, or upset she's back, for heaven's sake.'

She was breathless by the time the rant was over. Zoey was staring at her as if she'd announced she was an alien. It gave her a moment to catch her breath, though it didn't change the hurt and anger churning in her stomach.

'You don't get it, Zo,' she said eventually. The words came in a heartbroken voice she had no idea existed in her vocal range. 'Tell Mom I'm… I needed… Tell her I'm in the bathroom.'

She walked away, ignoring Zoey's hoarse call. She couldn't stay there. She was afraid that like blood from a damn stone, her hardness might produce tears.

'She's asleep.'

It was the first thing his father said to him when Parker walked into his mother's room. When he'd seen Wade Jones's hulking figure, he hadn't even been surprised. The last six years had been a lot of him walking into rooms and seeing his father there. Surprise had only come the first year. Now, it barely fazed him. Which was a disappointment. He would have liked at least twenty years to balance all the times he'd walked into a room and wished for his father to be there, but he wasn't.

He acknowledged Wade's words with a nod, looking at his mother. Her left arm was in a cast. There was an ugly bruise crawling out from under the plaster and creeping up to hide under her hospital gown. There was a lighter bruise and some swelling on the right side of her face, which Parker assumed was what she'd landed on. His fingers curled, and he folded his arms, not wanting his father to see how upset he was.

Allowing Wade to see his emotions felt like weakness. His mother would have slapped him if he ever admitted that out loud. To her, emotion was never weakness.

'People are going to try to make you believe that because you're a man,' Penny had said. 'But don't believe it. It's bullshit. If you have feelings, feel them. Show them. You have them for a reason, and if you don't let them out, they're going to come out in ways that'll be a hundred times worse.'

He believed that, too. Except when it came to his father. No, with his father, it felt as if everything his mother had taught him went up in smoke. *She'd be thrilled to hear that if she wakes up*, a voice in his head said. *When she wakes up*, he corrected it with a frown.

'She's going to be okay, son.'

Parker met his father's eyes. He could see that Wade believed it. With a smile that held no humour, Parker turned and walked out of his mother's room. He heard a chair scrape back and held his breath when he felt his father following him.

'Parker—'

'Why are you here?' he asked quietly. 'Is it because of the room? Because I'll reimburse you.' His mind scrambled as he tried to think about how much of his savings he'd have left once he paid his father.

'I don't care about the money, Parker.'

'Yeah, I forgot. When me and Mom were struggling to pay our bills, you were out building your own business.' He locked his jaw. He didn't need the echo of his mother's voice telling him this was what happened when he didn't let his emotions out. 'I'm sorry,' he said with a small sigh. 'The pressure.'

It was all he offered, but his father seemed content. 'The doctors are positive about her recovery.'

Parker frowned. 'Why are they telling you that?'

'They told your mother. I was there and she wanted me to stay.'

'They told me I couldn't see her until visiting hours.'

'They probably would have let you, had you been here.' Parker gave his father a look, and Wade immediately backtracked. 'Not that you should have been. They told her you were here all evening. She probably figured you needed some sleep. She would have wanted you to get some sleep.'

It took him a long moment to figure out how he could navigate through the minefield of his emotions.

'Did they only talk to her about the accident?'

His father's silence was answer enough. Parker closed his eyes. When that didn't magically take the emotions away, or transport him into a far-off land, he opened them again.

'I need a moment.'

'We need to talk about your mother's diagnosis.'

'No, I need to talk to *Mom* about her diagnosis. Not with you, Wade. Not when you haven't been in our lives for long enough to know what this diagnosis is going to mean.'

'I've been around for six years.'

'I'm twenty-six,' Parker told him. 'There are twenty more years you've missed out on.'

'I understand that, Parker.'

His brow knitted, and for a moment, Parker felt as if

he were looking in a mirror. He'd seen that exact look on his own face countless times. When he was concentrating on shaving or doing his hair. Parker didn't know what his father was concentrating on.

'I'm trying,' Wade said eventually. 'I know I was a bad father the first part of your life. I'm trying to make up for it. I'm trying to be a better support system for your mother, too.'

'And how does Kelly feel about that?' Parker asked sourly. 'How does she feel about you spending hours with your ex-wife?'

'She understands they're hours I'm spending with my son, too.' The words were careful. 'I know you want me to be the villain. I get that I was for a long time. But don't I deserve redemption?'

'What do you think this is?' Parker asked in disbelief. 'A comic book? This is real life, Dad. You weren't here. You can't just swoop in and save the day like a hero would.'

'Parker,' his father said, frustrated now. 'Think about your mother. You can't take care of her alone.'

'But I have,' Parker replied flatly. 'I've been taking care of her alone my entire life. And she's been taking care of me. She and I will figure this out, too.'

Chapter Eight

'What are you doing here?' Parker asked when he got to his car and found Sophia leaning against it. She didn't bat an eyelash at his curt tone.

'Distraction. For a day. The rest of today.' She released a breath. 'I desperately need to get out of here.'

Parker studied her. 'Get in the car.'

They were driving before long, the air tense and heavy though not because of anything they'd done to each other. Everything that had kept them lingering in the car before that hour in the hospital had caught up to them. Confirmation, he thought, that they should have lingered longer. Perhaps she was onto something with proposing they distract one another for the day...

Which meant they needed to do something that would distract them. He needed to take his mind off the fact that his father was currently inside his mother's hospital room. Waiting as if he'd been there when she'd needed him most.

He gritted his teeth and took the off-ramp toward the city. He could only really think of one place that would calm him, and that meant driving through the steep hills of Cape Town's main roads to get there.

It was busy. People had woken up to a sunny weekend day and were going to the beach to enjoy it. They spent hopelessly too long in traffic, before spending hopelessly too much time trying to find a parking space once they got to the beach.

Eventually, Parker pulled into a paid parking lot, ignoring the inner voice telling him he would need to start saving his money if he wanted to take proper care of his mother. With Penny losing her job, his was the only income. Despite his two jobs, they would struggle. Particularly once they'd have to do something about his mother's sickness.

'Parker.'

He turned his head slowly, as if he were in a dream. 'What?'

'We've been sitting here for fifteen minutes. You've been *staring* for fifteen minutes.'

'That can't be true.'

She smirked. He could see the expression clearly despite the fact that they were in underground parking.

'I'd like to assure you it isn't, but it is.'

'Why would you let me sit here for fifteen minutes?'

'You needed it.'

'You're right,' he said after a pause. 'Come on, let's go.'

Usually, Cape Town's beaches were a double-edged sword. On the one hand, they were pretty damn close to idyllic. Long stretches of light brown sand; dark blue water crashing on the shore against rocks on random points in the ocean. There were hills that rose and dipped; people selling ice creams; stores offering cold beverages.

On the other hand, there was the wind. It whipped sand so hard against skin that it felt like an exfoliation. Some people would brave the wind and set up their beach gear only to be rewarded with umbrellas that flew away, towels following shortly after. Today though, the beach was quiet. There was a slight breeze, but it wasn't threatening, and the sand stayed safely on the ground as they walked.

'This is nice,' Sophia said after a moment.

'I thought you might like it.'

'Why?'

'It's peaceful. I figured we could both do with some peace.'

'We could probably both do with some sunscreen, too,' she noted absently.

'We won't stay long enough to get burnt.'

'Okay.' There was a pause. 'Thank you. You're right about it being peaceful. And me needing peaceful.'

'Want to tell me why?' He couldn't help himself.

'I had a fight with my sister.'

'The one in labour.'

'No.' She pulled her face. 'What kind of person do you think I am? I wouldn't fight with my sister while she's in labour. Please. I haven't seen Angie since we got to the hospital.' She fell silent for a few seconds. 'My younger sister, Zoey.'

'What happened?'

'She said some stuff about me.'

He waited for more. Nothing came. 'Do you want to elaborate?'

She let out a little breath. 'She told me I was mean.

That I've become meaner since Angie came home from teaching in Korea.'

'Have you?'

'What do you think?'

'I think there's no good way for me to answer this question.'

He caught the twitch of a smile on her face before it sobered.

'I think I'm mean in comparison to Angie.'

'And do you often compare yourself to Angie?'

There was a long pause. Longer than, he thought, either of them could have expected.

'I probably do,' she admitted quietly.

The ocean crashed over their feet. If it had been seconds earlier, he wasn't sure he would have heard her answer.

'But not out of my own volition. I was compared to her so often as a child…' She trailed off. 'It wasn't ever done purposefully, I don't think. My parents never stood in front of me and said "Sophia, you should be more like Angie" or anything. I think…' She sighed. 'I felt that way because I'd look at her and how they treated her and the responsibilities they gave her and I… *I* felt that way.'

He wanted to ask questions, but he didn't know how much she'd reveal to him. She hadn't tried to hide anything from him, but she only told him things she wanted to tell him. That much was clear. If she wanted him to know this, she would tell him. So he didn't speak, giving her space to pace herself instead. To actively decide what she wanted him to know as she went along.

'I don't think I'm mean. I do think she's comparing

me to how sweet and kind Angie is. Angie would do whatever she could for them without a word of complaint.'

'She also left.'

'Yeah. For three years. But after my dad died.'

'Are you excusing her behaviour?'

'I'm telling you she left because my dad died and she loved him.'

'So did you.'

'That's not what you thought earlier.'

She had him there.

'Earlier... Earlier I think I was still under the illusion that love only looked one way.'

She stopped walking, and they turned to face one another. Her eyes were bright with emotion, the light breeze fluttering through the round short curls on her head. She had the perfect face, he thought idly. Not in the conventional sense—her nose was too sharp, her lips too plump—but she was striking. Her face suited her personality. Which, to him, was perfect, too.

'It doesn't, you know,' she said softly. 'My father and I didn't have a great relationship. He was too stubborn, and he expected too much from us. Angie gave in to him, which I guess made him believe that I had to, too. Zo didn't have to, because we protected her from it.'

'How about you? Did you give in to him?'

'I think I fell somewhere in between. I did what I had to do, but I didn't pretend like it was all fun and games.'

'Did Angie?'

'She didn't complain. She wouldn't. She was too concerned about what my parents would say.' There was a pause. 'She never wanted to upset them, even though

I could see it upset her. What they were doing to her. I couldn't let that happen to me, too.'

'So you're mean because you have boundaries?'

Her lips curved as if he'd amused her. 'Yes. Funny how that happens.'

'I'm sorry you have to deal with this.'

Silence stretched.

'Honestly, Parker,' she said. 'I could have sworn you were a lot harder than you turned out to be. It's not a criticism,' she added. 'I like people who are in touch with their emotions.'

'Why are you saying it like you're disappointed then?'

'Maybe because I'm going to miss letting you piss me off.'

'Don't worry,' he said with a grin, 'I don't intend to stop.'

'Good.' She narrowed her eyes. 'What was your drama at the hospital?'

'My father.' He angled his head, asking if she wanted to keep walking. She began to move in answer. 'He was at the hospital.'

'Why?'

'I told you things changed six years ago. He had…a change of heart, I guess. A new wife, a stable job. He started visiting my mom again. He started visiting my mom and me,' he allowed.

'Why would he visit your mom?'

'It's complicated,' he said, settling on the only description of his parents' relationship he could come up with. 'They were friends before they got married, and they really only got married because my mom fell pregnant with me. She didn't want to, but you know how things were back in the day. Their parents insisted, and they had me. Then my father realised he wasn't ready for the responsibility. Shocker at twenty-one, right?'

He rolled his eyes. 'Long story short, he built an electrical business that is doing incredibly well. He felt guilty enough to rekindle the friendship with my mom.'

'Wow,' she said after a moment. 'That's…some story.'

'Yeah.'

'Your mother is obviously a saint.'

'Why?'

'Besides the fact that she put up with you all these years—' she gave him an impish grin '—if a man ever did to me what your father did to her, I'd skin him alive and wear the spoils as a warning to all other men.'

His feet stopped walking before he realised it. She was metres away from him when she realised he wasn't next to her anymore, too.

'Are you okay?' she asked as she turned back.

'I have that visual in my mind.'

'What visual?' She looked at him innocently.

He had no doubt she'd do it. But then, he wasn't sure any man would walk out on her. Not when she was this scary—and he'd barely known her for a day. And if a man walked out on her, he would surely never walk back in again. Not when he knew what he would be returning to.

Parker had no doubt she'd be this scary if she were ever in a romantic relationship. She was one of those people who didn't feel the need to hide any part of herself. What she allowed him to see was who she was.

Those parts of her were carefully curated, but he had no problem with that. It meant he earned what he knew about her, which made the knowledge precious.

Which was scarier than the prospect of being skinned alive.

Still, knowing that didn't put him off. He was intrigued by her in a way he'd never experienced. The few romantic relationships he'd had tended to come second to his relationship with his mother. It wasn't entirely intentional; he wasn't obsessed with his mother. Didn't compare all the women he dated to her. But Penny didn't have anyone to rely on. And after what she'd gone through with his father, she needed someone reliable. She needed *him*.

He couldn't afford for his attention to be on someone who would inevitably disappoint him. Or worse: make him forget his priorities. Not that he'd ever say any of that to his mother though. She had no idea she was part of the reason he wasn't in a long-term relationship.

Which makes the fact that you're here, begging for distraction, the one thing you've always criticised relationships for doing, so interesting.

'Hey,' Sophia said softly. 'Get out of your head.'

'How?' he asked without hesitation.

She looked around, her hand gripping his almost effortlessly as she did. When she looked back at him, there was a glint in her eyes.

'How do you feel about playing tourist?'

Sophia understood Parker's desire to escape. She felt it when she looked into his eyes and saw the shadows there. They dimmed the gleam from his face. She'd initially found that gleam annoying, but now that it was gone, she kind of missed it.

Either way, when she'd seen the tall red bus with its open top and empty seats, she'd recognised it as a necessary distraction. Since that's what she'd asked for at the hospital—what he'd tacitly agreed to by telling her to get into the car—she thought he might appreciate it. It was a bonus then that sitting at the top of the bus would send wind ruffling through her hair. Perhaps it would even help her shovel out some of the sand that had weighed down her lungs since that conversation with Zoey.

Telling Parker what had happened hadn't helped her as much as she'd hoped. His understanding had, but it wasn't his understanding that mattered. She thought after decades of caring for Zoey, her sister would have a more nuanced view of her. But like she'd told Parker, Angie tended to eclipse things. Nuances. Layers. Sophia shouldn't have been surprised or hurt by it. She was both.

She refused to accept it. Which was why she was sitting on the top level of a sightseeing bus, earphones in, listening to a woman drone on about the city she'd grown up in and adored her entire life. It probably explained why her fingers were mingled with Parker's, too.

She studied their hands where they rested on his knee. The light brown of her skin, the darker brown of his. They looked good together. Almost like they fit.

The thought had her eyes lifting to his face. Again, she thought about how handsome he was. She'd never had creative impulses in her life, but she had them now.

She wanted to draw his face. To sculpt it, or paint it, or memorialise it somehow so that when this day was over, she'd have a memento of how kind he'd been.

She shuddered. Wondered where the fanciful notions were coming from. Parker released her hand and put his arm around her, drawing her in to his side. Then he stiffened, as if he hadn't realised what he'd done. He looked down at her. She looked up at him. Their gazes locked, the contact of their skin suddenly heating. It was as if someone had dropped chilli powder along the lines of it. It was as if she'd run her tongue along that line. Which made her think about running her tongue along those magnificent abs she'd got a glimpse of when he'd come out of the bathroom.

The lust didn't surprise, nor the memory. She'd wondered when the moment would come, quite frankly. When she'd think of that image that had been seared in her brain. How she'd pretended to seduce him, but had really been seducing herself.

She thought the moment would come when she was under the blanket of nightfall. Perhaps alone in bed, hidden from anyone's voyeuristic eyes. She had not expected it to come when she was tucked into his side, his abs—and, er, *other* body parts—only a short distance from her hands. She could just reach over and feel the rifts of it. Or the swell of it, depending on how far she went.

An intake of breath told her she hadn't only thought about touching Parker, she'd actually done it. Fortunately, she'd gone for his abs. She snatched her hand away, but he grabbed it before she could get far. Tentatively, without taking his eyes off hers, he placed it back on his torso. The muscles were tight underneath her fingers, tensed, as if preparing for something. Which was the problem. They couldn't prepare for anything. If they did, she was worried they might be arrested.

Abruptly, she stood. Parker's eyes widened. Slowly, he took his earphones out his ears. She did the same.

'Surely, this is an exaggeration,' he said mildly, though his voice was husky. 'You don't have to jump to your death because you touched me.'

'How tempting,' she replied dryly.

'Seriously, you're not supposed to be standing. You could fall over the edge.'

'At this speed?' she asked, as the bus crawled through traffic.

'You're still not supposed to be standing.'

His voice was testy now. She recognised it as the voice of sexual frustration. Hers would have sounded the same if she didn't have such excellent control. An evaluation she made based on everything she knew about herself… Except for the fact that she hadn't even been aware of her hand exploring Parker's abs.

'If I'm not supposed to stand,' she said slowly, looking around, brightening when she found exactly the kind of thing she was looking for. 'They wouldn't have put this in the bus.'

A few minutes later, she was speaking into a microphone that overrode the automatic tour guide in the passengers' ears.

'Good afternoon, everyone. My name is Sophia Roux and the Red Bus Sightseeing Company would like to welcome you all on this tour of Cape Town.'

Parker watched her, his mouth in a line that told her

he wasn't impressed with her. His eyes, however, told her he was amused and trying to fight it. The sweet spot she was going for.

'As you can see, today is the perfect weather for a day at the beach. For those of you who were able to enjoy a trip to Llandudno Beach, I'm sure you'll agree. Unfortunately, so does everyone else in Cape Town, and thus, we can't complain about being stuck in traffic. I'm talking to you, sir.'

She pointed to a man with a shock of white hair that was partially obscured by a black cap. He was obviously grumpy about the current speed they were driving. His frown deepened when she called him out.

'Why would you come to the most heavily congested city in South Africa if you didn't want to sit in traffic? Especially on a day like this?'

He said something to her, though she couldn't hear him because he was so far back. Based on his hand gestures, that something wasn't flattering. When she opened her mouth to respond, Parker stood, tapped her on the hip, and she turned to him.

'Are you trying to *discipline* me?' she said, still speaking into the microphone.

Parker didn't get a chance to reply when a middle-aged woman about two rows in front of them put her hand up.

'Yes?' Sophia asked.

'Correct me if I'm wrong, dear, but wouldn't this be more successful if you weren't so, um…' Her eyes fluttered over to Parker. Sophia thought she might have seen the woman mouth the word 'help' to him. She didn't get any, which pleased Sophia, but that didn't stop the woman. She continued. 'Aggressive.'

'You're right,' Sophia said with a smile she'd practised many times. It was the one she gave all the people who were uncomfortable with her *aggression*. 'Shall we continue the tour then?'

Sophia pointed to a random hill. 'Over there we have the hill the Dutch colonisers first settled on in 1652.' Utter rubbish, of course. But if they were so concerned about aggression, rather rubbish than what she actually wanted to tell them. 'They had breakfast on this hill every morning, as it gave them the perfect view of the ocean—' she pointed at the blue expanse '—from where they believed enemies might come.'

'Who were their enemies?' a voice called from somewhere in the back.

'Who *weren't* the colonisers' enemies?' Sophia asked. 'In fact, I think it could be argued that the colonisers were their *own* enemies.'

'Is that historically accurate?' another voice asked.

'Of course it is. If you don't believe me, please ask my esteemed colleague, Dr Parker—' She glanced at him, realising she didn't know his surname.

'Jones.'

'Dr Parker Jones.'

Up until that moment, Sophia hadn't checked to see how Parker was reacting to the rubbish she'd been spouting. When she met his eyes, she saw they were alight with laughter, his mouth no longer in its grim line.

Mission accomplished, she thought, and handed him the microphone.

Chapter Nine

'The problem is that you can never predict what's going to happen when you make so many enemies,' Parker ended his incredibly long-winded—and nonsensical—explanation of why the discussion of colonialism needed to be interrogated.

He enjoyed it more than he probably should have considering he was lying. But was it even lying when he didn't know what the truth was? Perhaps it was merely storytelling. Regardless, the delighted expression on Sophia's face made it worth it.

Also, the disgruntled gentleman with the white hair who was, he and Sophia had learnt, an actual historian. No one had believed him though. Sophia, Parker had discovered, was an excellent liar. So excellent that even though most of the passengers had been on the bus longer than they had, they believed that Sophia was a tour guide. That Parker was her associate.

He didn't know how he should feel about it. One part of him dismissed any concern, telling him it wouldn't matter once the day ended. Sophia had only asked him for one day, so they wouldn't see one another again, and he wouldn't have to worry about her lying.

Another, more primal part told him he did care. If he wanted a future with her, he would have to care. But he didn't want a future with her. How could he? His mother would take up more of his time now that she was ill. He hadn't been interested in relationships for as long as he could remember; neither had the women he'd dated, who didn't appreciate him being on standby for his mother. That wouldn't change now.

Sophia knew what it was like to take care of a sick parent. She wouldn't want to hang around for that again. And *he* knew that romantic relationships ended in hurt and disappointment more often than not. His mother had gone through that with his father. It had strengthened his desire to not want to go through it himself. It also made him want to show Penny she could rely on him in a way she hadn't been able to with his father. He wouldn't let her down.

But that would start tomorrow. Today, he needed the fantasy. The break. Yes, the distraction, though he knew how hypocritical that was considering his opinion on relationships. Perhaps that was why he was thinking about futures: he was immersing himself in the fantasy. Since there was a limited time for it, he probably shouldn't interrupt himself with something as trivial as logic...

'Well, this is where we get off,' Sophia said suddenly, taking the microphone from Parker. 'We hope you enjoyed your day, and we thank you for using Red Bus Sightseeing.'

She grabbed her handbag and his hand, and they made their way down to the bottom of the bus, where the driver was bobbing to music from his own earphones. Which explained why they hadn't been kicked off the bus. Parker nodded a greeting before he and Sophia exited.

'Why are you in such a hurry?' Parker asked, when Sophia pulled him to the side of the road. 'And do you realise you got the name of your tour company wrong?'

'Look,' she replied, nodding her head in the direction of a Red Bus employee making her way onto the bus. She was talking into her phone. When Parker looked up, he could see the old grey-haired historian speaking on his phone.

'He tattled on us?' Parker asked in disbelief.

'I think he was tattling on our besmirching of our colonial ancestry,' she said in a wry tone, before turning to face him. 'They're looking at us.'

'Yeah?' he asked. 'What should we do—'

Her mouth on his silenced him.

He'd been thinking about kissing Sophia again pretty much since their first kiss. But that had been exploratory, inquisitive, and she hadn't given him any indication that she wanted to do it again. Except when he'd come out of his bathroom. And that moment in the car before they'd gone into the hospital. There was also the moment on the bus, when she'd touched him and his body had pleaded with him to ignore that there was a thing like public indecency and he was very close to being arrested for it.

So perhaps she had given him *some* indication.

Not that it made this any less of a surprise. Her lips were as soft as the first time, even as inquisitive, but there was no exploration. There was a passion he could have blamed on her wanting to obscure them. He could have blamed the urgency on that, too. He didn't. No,

he thought the passion and urgency came from wanting something and resisting it for too long. Who cared
if too long was a few hours? Time was relative when
it came to lust, and he was glad both he and Sophia
seemed to agree on that.

Then she pulled away from him, her eyes moving to
behind him. She lowered to the ground.

'Did it work?' he asked, his voice hoarse.

'I think so,' she replied with a small smile. It made
her look extraordinarily pleased with herself.

He frowned. 'Why are you smiling like that?'

'Like what?'

'Sophia,' he said, looking behind her. The bus was
no longer there. 'Are you smiling because you kissed
me without reason?'

'Oh, I had a reason,' she said easily. 'I wanted to.'

His eyebrows rose. 'Okay.'

Her smile widened. 'Is that difficult for you to understand?'

'That you kissed me for no other reason than you
wanted to? After,' he continued, 'you made me think it
was because some woman was looking at us? After you
just about jumped off a bus to keep from touching me?'

'If I'd touched you, things would have got a lot worse
than a simple kiss.' She was completely serious now.
And then came the switch. 'And if you want more proof
that I kissed you because I wanted to, the bus is actually a few metres down there. I moved us behind this
pillar while we were kissing. To be safe.'

She grinned. He couldn't help but smile back.

'You're diabolical.'

'Thank you,' she said sincerely. 'Now, if we don't

continue this charade, we'll have to go back to the beach, then go back to the hospital.' Something flickered in her eyes. 'I'd like to postpone that for a while longer.'

He studied her. 'Are you sure? I know you care about your family.'

'Zoey knows I'm with you. And she's keeping me up to date on everything.'

'You're not answering my question.'

She sighed. 'I do care about them. But today, I need a break. I want to keep doing stupid things with you so I don't have to feel bad about needing a break.' She gave him a sly smile. 'So—shall we pretend to be art critics in this museum?'

For the first time since they'd climbed off the bus, Parker realised they were standing in front of a museum. It made sense. The bus was a sightseeing one, after all. It stopped at tourist attractions all over the city. Now, it was affording him the opportunity to pretend to be an art critic. And so was she, with her pleas that echoed his own desires almost exactly. He understood, and didn't judge her for it. Which was probably why he agreed to her suggestion and opened himself up to acting a fool.

He'd never had more fun.

'You know, this is so amazingly African,' Sophia said, her arms folded in the posture she'd assumed in her 'pretentious art critic' role. 'Do you see the bright colours, the slashes of the paintbrush? So bold, so inspiring.'

Parker struggled to hold back his laugh. She was looking at a plain blue canvas with some white strokes. He cleared his throat.

'What's most amazing to me personally is the depth of—' He stopped, unsure of where he was going.

'Of character?'

'Yes,' he said eagerly, grabbing on to the lifeline Sophia offered. 'You took the term right out of my mouth, Professor Roux.'

'Honestly, Professor Jones, it's the least I can do. You did, after all, inspire this piece with your article on depth and colour in African art.'

Parker laughed, turned it into a cough when a group of tourists moved closer. Sophia turned to them.

'Have you ever seen such depth?' she asked them, waving a hand toward the painting. 'I've always been jealous of the art Professor Jones has managed to elicit from his students. Brava, Professor. Brava.'

Because laughter was coming out in peals at this point, and the tourists seemed genuinely interested in the art piece, Parker walked away. In the distance, he heard Sophia identify it as him being overcome by the emotions of the piece. He laughed again, before entering into a new exhibit.

This one was nothing like the paintings he'd looked at and felt nothing about. No, the moment he walked into this room, reverence stole his breath. The walls were adorned with black and white photos of families. Different races, different cultures. Different definitions of family. There was a picture of four women, clearly of different generations. The plaque beneath the photo said that the men had gone off to fight in a war. They'd never returned. Next to it hung a picture of three young children. The oldest of them couldn't have been more than twelve. Their parents had died of AIDS, and though they lived with their grandmother now, she was too old to care for them properly. The twelve-year-old did most of the work.

He felt guilty then, that it was the third picture that choked him up. It was a picture of a mother and son. The father had died of cancer years before, and they'd been taking care of one another for most of the child's life. There was no resentment on either of their faces, only resolute emotion. Acceptance. They had no problem with it.

He wondered what would happen if a father walked back into their lives. Would it break their union? Would it change things?

He was worried—selfishly, if he thought about what they faced now with his mother's diagnosis—that that had happened to him and his mother six years ago. When he'd come home that one night to find his parents talking in the kitchen, his father's new wife sipping tea at the counter, he'd felt as if he'd interrupted something. Never in his life had he felt that way with his mother before. Worse yet was that it had been caused by a man who'd walked out on them. Who'd left them to fend for themselves when he'd had a cushy life.

Perhaps that was why his resentment for his father ran so deep. His reappearance had changed things. He'd learnt after that night that his parents had been talking for months before Wade had come to visit. Penny had met his wife and had, according to her, forgiven Wade for walking out. Which wasn't unbelievable. Despite what they'd been through, Penny hadn't blamed Wade for it.

'I was just as stupid as he was that night,' she'd told

him one birthday, when he'd been old enough to understand what she was talking about. The year after Wade
had stood Parker up.

'But you couldn't walk away,' Parker said softly.

She smiled. 'Well, there's the difference. I didn't
want to.'

Why did he? Parker almost asked. But he didn't. He
hadn't wanted to upset her. And then she'd welcomed
Wade back into their lives and Parker had wished he
had asked it. She might not have been so eager to let
him in if he had.

The disease isn't what will take her from you, an
inner voice whispered. He stilled. All amusement, all
humour that he'd cultivated with Sophia in the last two
hours vanishing.

'Do you like them?'

He started, not recognising the soft voice. When he
turned, he realised that was because he didn't recognise its owner. She was tiny, her head barely reaching his chest, her long dark hair in a plait that fell over
her shoulder. There was something soft about her, too,
something that told him the voice suited the woman
perfectly.

She was peering at him with piercing eyes, waiting
for an answer.

'Oh,' he said, then realised he was saying it in response to his own thoughts. Fighting a flush, he nodded.
'Yeah, they're beautiful. Chilling, actually.'

'Really?' She looked at the one behind him, beam-
ing. 'That's exactly what I was going for.'

'You took these?'

'Yes. I shouldn't ask people what they think, to be

honest with you. My husband says it's asking for trouble. Most of the time, I agree. But other times, when I see people looking at them so intensely, I can't resist.'

He laughed. 'I agree with your husband. Though I suppose I'd feel the same way if I saw someone reading my work in that way.'

'You're a writer?'

'A journalist,' he confirmed. 'Mostly digital stuff, and mostly human-interest stories. Hence the appeal of your photos.'

An idea sparked. 'Hey, would you be interested in letting me write a piece about you? About this?'

'Really?' She reached up, gripping the end of her plait. 'I would love that.'

'Great.' He smiled. 'Let's begin with your name.'

She found Parker talking to another woman.

They were standing around a table, a phone on the surface in front of them. Parker was taking notes. The woman's head barely made it to the top of the table. She was one of those annoyingly petite women who looked cute no matter what they did.

Not that she cared. Of course not. The fact that she'd never found a petite woman annoying in her life didn't mean anything. So what if she'd grown up in a house filled with women and appreciated the range of shapes they came in? It didn't matter. This didn't matter.

Oh, no.

She had to admit, it gave her pause. She was *jealous*. The unfamiliar feeling clawed its way up her spine. It felt exactly as petty as she imagined it would, and she knew she couldn't allow it to grab hold of her tongue.

She couldn't imagine what it would do with such power. Especially in a woman who was already considered mean, even by the people who knew her best.

Identifying it had allowed her to see beneath that petty layer of it though. She wasn't jealous merely because he was speaking to another woman. Fortunately, she hadn't ventured so far beyond what she thought she knew about herself. No, she was jealous because for a brief moment, she'd wondered if this was the kind of woman Parker should be with.

It made no sense since she and Parker weren't…anything. It made no sense because the question had echoed through her head in Zoey's voice.

She isn't mean, Soph, Zoey's voice said. *She's like Angie. Parker should be with someone like Angie.*

Her spine stiffened, but she forced herself to look at the woman again. She looked nice. It might not have been a description Parker believed could be used on people, but it felt exactly right with this woman. She smiled a lot. Made gestures with her hands. Her face was animated, and she laughed when Parker said something. The laugh was nice, too, like the music of a xylophone. None of it seemed pretentious, or like she was interested in Parker.

It should have soothed Sophia's ruffled emotions, but it only served to make them worse. She didn't like comparing herself to random women. It was a recent occurrence—something she did as of five minutes ago—and it pissed her off. Comparison implied a feeling of inferiority. But she was who she was; there was nothing inferior about her.

'Soph,' Parker said, finally lifting his head. 'I'm sorry, I didn't see you.'

She didn't reply.

'How long have you been standing there?'

Again, she didn't reply. Quite honestly, she didn't know. She'd been lost in her head, in her observations, and she hadn't been keeping track of time. But the woman at Parker's side said, 'We've been talking for at least forty minutes.'

'Forty?' Parker repeated. His eyes widened. 'I'm sorry. I didn't realise.'

'It's fine,' she replied, finally able to speak. 'What were you doing?'

'I got Lisa to agree to an interview. She took all of these photos.'

Sophia looked around, talent jumping out at her before her mind could taint the observation with jealousy.

'Wow,' she said. 'You're good.'

Lisa blushed prettily. 'Thank you. I'm sorry—did I hear Parker call you Soph?'

'It's Sophia,' she said, moving forward. She held out a hand. 'It's nice to meet you, Lisa.'

'Likewise.' Lisa shook her hand and turned back to Parker. 'I think we're done here?'

'We are.'

'Great. Send me the link when the story comes out.'

'I will.'

Lisa greeted them both and left the room. There were other people walking around, though not nearly enough to ease the tension between her and Parker. He didn't say anything, only gathered up his things on the table.

When he met her eyes, he opened his mouth, but she cut him off.

'If we leave now, we can get the bus that'll be here in five minutes.'

She turned around and walked without checking that he was behind her. A part of her told her it was petty. She ignored it. Her mind couldn't saturate her with jealousy and then have parts that wanted to be reasonable. That wasn't the way it worked.

You're being stubborn.

It was her father's voice in her head this time. It said the thing her father had told her time and time again, though never did it entail her being stubborn with herself. Which didn't matter. What did was that he was calling her out. Again. Even though he was dead.

She smiled. Thought that anyone looking at her might have thought her unstable because of it. She didn't care. If she couldn't amuse herself with the memories of her father, then she couldn't give the anger, the frustration, the love the time of day either. Besides, it reminded her of the nuances again. Her relationship with her father wasn't conventional, but it was interesting. And she missed it. Even on the days she hated him for causing the complicated dynamics in their family, she missed him.

He would have told her the truth now.

She might not compare herself to random women often, but she did it with Angie all the time. The fact that it was spreading to random women told her she was letting it mess with her head. Or that she was letting Parker mess with her head. Either way, she couldn't get upset with Zoey for doing it when she did it herself.

She knew she wasn't doing it because she thought less of herself, or expected more of herself. It wasn't for the sake of her self-esteem. Rather, it was for the sake of her family's needs. She thought they needed Angie and what she offered them. They implied it all the time— but perhaps they only did because she allowed them to. Perhaps they were simply following her example.

Thinking about it kept her occupied for the first few minutes of the bus trip. The bus struggled up the winding hill that led to Table Mountain, the traffic not helping the situation. Sophia didn't try to speak with Parker, or distract either of them by speaking over the microphone. Since the bus was a hop-on, hop-off bus, none of the passengers were the same as their first trip. The day was drawing to a close slowly, early afternoon turning into late afternoon. Sophia wondered if her niece had been born yet.

Would it change things, having a niece? Would she be a different person as an aunt than she was as a sister? A daughter? The answer should be yes, since she wasn't at the hospital, waiting for her niece to be born. As a daughter and sister, she usually set aside her own feelings and let theirs take precedence.

Today, she wasn't doing that. Maybe the answer *was* yes then; maybe her not being at the hospital was a symbol that she was putting up boundaries. Would she do that with her niece, too? Did that make her selfish?

'You're upset with me.'

She was shaking her head before she realised what she was doing. It had been to clear out her thoughts rather than to deny his words. She didn't clarify that to him.

'Look,' he said with a sigh. 'I saw those incredible photographs and couldn't resist the opportunity to write about Lisa's experiences taking them. I...needed to hear her stories.'

'Good eye.'

'Oh,' he said. There was a long pause before he said, 'You're not upset about that?'

'Why would I be upset by that?' she asked easily. 'You were doing your job. And you weren't trying to kill me in the process this time.'

Parker rolled his eyes. 'Why are you acting so aloof then?'

'Aloof?' She tilted her head. 'I don't think I've ever been described that way.'

'I don't think that's true.' When she looked at him, he elaborated. 'When you don't like something, or you're uncomfortable, you get distant.' He frowned. 'It must have come up? With your family? At your job?'

'My family doesn't see distant. They see mean,' she reminded him. 'And I'm in Human Resources for a finance company, so no one's going to evaluate me based on my personality there. At least not to my face.'

His frown deepened. She sighed.

'Once again, you're thinking about how that career doesn't suit me.'

'Actually, I was thinking that might be the perfect career for you. You get to tell people what to do without being responsible for them doing it.'

It was her turn to frown. 'I don't know if you're insulting me, or complimenting me. Also, how do you even know that?'

He gave her a serene smile. 'You take care of your family, but they exasperate you because they see you as a drill sergeant, not a human being. Inference,' he said with a smirk now. 'I pay attention.' There was a brief pause. 'That's how I know you were upset back there.'

'Back to this?' she muttered, though she was still trying to wrap her head around how he was able to see through her.

'I'd like to know.'

She wanted to answer, but the idea of admitting what had happened—her jealousy and her revelations—made her feel oddly vulnerable.

'Sophia,' he said softly. 'Tell me.'

To her horror, her cheeks began to burn.

'Are you blushing?' he asked, the tone of his voice changing. 'Why would you be—' He broke off, and a wide smile claimed his lips. 'Soph, were you *jealous*?'

She didn't reply.

She did bristle.

'You *were* jealous!' he exclaimed. 'Amazing.'

'Don't be obnoxious, Parker,' she said, refusing to look at him. 'It's unbecoming of a gentleman.'

'I'm not a gentleman.' He grinned. He was too happy about this. 'I can't believe you're jealous.'

'Me neither,' she offered darkly.

'Why are you?'

'I—' She hesitated. 'I don't know,' she replied, going for the safe answer.

'Should we try and figure it out?'

'No.'

'You're in love with me.'

She snorted.

'Fine, not in love, but in lust.'

She pulled her face.

'You're interested,' he finally settled on. 'Regardless of what you say, you're interested.'

Sighing, she nodded.

'Wow,' he said, sitting back. 'I didn't expect that.'

'Don't worry, nothing will come of it.'

'I'm not worried.' He paused. 'Why not?'

'My life became infinitely more complicated this morning. So did yours.'

His expression locked, but not before she saw the hurt it hid. She sighed.

'Look, Parker...' She tried to formulate the words, then figured nothing she said would sound right anyway. So she just said it. 'Dating is the last thing you think about when you're taking care of someone.'

'Speaking from experience?'

'*Yes*,' she said empathically, grateful he saw it. 'I haven't dated in the last five years. My last boyfriend—'

She broke off. It felt strange talking about her last relationship with Parker, though it was how she knew they didn't have a future together. Besides, with all the things going through her head at the moment? She couldn't figure out the dynamics of a new relationship in all that. Hell, she could barely figure out the dynamics of her current relationships. Sure, those were with her family, but she couldn't imagine a new romantic relationship would be easier. Especially when she added family complications—his and hers—to that.

She met his eyes. 'A relationship needs time and

work. It won't be a priority for either of us when we get back to the hospital. Less so when you get home and realise your mom needs time and work, too. Trust me.' The bus stopped with a slight lurch. Sophia looked up. 'Come on. Let's go see our city from the mountain.'

Chapter Ten

They were at the top of the world. So why did he feel like everything was crashing down around them?

He was being dramatic, he thought, looking at the spectacular view of Cape Town from the top of Table Mountain. It had taken them an hour to get there, the line had been so long. It had been made longer by the silence he and Sophia had stood in. But now it felt worth it.

Vast blueness stretched out on his left, the city and its building and infrastructure on the right. He'd been there all of twice in his lifetime. Once, when he'd been a kid and they'd gone as part of a school trip. The second had been two years later, on his birthday. The birthday his father had stood him up at.

He'd begged his mother to take him. His father had had a client in town, and he wouldn't be able to pick them up in time. His mother had been reluctant, not more so than usual since his father's reappearance on his birthdays. At least it hadn't seemed that way to him. But she must have known something was up because she'd called Wade before they'd left. The conversation had quickly gone from normal conversational tones to hushed whispers.

By then, Parker had known what those whispers meant. He'd gone to his room, put on some music, and ignored his mother's calls. When she'd knocked on the door, he hadn't answered. She'd opened it then—Penny had always been a 'my house, my rules' kind of mother until he'd become an adult and begun to help pay the bills—and lowered to her haunches in front of him.

'We're going to the mountain,' she'd said.

'No, we're not.'

'Yeah, we are. You get to go for free on your birthday. Do you think I'm going to give up a free trip? Get ready. We're leaving in five.'

She'd got up, but he didn't move.

'Parker.'

'He's not going to be there.'

'So, what, baby? That doesn't mean you and I can't go. We deserve to go. You deserve to have a good birthday.' She lowered, kissed his forehead. 'I can show you the world, too, kid. Your dad isn't the only one who can go big on your birthday.'

A pang vibrated through his chest, and it took him a while to realise it came from the memory. He felt like there'd been so many memories that day. Perhaps he was making up for his mother. For the fact that before long, she wouldn't have them.

'Parker? A cable car's going down now. Do you want to leave?'

'No,' he replied. He walked a few metres away from her and sat on a bench that overlooked the ocean. He didn't comment when she lowered next to him.

'This is exactly the reason I don't date, by the way,'

she said nonchalantly. 'Some men get so precious about commitment when all I'm offering is to bone.'

'*What?*'

'I wanted to know if you were paying attention.'

'I was.'

'So I see.'

'What's the real reason you don't date?'

'Hmm.' That was all she said for a while. 'Priorities, I suppose. I was taking care of my father, and then Zoey and my mom. Dating… I don't know. It felt like another form of taking care of someone.'

'You've never had a boyfriend?'

'I told you I did.' There was another long pause. 'Lyle Carstens. We met during my first year at university. He was studying engineering; I was studying human resources. We had one class together—introduction to computers—which was compulsory for all first-year students. We sat next to each other and had basically the same facial expressions at the lecturer telling us how to use headings in Word.'

'That bonded you two together.'

'Initially.' She exhaled. 'Turned out we had some mutual friends, and we kissed at a party one night. We kind of fell into it after that, to be honest with you.'

'What changed?'

'My dad got sick.' She looked up, out into the distance. 'Things changed drastically at home then. Angie went into fix-it mode, which was her way of dealing with it. Mom didn't deal at all, spent all her time with my father, which had already been happening.' She took a breath. 'Zo was in her last year in school, so we wanted things to be as stable for her as we could. Angie and I picked up a lot of the slack at home with simple things like cooking and cleaning. Then more complicated things like my dad's hospital visits and so on.'

Ah, so this was why she'd been so unwavering about his mother's illness changing his life. About the priorities. He suspected he already knew the rest of the story, but he didn't push her. Only said, 'So you dealt with it by fixing things, too.'

'Yeah, I guess so.' She paused. 'It meant I was spending all of my free time at home, and anything outside of that wasn't a priority.' She shrugged. 'Lyle didn't like that. Which felt like evidence that dating was another form of taking care of people's feelings. We broke up.'

'It's not taking care of people's feelings. It's respecting them. It's a choice to care for them and have them care about you in return.'

Sophia pulled her face. 'See, time and work.' She let out a small huff of air. 'I don't do either of that well.'

'You did fine with your family.'

'I'm here with you instead of with my family, Parker. Does that seem fine to you?'

'I'm here with you instead of with my mother. I guess I'm the last person to talk.'

There was a long silence.

He knew he was being a hypocrite, giving Sophia advice on relationships when he shared many of her views. Except his opinion centred more on wanting someone to show they cared—and being disappointed when they didn't. Having that disappointment throw emotions into disarray. Fighting to get them back on track.

Maybe he wasn't giving advice because he disagreed.

Maybe he simply knew what relationships were supposed to look like.

When the silence extended, he kept waiting, because he knew Sophia wanted to ask him something, but was fighting her natural instinct to let him brood. He wasn't sure how he knew that with such certainty. The fact that he did should have pushed him further away from her. Instead, he wanted to pull her in close and plug fingers into the holes she'd poked into the future they couldn't have together.

'Okay,' she said after a moment. 'You're waiting for me to ask the question, and I'm waiting for you to answer it. I'm going to ask because it's annoying to keep waiting and I'm tired of constantly being annoyed with you.' There was a quick beat. 'Well, not tired of it entirely. There's a certain kind of annoyance that's not too much, not too little. That's my comfortable place with you.'

'You're talking a lot,' he noted with a grin.

'Yes, keep doing that. It's taking me right to my sweet spot.'

He opened his mouth, but she lifted a hand.

'I'm aware of how that sounds. Just answer the question.'

'You didn't ask a question.'

'Yes, I asked—' She broke off. Rolled her eyes. 'Okay. Why don't you want to go back down?'

'It'll mean returning to reality.'

'What specifically? I mean, I know the stuff with your mom is a lot. And I'm not judging you, considering I'm with you and literally asked you to distract me. But you know we can't run forever.'

'I'm not running from it. Not really. My mom was sleeping this morning when I left. She was sleeping when I got back. I didn't have the chance to speak with her, so I'm not abandoning her.'

'But you are running from something.'

'The anger,' he answered, because it was right there, on the tip of his tongue. 'I'm angry at her.'

'Because she's sick?'

'What? No.' He emphasised it with a shake of his head. 'No, I'm not angry because she's sick.'

'Are you sure?' she asked quietly. 'With my dad, I was angry. At him for getting sick. And then for dying.'

Her head jolted to the side, a quick, slight movement. He waited for her to figure it out. Tried to figure out whether his anger had anything to do with his mother's illness.

It did, he thought. Though it made absolutely no sense, he was. Upset that she'd got one of the worst illnesses possible. He'd seen too many television programmes to pretend like he didn't know what was coming next. She would begin to forget small things at first. She already had.

To check the time so she would get to work punctually. Or to put on an item of clothing that would put her morning routine out of sync and cause her to be late. She'd forgotten some of the routine at the store, too. It would disorientate her at first, panic her soon after. She'd forgotten her favourite recipes. Small things that didn't really matter in the larger scheme of things. Small things that eventually added up.

They were a precursor to big things. She'd forget their time together. She'd forget what they'd been through together. There was a part of him that wondered if she already had. Having his father in the mix would make a lot more sense then. She'd forgotten what his absence had put them through. Him through. Maybe that was why she was welcoming Wade back.

And when she was gone, she'd leave Parker to welcome Wade back in her stead. He wasn't sure he could do that. Didn't know if he wanted to. He was anticipating her asking the question, and he worried that he wouldn't be able to tell her the answer she wanted to hear.

All of it made him angry. Anger was better than the sadness, the complete panic at the thought of losing her.

'I'm sorry,' she said eventually. 'I got…lost.'

'Want to talk about it?'

She took a breath. 'If I say no, are you going to keep what you've just realised to yourself and continue brooding?'

He almost laughed. 'If I keep it to myself, I promise I won't brood.'

'Then no, I'd rather not talk about it.'

'Sure.'

She shifted, looking back at the line to get the next cable car. Then she turned, looked back over the ocean, and relaxed.

'Take your time,' she said.

'You're not in a rush to get back to reality?'

'Reality's overrated.'

He laughed, and they sat in silence.

He didn't realise how much he needed it until they were doing it. Here, on top of the world, there were none of the sounds that punctuated even a quiet day. Traffic noises didn't come up that high, nor did the busyness of people going about their lives. There was some shuffling around them, some conversation, but it was rare, as if the mountain weaved a spell of silence over its visitors.

At some point, their hands found one another and linked. At another, Sophia shifted into his side. His arm lifted easily, automatically, drawing her closer until he could feel the softness of her curved around his upper body. His breathing changed, grew heavier, as if his lungs understood that there was magic happening between them, too.

He wanted to blame it on being under the mountain's spell again, but the truth was that he was under Sophia's spell. She was a cranky witch, stubborn and contrary, but she made a potent potion. Powerful, too.

'Even if I wasn't doing a story with Lisa,' he said softly, deeply enchanted, 'you would have no need to be jealous.'

'I know.' She straightened, curling her legs under her. Their hands were still linked. She made no move to pull away. 'There's no reason to be jealous.'

He lifted a hand, brushed at the curls flopping over her forehead. 'Exactly. How could I see her when my eyes are stuck on you?'

Her lips curved. 'I meant that there's nothing here, between us, so there's no need to be jealous. And that was too cheesy for you to have said with a straight face.'

'You're the one who told me you were interested,' he reminded her. 'And I said it with a straight face because it's true. I'm…interested.'

'Interest isn't enough.'

'What about interest and attraction?' he asked, leaning closer.

Her eyes dipped from his eyes to his lips, then lifted again.

'Maybe we should test that attraction one more time…'

She had never been the pursuer. In her relationship with Lyle, she let him do the work. In the brief flirtations she'd shared outside of that, she hadn't participated much. Partly because she hadn't been interested in doing more work, and partly because it served as a great test. If they were eager enough to wade through her boundaries—the ones she constructed with sarcasm and, she easily admitted, annoyance—it meant they'd be willing to put in the work elsewhere.

She rarely got the opportunity to prove that hypothesis. If they stuck around, they often said something so stupid that she couldn't, in good conscience, reward it. She wouldn't claim that her body was a reward out loud, of course. She was aware of the implications. She also knew that she was worthy of whatever the hell she wanted, and that it was her body, so she could think of it in any way she wanted.

But none of that mattered now, with Parker. Both of the two times they'd kissed before had been because she'd pushed it. They were about to kiss now because of her. If her body was a reward, she hadn't made Parker work very hard to earn it. Or perhaps it was simply because he hadn't expected it that made her want to give it.

She pulled back. 'Do you want to do this?'

He looked at her as if she'd asked him to help her cook a meal on the mountain. 'Yes.'

'Are you just saying that, or do you mean it?'

'Soph,' he said with a soft smile. 'Shut up and kiss me.'

She smiled and leaned forward. Their lips touched. She could have sworn the mountain parted beneath her and she was falling into a hole of contentment.

She had that same feeling in her stomach that she had whenever she fell. That drop, that anticipation of landing. His tongue swept into her mouth and the shock of it, still, after two times, told her she'd landed. It reverberated through her body, sending tiny jolts of pleasure through her. The hair on her skin stood on end, the cells of it eagerly waiting to be rewarded for their attention. But Parker touched only her face with his hand, not acknowledging the extent of her desire for him.

She didn't rush it either, curious as she felt the shift between them. He was in control now; he set the pace. Before, it had been eager, desperate. Now, she tasted only patience in the strokes of his tongue.

Had he been lured in by the steadiness of the mountain? Of sitting above the world, gaining a perspective that dictated appreciation? Or perhaps he was sweeping them into a romance she hadn't known she wanted until that moment. For an hour, she'd been granted the gift of seeing the city she loved in a completely different way. It reminded her of how fragile things were; of how trying to control it meant nothing. Not when she was so far away from her life. When all the things she'd been hurt by, or offended by, sat kilometres away.

Parker changed the angle then, and her brain went

blank. His tongue stroked more leisurely, more deeply. A low, hungry groan rumbled from his mouth. His free hand rested on her waist, just below her breast. His thumb shifted up, touching the underwire of her bra, barely pressing into the swell that fell over the wire. It was a tease, and it immediately made her want more. His hand on her breast, teasing. Showing her skills she had no doubt he had. Or no, his thumb, brushing over her nipple. Then again, and again, before his mouth followed, and his tongue.

She drew back with a gasp, but not far enough to break the intimacy.

'Are you a wizard?' she said, her chest heaving in and out.

He smiled, his hand sliding down to the middle of her waist, his other brushing her hair again. 'Strange you should ask.' There was a hoarseness in his voice that pleased her. 'I was thinking the same thing about you, though I'd called you a witch.'

Her cheek lifted. 'I'm whichever one is more powerful.'

His smile widened. 'Which spell did I cast?'

'You put…images, into my head.'

'In that case, I am a wizard.' The smile went from flirtatious to self-satisfied. 'That's exactly what I was trying to do.'

'It worked.'

'Were they vivid?'

She knew the game he was playing. She thought by now he'd know she wouldn't let him win.

'Very.'

'What did they entail?'

She leaned forward, put her mouth next to his ear. 'How good are you with your tongue?'

She angled her head so she could look at him, and smiled at the shock on his face. When she sat back, she patted his knee.

'I'm happy to take the answer when you have it.'

He still didn't reply. She grinned.

'Come on, let's get in line to go back down.'

He followed her wordlessly. She hadn't thought she'd been that provocative, but clearly she underestimated herself. Again. Apparently, she didn't realise how what she said was perceived by people. According to her sisters, at least.

Angie had always told her that, with Zoey agreeing in the background. Though Zoey hadn't been so much in the background today. Sophia tested the thought. She expected the resentment or anger she'd been experiencing that day whenever she thought of her sisters to come. Either about what Angie represented to her family, what they compared Sophia to because of it, or about Zoey's newfound attitude. But those emotions didn't come. Instead, there was an acceptance. A resignation, even. She didn't know what it meant. Or how Parker had helped. She only knew he had.

They got the next cable car down the mountain in silence. Somehow, a switch from attraction to emotion had been made. Unsurprisingly, her emotions were tangled up in her family. In Parker, too, but she ignored those knots. She thought about how her mother must have been wondering where she was. Charlene might have been focusing on Angie that day, but Sophia had pushed the boundaries. She also left Zoey alone to deal with their mother. Angie probably wouldn't know that Sophia wasn't there though. If she did, she wouldn't care. She'd be thinking about her baby. About becoming a mother.

She shook her head at the enormity of it. Her sister was going to be a mother. She might even already be a mother, since Zo had messaged that Angie's labour had begun to progress more rapidly. Sophia had no reception on the mountain, so she might get back to the ground and discover she was an aunt.

Holy crap.

Her hands had already been on the railing of the cable car; now her grip tightened. The car was entirely enclosed by glass, allowing its passengers a stunning view of the city.

The misshapen buildings became more focused, the traffic less like ants, more like discernible vehicles. When they reached the bottom, they had to take stairs back down to the road. It was only when they were on the ground, waiting for the bus, that Parker spoke again.

'Let me show you.'

Chapter Eleven

'What?'

'Let me show you,' he said, lowering his voice.

People were milling all around them since Table Mountain was such a popular tourist destination. There were some people who had no conception of personal space either. He assumed they were waiting for the bus, but did they have to wait so close to him and Sophia? He was trying to seduce a woman here.

He didn't take a moment to feel the emotions rippling in his chest at that admission.

'Again, I have no idea what you want to show me.'

He dropped his head until his mouth was next to her ear. 'How good I am with my tongue.'

'Oh.'

It was all she said. She blinked a lot though, a range of comical expressions crossing her face. Well, they'd be comical if she weren't responding to his suggestion. If his stomach wasn't doing loops, a feeling of dread bouncing there.

She swallowed, opened her mouth, but the bus arrived then, and they got on it, taking the stairs to the top level.

'I have thoughts,' she said when they were seated and the bus started moving.

'Okay?'

'There's a big part of me that feels guilty about not being at the hospital.'

He nodded, because he understood. Felt the same.

'There's a bigger part that knows Zoey will message me when Angie's baby's born.' Her eyes were bright. He couldn't tell if it was from emotion or anticipation. 'If I go back now, I'll probably wait for an indefinite amount of time. Again.' There was a brief pause. 'And I'd be thinking about you, and how much I would have liked to agree to your proposition.'

'What are you saying?'

'I think… I want to agree.'

'You think?'

'Well, yes. Because I'm not one hundred per cent sure this decision is the best one. Not because I don't think what we'd do wouldn't be amazing, but because we both know it can't go anywhere.'

It was a lot to think about, and he gave her props for being able to do so. In all honesty, he'd lost some of his brain functioning when he'd started considering how he could convince her he was good with his tongue. Now that he could process what she was saying, he knew her concerns were valid. Familiar. And he wanted her to make the right decision, regardless of what that would be.

'You don't have to say yes.'

'I want to,' she replied softly. 'I have to, actually.'

'No, you don't.'

'Not because I feel coerced.' She bumped her shoul-

der against his. 'But because I need to do things for me.
I need…boundaries.'

'And making out with a guy you met today is you
establishing those boundaries?'

She smiled. 'Yeah, I think so.'

His lips curved in response. Somehow, her figuring things out had made him want her more. Which
encouraged him to forget his own reason to say no.
'Okay then.'

'Okay. Unless…' She turned to him, narrowing her
eyes suspiciously. 'Unless this is one of those times
where you're proposing something to see if I would do
it, and not because you really want to do it.'

'No,' he said with a choked laugh. 'I don't know
why you'd think I'd do that. No,' he repeated. 'I really
want to do it.'

'Okay,' she said again, breath shuddering through
her lips.

'Sophia.' He waited until she looked at him. 'This
isn't a test. For either of us.'

'Isn't it?'

'No.' He took her hand. 'We can want each other and
still love our families.'

She squeezed his fingers. 'I know.'

'And I was asking your permission because you don't
have to do anything you don't want to.'

'Permission? Was that what that was?' she asked, her
voice back to its usual dry tone. 'And here I thought I
was being propositioned.'

'They aren't mutually exclusive.'

She turned her head, eyes sweeping over his face. 'I
see that. With you,' she clarified.

He wondered how many others hadn't given her the opportunity to see it. It took all his self-control not to clench his free fingers into a fist.

'Are you nervous?' he asked.

'Aren't you?'

His hand almost lifted to that spinning in his chest. 'Yes.'

'And you still want to do this?'

'Yes.'

'Me, too.' She paused. 'Is that why you asked me whether I'm nervous? Because you are?'

'Yes. And in case we weren't nervous for the same reasons.'

'Why are you nervous?'

'I…like you.'

The skin between her brows creased. 'That makes you nervous?'

'It makes me worry about wanting you and liking you.'

Especially when he couldn't afford either beyond that day.

'You know,' she said, after a few minutes had gone by. 'You've never told me about your dating life.'

'I didn't have much time for it,' he answered. 'My mom needed help at home. I work two jobs to help pay the bills. I try to pull my weight with the chores. Relationships take time.'

'*Now* you think so,' she said wryly. 'Was there no one while you helped your mom?'

'I didn't say that,' he said with a curve of his lips. 'There were women who came and went. Some stayed longer than others.'

'What does longer mean?'

'Eight months? Ten?'

'Ten months?' she repeated.

'How long did you date Lyle?'

'Eleven months.'

'So your longest relationship beat mine by a month. You can hardly claim superiority because of that.'

'I guess not.' She went quiet for a while. 'But my life changed very suddenly, and very obviously. My dad got sick. There was no event in your life that changed things for you.'

'No one event, maybe. But I had a string of examples— Wait, how has this turned into a judgement of my character?'

'It's not. It's just…'

'Yeah,' he said when she didn't finish. 'It's that *just* part that makes me think you're judging me.'

'I'm not judging you.' Her voice was sincere. 'But I am glad to know that interest and attraction aren't enough to build a relationship on.'

He locked his jaw. He was thankful for it, though it was a little painful, because it kept him from pointing out that there was more between them than interest and attraction. There was an emotional connection that had them talking about things strangers didn't talk about. There was a slight animosity that ramped up the tension and kept them both on their toes.

But pointing that out would imply he thought she was wrong. He didn't. Nor did he want a relationship with her. He had too much on his plate to forge a new relationship. And his views on relationships hadn't changed—despite the fact that she tempted him. The only temptation he would give in to was physical. There could be nothing else.

There *would* be nothing else.

They didn't speak for the rest of the trip. It was longer than the others they'd had on the bus since they didn't get off at any of the tourist attractions. It took an hour to get back to the beach. The traffic had subsided by then, so they got to the main road fairly quickly.

'Where to?' Parker asked into the silence.

'The hospital, I guess. What?' she asked after a pause.

'I didn't say anything.'

'Yeah, but you made this sound…' He couldn't recall making any sound. 'Say what you're thinking, Parker.'

'I wasn't thinking anything.'

'Parker.' Her voice had gone so low he would categorise it as a growl.

'Honestly—' He broke off with a sigh. 'I think it's funny that you got into my car because you didn't want to be with your family, and now you're heading back to your family because you don't want to be with me.'

'That's not it.'

'No?'

'No. You've been acting weird and I figured you'd retracted your offer from earlier.'

'My… Oh.'

She snorted. 'Nice try, pretending you forgot.'

'I did.'

He hadn't, but he thought it was the gentlemanly thing to pretend he had. He was rarely a gentleman, though his attempt was mitigated by the fact that pretence only seemed to add to her frustrations. Life was all about balance, after all.

'Hmm'

'What?' he asked.

'I'm trying to figure out whether I want a commitment-phobe *and* a liar in my bed.'

The car swerved, but he changed lanes and hoped it seemed natural. 'I'm neither of those things.'

'And this lying thing seems compulsive, too. Like you can't help it.'

'Where am I driving to, Sophia?' he asked, more harshly than he'd intended.

'My house.'

His grip tightened on the steering wheel. 'Can you tell me where your house is?'

She rattled off an address, before telling him she'd give him directions as they went along. But that wasn't for the longest time, and with each passing second of silence, the ball of nerves in his stomach grew. There was an ache lower in his body as well. It seemed to be anticipating the possibility of being soothed.

The thought made him grip the steering wheel even harder.

He wasn't the kind of guy who gave in to his physical compulsions. He'd never had a one-night stand before, which was what this would essentially be. Probably because he liked to make sure everyone's expectations were where they needed to be: no future, no long-term relationship. Just a short-term, 'you scratch my back, I scratch yours' kind of thing. He learned from the eight—or was it ten?—months he spent with his ex-girlfriend that expectations should be managed as early as possible to avoid disappointment. Since that didn't generally happen over the course of one night, one-night stands weren't a go-to thing.

What was different about Sophia, then? Something must have been for him to have met her that day, and now be driving to her house. Was it that he knew she was honest? That she'd been clear about her expectations and he believed her? Maybe it was that they had so much in common. Their other responsibilities that took preference over a relationship. Yes. That must be it. So why didn't it ring entirely true?

His basal desires told him he needed to stop overthinking things. Who overthought things when they were about to get laid anyway? He snuck a glance at Sophia. She seemed surprisingly calm, considering the nerves she'd shown on the bus. Considering the concerns she'd articulated on the bus.

'You're not nervous anymore?'

'What do you think we're going to do once we get to my house?' she asked, shifting toward him.

'I…um…we…'

She laughed softly. His skin prickled.

'Don't be afraid, Parker,' she said. 'I'll be gentle.'

'Stop screwing with me.'

'I thought that's what you wanted me to do?' she asked lightly. He gave her a dark look. She sighed. 'Okay, look. I am nervous. The way I deal with my nerves is by pretending not to be nervous. And with sarcasm and all that.' She waved a hand.

'We don't have to do this.'

'I've already told you I'm in,' she said.

'I want you to know your options.'

'I do.' There was a small break in tension when she pointed out a turn he had to take. 'I'm partly asking you to take me home because I need a shower. And maybe a nap.' She paused. 'I need to be somewhere comfortable.'

He softened. 'I'll drop you off.'

'No,' she said immediately. 'No.' She took a deep breath. 'I need you there, too.'

She'd admitted to needing Parker. She'd told him he made her feel comfortable. She'd asked him inside of her house, told him to wait in her bedroom, and had taken a shower. Yet *now* the nerves were catching up to her. *Now*, standing in her towel with only her underwear on, she was wondering if she'd done the right thing.

To be fair, the fact that the underwear was even with her in the bathroom told her that she'd been nervous before. She put a bra and panty on—simple cotton, though they were a cute turquoise colour that popped against her skin—as protection. Not the kind they might need in a couple of minutes, she thought, as her brain self-destructed, but it was armour.

There was nothing wrong with a bit of armour.

The towel was wrapped around her; still, she gripped it between her breasts, holding on for dear life. She made her way to her bedroom, trying to ignore the pictures in the hallway. It had been Angie's idea when she came back. Her sister had put up a variety of pictures, some from when their parents had been dating, from their wedding, their marriage. Others were of her, Angie, and Zoey, at various ages, being forced to take pictures together.

Unavoidable, Sophia thought, as their ages were so

close. There was a two-year gap between her and Angie, and a one-year gap between her and Zoey. It translated to lots of pictures of the three of them wearing identical outfits, being forced into the same activities, and all around being treated as if they were the same children.

When she reached her bedroom, she sighed, relieved to be away from the judging eyes of her past self. She was sure her future self would judge her, too, but that wasn't Present Sophia's concern. Present Sophia wanted to make out with a man she'd met that day. She also didn't want to think about the fact that what she was about to do was probably a mistake. Present Sophia was all about feeling and not thinking.

She found Parker examining the jewellery on the shelf above her computer. It had been out of necessity since she owned too many earrings, but not enough space. She'd taken a piece of polystyrene foam, prettied it up, and hung her earrings there. Occasionally, an earring would drop on her head as she examined CVs, but she considered it an occupational hazard.

The hazard was working from home.

She leaned against the doorframe, studying him. He was so very tall, his body taking up so much space in her room. His shoulders were broad, and since his back faced her, she was granted a look at his spectacular butt. She had to give props to his jeans—well-worn and generous in affording spectators a view of said butt.

Nerves gave way to something more intoxicating, interrupted only when he began to speak.

'Did you intend on telling me you were standing there?' he asked. 'Or were you going to keep staring at me?'

'The latter, probably,' she replied with a smile. The nerves slowly returned, and her grip once again tightened on the towel. 'I see you've discovered I'm crafty.'

'Is this the only proof?' he asked, turning fully toward her and leaning against her desk. If he folded his arms, he'd look like a man at ease with seduction.

He folded his arms.

'I thought it was quite good,' she teased, despite the nerves in her tummy. 'Particularly since I'm not in the least bit creative. The very fact that I thought about it is a feat, honestly.'

'I'm not sure I would describe it as good, or that I'd call you crafty. I do think you're pragmatic, which in my opinion is better.'

'You're right, it is better.' She smiled. 'Do you like the rest of my room?'

He looked around at the blue walls; the canvas she'd put up that was mostly white, bar three different coloured tulips; the desk in the corner; her bed on the opposite side of the room; windows just above it.

He met her eyes. 'It's nice. I'd like it better if you were in it.'

She looked down at her feet, which were still standing on the threshold of the door. They took one small step forward.

'Happy?'

'Are you?'

'Please don't tell me this is how the entire—' she hesitated '—thing is going to go.'

'This *thing*—' his voice was heavy with humour '—goes however you want it to.'

Her feet moved again. And again, and again. Because

she was looking into his eyes and they shone with sincerity. And she trusted it. She *trusted* him. Which, if she was being honest with herself, was the reason she was standing in front of him at all. A short distance away, actually, her breath catching as she looked up and found his face not so far from hers.

'Slowly.'

The word burst from her mouth at, ironically, top speed.

'Show me.'

Her hands left the safety of her towel, reaching up and taking his face in her hands. His skin was warm. Her thumbs skimmed over his cheeks, as if brushing something away. She looked at him, wondering if he thought her strange for doing it. He didn't. There was no judgement in his eyes, only a surprising steadiness that had the attraction she felt for him turning into a whip.

She felt the first strike of it when she lowered her hands to his chest. It was magnificent, the broadness, the muscles beneath her fingers. A second strike came when she ran her hands down his torso, hooking her fingers into his jeans. She pulled him close in one quick movement. It had his body hitting hers with a force that took her breath away. But as her eyes rose to meet his, she knew her breath wouldn't have had a chance anyway.

'I think,' he said, his laboured breathing undermining the calm he spoke with, 'if we were in prison, this would mean I belonged to you.'

She smiled. 'That's the back pocket.'

'Is it?'

'Yes. Also, I think it would mean you're my bitch.'

His eyebrows rose. 'Is there a difference?'

'Maybe.' She pulled him closer, feeling his arousal against her belly. 'One of those things is happening here.'

He laughed lightly, lowering his head until their foreheads touched. 'This is a bad idea.'

'Which part?'

'All of it.'

His eyes lowered to her mouth. Almost automatically, her tongue pushed through her lips, wetting them. Desire claimed his features, giving him a primal look that had her looking for her breath again.

'I can't help you decide that,' she whispered. 'I think my brain…went on vacation.'

'How about we see if we can do that for your body, too?'

He slid an arm around her waist, closing the tiny space between them. The other lifted. He traced her hairline, her lips with his finger. Down, over her collarbone. He touched the skin just above the line of the towel. Her breasts were barely visible, but his fingers followed the swell of the top of them.

His head lifted. 'You're wearing a bra.'

She swallowed. 'Yes.'

'Why?'

'I…wasn't sure if I wanted to do this.'

'Are you now?'

'Eighty per cent.'

It had slipped from her lips, though she had no idea where it had come from. Though her mind had gone on vacation, it was still offering her images. Most of them entailed her lying on her bed, looking up at Parker as he looked down at her, and they took the plunge, so to speak. That didn't sound like someone who was only eighty per cent sure they wanted to make love to someone else.

Panic mingled with need, with desire. It probably came from the stupid twenty per cent.

'Hey,' he said, lifting her chin. 'There's nothing wrong with eighty per cent.'

'Yes, there is. This should be one hundred per cent.' Her frown deepened. 'Or doesn't that matter to you?'

He blinked. 'I didn't mean it like that. Do you want to stop?'

'How did you mean it?' she asked instead of answering. The truth was that she wasn't sure how to answer.

'It's stupid.'

'Tell me,' she urged softly.

'Promise not to laugh?' he asked. She nodded. 'Fine. I thought… I thought maybe you meant you only want to go…eighty per cent of the way.'

There was a long pause.

'Like, eighty per cent of the way *in*?'

'You promised not to laugh.'

'I'm not laughing,' she said, though she was. 'No, I'm sorry, I'm sorry,' she said again when he took a step back. She closed the space. 'For what it's worth, if you went eighty per cent of the way in, I'd probably give you the last twenty per cent for free.'

He groaned and she laughed again.

'You know that's not what I meant.'

'I do,' she said, her chuckles fading. 'How about we take it percentage by percentage? See where that gets us?'

He opened his arms. 'That sounds good to me.' He lowered his head, but before he kissed her, he said, 'We can stop whenever you want. Even if it's eighty per cent in.'

She grinned. 'Ditto.'

He smiled, then his lips were on hers.

Chapter Twelve

She was opening her mouth to him before their lips had fully touched. Surrendering the first percentage because she was sure it would be the toughest.

She wasn't sure why she was worried. It was like they'd kissed a million times before, though this was only the fourth time. But that didn't matter. Not as their tongues tangled, fighting a duel where they'd both emerge the winner. Especially as his hands tightened at her waist, gripping the flesh there.

She waited for the towel to fall off as it always did. Though it usually annoyed her, now it offered an excuse to reveal herself when pulling it off seemed too... active. In the end, it didn't matter. Parker took the ends of the towel at her front and parted them as if he were opening a gift.

She was never self-conscious in front of men, largely out of pure will. It had always felt like she was conceding power to them. She had been born into a society that did that anyway, and zero part of her wanted to play along. So it wasn't Parker seeing her body that was the problem; it was his expression that bothered her.

His face brightened as his eyes swept over her body.

There was a kind of awe there she'd only seen on tele-vision. Usually, the person was looking at something materialistic, like a car, or a piece of jewellery. Seeing it in reality now, while he looked at *her*, made her want to shuffle her feet. Or punch him in the face.

'How is it possible that you're so beautiful?'

'It's my witchy abilities,' she answered, though her voice was breathy and didn't at all belong to her. 'I'm very powerful. I can make you see perfection if I want to.'

'Are you doing it now?'

'Do you see any imperfections?'

His eyes went dark, and for a moment, Sophia wor-ried she'd said the wrong thing. The moment extended when his gaze lowered down her body again, somehow more intense than before.

'You have stretch marks,' he said softly. 'On your breasts.' He traced the light brown lines. 'On your hips.' He traced the lines there. 'There are these little dimples here, too.' His hands spread, taking the roundness of her hips in his palms.

He squeezed, and her breath, with its already tenuous occupation of her lungs, rushed through her lips. She sucked air in again, quietly, then forced herself to speak.

'Those dimples are called cellulite.'

'I know.' He kissed both hips. 'They're great for holding on to.'

'And kissing,' she said breathily.

'And kissing,' he repeated with a smile. 'You have a scar on your knee.' He knelt before her, pressing his lips to the white mark. 'What happened?'

'I fell. When I was seven. Zoey was trying to catch me on the tar outside.'

'Did she?'

'No,' she said with a smile. 'I got up and ran away immediately. Only dealt with the wound hours later.'

'Your parents couldn't have been impressed.'

'No,' she agreed. 'But let's not think about my parents now, shall we?'

He chuckled, running his hands down her calves, then back up as he stood.

'Can I see the back?'

'Of me?'

He only gave her a look.

'I'm not a car, Parker.'

'I can't answer your question without seeing the back of you.'

'Oh, for heaven's sake.'

She turned, almost lifting her hand to her hair as she did. Then she remembered that she cut it when Angie came back.

Before, her hair had been long, falling to her mid-back in an unruly curtain of curls. She supposed there was some significance in the desire she'd had to cut it off almost as soon as Angie had returned. But she hadn't lingered on it since the shorter style suited her better—and was much easier to maintain—anyway. Now though, she missed the comfort of clinging to it. She wanted something to do with her hands, so she didn't have to twiddle her thumbs while Parker examined the back of her.

'You know,' he said, his voice close, 'I like you obedient.'

Her head whipped toward him. 'Excuse me.'

'Only here,' he clarified, coming closer. 'I wouldn't dream of asking you to do what I say outside of this room.'

He was right behind her now, though not touching her. She could still feel him. His body radiated heat— or was that her own? Her temperature was higher than it had ever been before. If she wasn't almost naked already, she would have thrown off her clothes to get some relief.

'I'm not doing what you say because I'm obeying you.'

'Of course not.'

His breath was on her neck. Her skin pricked. Her body yearned.

'I'm doing it,' she continued deliberately, albeit softly, 'because I really want to know your answer.'

'Hmm.'

It was all he said for a long while. Which she didn't mind since he'd replaced the talking with touching. Light touches that felt as if he were trailing her body with a feather. Touches that had her heart racing, and her body pulsing with need. Then his hands gripped her hips and he pulled her back against him, fitting himself between the cheeks of her butt.

Her breath caught.

'You're perfect.'

'The stretch marks and the cellulite didn't put you off?' she whispered, unable to use her voice. She was fairly certain it had been sacrificed in the spell of his seduction.

'They're what make you perfect.' Gently, he spun her

around. 'You're real, and you're confident, and that's sexy as hell.'

His mouth met hers, and with the words that had just come from his mouth, Sophia expected him to rush. But the meeting of their lips was soft, gentle almost, as if he were leading her to something he knew she feared. It wasn't a bad description, she thought, as her head went cloudy from his kiss.

She was terrified of the way he'd changed in this room. He'd gone from an easy-going, arrogant man to the consummate seducer. A witch or wizard or perhaps warlock, since the latter had the kind of wickedness that Parker skilfully managed with his words, his touches.

But it was the tenderness, the awe that got to her. The patience as he waited, just a beat, every time his hands moved to a new part of her body. She didn't know how, in her heady state, she knew he was asking for permission. She could almost hear the words 'Is this okay?' come from his lips. Skill, she thought again, that she could hear it without him even uttering the words. That she could *feel* it.

He brought both his hands to cup her face, angling her head, deepening the kiss. It sent an electrical current through her body. It went directly from her mouth down to between her legs. She hadn't believed the pulsing could become more urgent. Or that the tightening could become almost painful in its need.

Impatient with it, she took his hand from her face, and placed it there, in that spot.

He pulled away. 'Are you okay with this?'

'I put your hand there, didn't I?' she asked hoarsely. 'And are *you* okay with this? Your face looks…pained.'

He chuckled, the vibration travelling through his body to his hand. She swallowed.

'I am in pain. It's the good kind, and I can handle it.'

The words stopped her world. Quite literally and quite abruptly. Their gazes locked, but something unlocked inside her. She swore she heard a key turn.

She stepped back on unsteady legs. His expression immediately turned guarded. He made no move toward her, only looked at her. Taking her lead, she realised.

Her world began to move again, but it was irrevocably changed.

For all his talk, all his 'we can stop at any time', Sophia hadn't comprehended what he'd meant. This made her see. He was painfully aroused. She was, too, and he'd felt the proof of that. But the moment she'd stepped away, the moment she'd given some indication that she wanted to stop, he'd taken her lead.

The rush of feeling that came with the realisation made her legs go even weaker. She lowered down to her bed as emotion crashed over her in waves. She felt him sit beside her, but not close enough that they were touching. He was giving her space. To breathe, to think, since he didn't say anything either.

Her mind went over the day, over the things she'd told him and things he'd told her. They were messes, the two of them. Perhaps not as bad as liquid spilled over a carpet. More like crumbs on a kitchen table. But they still needed cleaning up. He, more than her, she knew. Except that didn't keep her from wanting to cook in that untidy kitchen. The metaphor was getting messy in her head, too, but the silliness of it allowed her to think it through. She wanted to cook. Hell, she wanted to make something out of those crumbs. But there was no certainty that what she made would be edible.

She'd spent her entire life making food out of spoilage. She'd been forced to, with her family. And now she was choosing this? She got to choose her ingredients now, and she was choosing *this*?

Because that unlocking, that click she'd felt inside herself as she'd stepped back from him, told her she wanted him. More than the pulsing between her thighs, the prickling of her nipples demanded. She wanted this man who annoyed her, but took care of her. Who cared enough about a stranger to make sure they were safe in a park early in the morning. A stranger who pissed him off, chewed him up, and spat him out.

He listened to her in a way she hadn't realised she needed. He didn't push her, content with whatever she offered him. He was funny. Dry. Gave as good as he got. He cared about his family, and she knew that if he'd been her boyfriend when she'd found out her father had a brain tumour, he wouldn't have reacted like Lyle had. He understood family responsibility in only a way someone who went through it could. And that mattered to her.

He mattered to her.

'What's wrong?' he asked, as if he knew her thoughts had come to some kind of a conclusion.

'I like you.'

'That's a problem?'

'Yes.' She turned to face him. 'I like you. That's more than interest, Parker. It sits somewhere here.' She waved in the vicinity of her chest. 'And not, you know.' She did the same wave over her groin. 'I trust you. Enough to tell you this when it makes me feel vulnerable. Enough to tell you this in my bra and panties, which makes me feel even more vulnerable. I mean, you can see my nipples!' she exclaimed.

To his credit, he didn't look down.

'There's nothing wrong with liking me.'

'Yes, there is,' she said quietly. 'This is a bubble we've created. Outside of the bubble, your mom is sick and you have to deal with your dad. Neither of us want a relationship. And I have to go back to a family and deal with a ton of unresolved feelings. I have to wonder if they want me for who I am, and it'll make me wonder if you want me for who I am—'

She broke off when she realised what she said. But before she could say anything else, there was a knock on the door, followed quickly by Zoey appearing in the doorframe.

'Am I interrupting something?'

Yes, he wanted to answer. That was before he'd even processed that the question had been asked. When he did, he realised that someone had had to ask the question.

His first reaction was to hand Sophia the towel he'd unwrapped earlier. She'd have something to cover herself for the moment, until he got the nightgown that was hanging behind the door. He gave that to her, too, and she thanked him softly before wrapping herself in the material.

Disappointment echoed through him. At losing the sight of her beautiful body; at the fact that she no longer looked at him.

'What do you think, Zo?' Sophia asked tiredly. There was no bite in her tone, which worried him even more. There was always bite in her tone. Seeing her sister unexpectedly after Zoey had interrupted a personal moment should have at least inspired annoyance.

'I think you should come up with a reason there's a man in your bedroom when Mom's downstairs.'

Sophia's face tightened, which was the same reaction he had in his chest. Did he want to meet Sophia's mother? Did he want to meet her when he was in Sophia's bedroom and Sophia was half-naked? He didn't have answers. Probably because everything except his brain suddenly felt hyperalert.

'Mom's here?' Sophia asked. 'Did Ange have the baby?'

'Nah.'

Sophia's eyes narrowed. 'Nah, what?'

Zoey grinned. 'Mom's still at the hospital with Angie. She's eight centimetres dilated. They say this last part will go fast.'

'So you thought it would be fun to come here and pretend like Mom's downstairs?'

Zoey's smile turned sweet. 'It was fun.'

Sophia didn't reply to that, but she turned to him. 'Do you want me to introduce you to her? Honestly, you wouldn't be missing out on anything if you said no. As you can probably judge based on the interactions you've witnessed.'

He smiled. 'I believe in second chances.'

'Funny how she needs it and she's only been here for five minutes,' Sophia said darkly. She turned back to her sister. 'Zoey, this is Parker. Parker, Zoey.'

'Hi, Parker,' Zoey said, moving deeper into the room. She was smiling at him, a happy, genuine smile that had his own smile widening even though her entrance had nearly given him a heart attack. 'It's nice to meet you.'

'It's nice to meet you, too.' He held out his hand, but Zoey shook her head.

'Oh, I don't think I should take your hand right now. Considering my sister's state of undress…' She trailed off with a wicked gleam in her eyes, and he pulled his hand back.

He felt his cheeks heat, but he kept the eye contact, not wanting her to win. Besides, she was right. The hand he'd offered her had been between Sophia's legs moments ago. Although it wasn't as condemning as Zoey had made it sound, he couldn't blame her for being cautious.

In fact, once he thought about it, it was actually quite funny.

'You didn't tell me she had such a great sense of humour.'

'I try not to talk about her if I can help it,' Sophia answered.

'She's…cute.'

'If you think demons are cute.'

'You shouldn't call your sister a demon.'

'She is.' Sophia's eyes turned into slits as she looked at Zoey. 'Demons who don't understand the concepts of boundaries and privacy.'

'The door was open,' Zoey defended herself. She'd been watching the interaction between him and Sophia with bright, interested eyes.

She was shorter than Sophia, though only slightly.

Her hair was in long, long twists down to her waist, dark brown against the lighter brown of her skin. Her expression lacked the sternness of Sophia's, and her nose was a little rounder, her lips a little less plump, but otherwise, her face was a copy of Sophia's. At least to his eyes, and at his first impression. He was sure as time went on he'd find more differences.

As time went on? a voice in his head asked. He frowned. Things were becoming more complicated. Perhaps he should have been the one stopping them, not Sophia.

'I was talking about what you were saying,' Sophia told Zoey. 'It was inappropriate.'

'So was taking Parker's hand when I don't know where it's been.'

'Do you do that with every person you meet?' Parker interjected before Sophia could respond.

'If I've seen them do something dodgy, yes.'

'Piece of advice? You should probably carry hand sanitiser. People do dodgy things all the time, not just when you're watching.'

Sophia smiled at him, and then aimed it at Zoey. 'He's got you there.'

Zoey shook her head. 'I hope I didn't walk into an alternate universe where there are two of you.'

'Trust me,' Sophia said after a beat, 'there's no one like me.'

The words were followed by a long, awkward silence, before Parker cleared his throat. 'Maybe I should give you two some privacy.'

'Yeah, thanks,' Sophia replied. 'You can go to the hospital if you like. I'll find you there.'

'Oh.' He wanted to think it through, but with Zoey staring at him, he said, 'Okay.' Then couldn't help himself. 'Are you okay?'

'Fine.'

'Are you sure?'

She met his eyes. Bit her lip. Nodded. 'I'll be fine. I'll see you at the hospital.'

I'll be fine. Which meant she wasn't fine at the moment.

It took every last bit of his strength to greet the sisters and walk out of the room. He desperately wanted to talk about what had happened. One moment, they'd been sharing the most intimate experience of his life; the next, she'd stopped and told him she liked him. He'd already known that. He thought she had, too. Wasn't that why they were in the position they were currently in? Because they liked one another? But she looked genuinely disturbed by it. Maybe because she knew things couldn't extend past that day?

He didn't know. He hadn't got a chance to process any of it.

He wondered if that was what was happening now. His mind felt as if it were running in place, but getting nowhere. Which he supposed was the exact opposite of processing. Usually, that entailed moving forward. Figuring things out. Having answers. None of which was happening.

He drove home instead of the hospital. It happened automatically, though he only realised that when he pulled into the driveway. He wasn't mad he'd done it. His autopilot must have known he needed the break. He needed his bed. A moment to think. Alone. If he went to the hospital, he'd need to control his responses. People would be watching him. His parents would be watching him. No, for one moment—even if it was for a short moment—he wanted to feel what he felt and not have to worry about who was checking on him.

He fell into bed minutes later, face first into his pillow. When breathing became harder, he rolled onto his back, and stuck his arm under his head. It was his go-to position when he needed to think. It made no sense then that ten minutes later, he was still lying like that. But instead of thinking, he was staring at the ceiling.

His body was sinking into the mattress. Of that much he was sure. It had been a long day, and his lack of sleep was finally catching up to him. He thought he'd have a moment to nap when he and Sophia had... After. An intense longing had gone through him when she'd proposed it. A residual wave of it went through him now. His arms physically ached at not having her in them.

What's happening to you? that inner voice asked again. He thought he'd agreed there could be no future for him and Sophia. That *they'd* agreed. But did this longing mean he wanted one? Did her reaction back at the house mean she wanted one, too?

If it did, her inner voice must have asked her the same question his had. So they'd stopped, and now they were two people who wanted to be together, but couldn't be. He couldn't invest in it. He had too much to prepare for.

That was at the heart of his reluctance. He felt as if he were standing in front of the door that would lead to his new life. The door had opened with his mother's diagnosis, giving him a glimpse of what it would entail.

Work, so he could get his mother the care she needed. Doctor's appointments, live-in help, dealing with his mother's stubbornness as she faced a disease that would make the stubbornness worse. His father would likely be around more, pretending to help but really only getting in the way. He'd have to deal with Kelly, too, because his father's wife wouldn't allow her husband to face this alone.

If he was being honest, he was relieved his mother had been asleep both times he'd gone to see her. Once he spoke with her, confirmed what was happening to her, he'd take a step through the door. It would shut and lock behind him, and he'd never again go back to what his life was in this moment.

In this moment, he had Sophia. She was tethered to him. He didn't want to walk through the door and away from her. And he would be, because she wasn't on the other side. She had enough to deal with in her life. It would be selfish to expect her to deal with him and his family; to have her support him as he took care of his mother, reminding her of what she went through with her father. No doubt, at some point during all that, she'd feel as though she was taking care of Parker, too. She'd leave him then, just like his father had left his mother when things got hard, and he'd be as disappointed as his mother had been.

He frowned at the clarity of the thought—the jump he'd never made before between his resistance toward relationships and his parents' relationship. The end of it. Of course, he knew their relationship hadn't made him want one himself. But he thought the why of it was clear: their relationship hadn't worked out, so neither would his. His mother had been disappointed, so he would be, too. He hadn't once realised that fear of disappointment had come from a fear of abandonment. Which, he supposed, made sense considering how his father had made him feel as a child.

The newness of the realisation made him wonder if it was better or worse that he and Sophia had barely got past kissing. Now he wouldn't have the added complication of the memory of making love to her. And then he laughed at himself because not having the memory wouldn't keep him from imagining it, which was a complication in itself.

The picture of her body was seared into his mind. A standard he'd compare anyone in the future with, though it was neither fair nor realistic. Partly because no woman looked like another; partly because no one looked like her.

He meant it when he said she was perfect. The way her hips and shoulders aligned with one another, one sharp lines, the other generous curves. Her waist that linked the body parts together in a wave that wasn't perfectly shaped, but offered a scenic route. She had wide hips and a generous butt, which made the back of her as desirable as the front. Her back was a fascinating combination of strength and pudge; which was probably a good description of her entire body.

And the way she stood in front of him unashamed, confidence there despite the clear vulnerability…

Oh. He liked her. *Really* liked her.

And he finally understood why she thought that was a problem.

Chapter Thirteen

Zoey waited until they heard the front door slam closed before she whirled around to Sophia, her expression both curious and excited.

'Who was that? And why did I catch you two on your bed *not* doing what I'd expected you to be doing considering you're in your underwear?'

Sophia studied Zoey for a second, wondering how she should answer. When no clear strategy came to mind, she went to her cupboard and took out comfortable clothes.

'Why are you home?' she asked, pulling on a T-shirt and cotton trackpants.

'Oh, no, you're not dodging my questions.' Zoey folded her arms. 'Who is he?'

'He is Parker. I introduced you to him.'

'Yes, but having his name isn't exactly the information I wanted. How do you know him? How have things escalated to a point where you're almost naked with him and I don't know who he is?'

'He's the driver of the car I took this morning.'

'This morning… As in, you only met him today? No, wait—as in the guy in the picture?' she asked incredulously. 'Wow, he looks a million times better in person.' She scrunched up her nose. 'His side profile isn't as flattering as his front.'

Sophia resisted the urge to roll her eyes. 'I'll be sure to mention that the next time I see him.'

'Are you seeing him again? Oh, yeah, of course. You said you'd see him at the hospital.'

'Yep.'

Though now that Sophia thought about it, she wasn't sure she would be seeing him. Maybe it would be easier for both of them if they didn't meet up at the hospital. They could pretend this day hadn't happened and go back to their normal lives.

Except she wasn't sure she could go back. This day had changed her. Opened her eyes to things she'd been keeping outside her field of vision. It had also instilled a desire unlike any other she'd experienced before. She wanted…a chance. A future. With a man.

She felt ridiculous because of it. When had she ever been interested in having a romantic future? She'd brushed off the experience with Lyle so quickly she'd questioned whether she'd simply been wasting her time. When she'd determined she had been, she'd channelled her energy into her family, as she always did.

But that relationship was changing, too. Had been for longer than she'd allowed herself to see. It had started when her father had got sick. Changed again when he'd died; and again, when Angie had got back. Maybe her dissatisfaction now was teaching her that *she* had to change, too. Not who she was, even if her sisters believed she should, but how she saw things. How she handled things.

Her strained relationships with her family members seemed to prove that. Perhaps not with her mother, who wasn't an easy person, so naturally a relationship with her wouldn't be easy. But with Angie and Zoey? She didn't want things to continue this way. And maybe she had the power to make sure of that.

'Can we talk about what you said at the hospital?' Sophia asked, suddenly tired. She lowered onto the bed.

Zoey's eyes widened. She came to sit next to Sophia.

'I shouldn't have called you mean.'

'But you think it?'

Zoey opened her mouth, then closed it on a sigh. 'Sometimes.'

'That's such bull, Zo,' Sophia said quietly.

'You asked, Soph.'

'Did you think it was mean when Angie moved away when you needed her?'

'It's not the same thing.'

'Why not?'

'I... She left for a job.'

'There are jobs here.'

Zoey shook her head. 'She needed to go. She needed to clear her head.'

She said it with such certainty that Sophia knew she was repeating what Angie had told her.

'My head was fogged up, too,' Sophia pointed out. 'You don't think I would have liked to go away? To clear *my* head?' She didn't give Zoey a chance to answer. 'But I didn't have a choice because Angie was gone and then you left.' She angled toward Zoey. 'Is that why you're defending her? Because you did it, too?'

Zoey blushed. 'No, I just... I understand.'

'But you can't understand that I'm different to Angie.'

'I get that, Soph. I do. But you're…harsher. You're—'
She lifted her hands in a helpless gesture.

'Meaner?' Sophia supplied when Zoey didn't finish her sentence. Zoey nodded. She took a moment before she continued. 'You know, you're using the comparative form of those adjectives. Harsh*er*. Mean*er*.'

'That last one was you.'

'Yeah, but I took my cue from you,' Sophia replied. 'You're comparing me to Angie, which is why you're using that form. You see me through an…an Angie filter. She's sweet and caring and soft. And I'm… I'm not.'

Sophia was horrified when her eyes started burning. She swallowed, then shifted back into her pillows. Grabbing one, she held it in front of her like a shield.

'Soph, you're overreacting,' Zoey said. 'I'm not trying to insult you when I say it. I'm stating a fact.'

'A fact you've come up with because you're comparing me to Angie.'

'No, *you're* comparing you to Angie,' Zoey exclaimed. 'This entire conversation has been you comparing yourself to her. It has nothing to do with me.'

'Maybe not,' Sophia said after a pause.

Zoey wasn't the first person to tell her that, she thought, remembering Parker's question earlier that day. Even then she'd known the answer was significant. More so now was that she wanted to share her discovery with Zoey. A different angle of it, at least.

'You're right. I have been comparing myself to Angie.' She waited a beat. 'I've been thinking about how I stayed when Angie went to Korea. How I helped you after you went missing for three months during your final year at university when Angie didn't even know about it.'

Zoey's colour deepened. 'Dad died.'

'Which I told the university administration. I demanded they give you a chance to pass even though they were right, and you should have repeated the year. They gave in, though they probably wouldn't have done that if Angie had gone, too. She would have been perfectly polite and accepted their recommendations, and you'd probably be a year behind on everything you've achieved.' Sophia waited a beat. 'That's how this comparison thing works, right? I make myself feel bad because I'm not Angie? Oh, no, wait,' she said dryly. 'It's not. Because when I compare myself to Angie, I see who I *am*, not who I'm not.'

Zoey's brow knitted. 'I see you.'

'No, Zo,' Sophia said, tightening her grip on the pillow. 'You don't.'

There was a long silence before either of them spoke.

'Okay,' Zoey said, shifting to face Sophia. 'You're obviously going through something. Tell me what you need me to do and say to make you feel better.'

'Leave me alone.'

'I can't leave you alone, Soph. You've never left me alone when I was going through something. I... I won't leave you.'

Sophia's heart ached at the words, but she clenched her jaw, refusing to speak. She didn't know how much time passed, but she was stubborn. She wouldn't speak for however long it took for Zoey to give her a moment to process.

The problem was that Zoey was stubborn, too. She

waited. And waited, and waited. Eventually, she let out a little breath.

'Okay. Maybe you're right. Maybe I have been comparing you to Angie.'

Sophia didn't answer.

'I guess we got used to having both you and Angie around. She…she balanced you out, I guess.'

You mean you didn't notice me when she was around.

Sophia didn't say it. It wasn't important. After the day she'd had, after this conversation with Zoey, Sophia realised she was confident in who she was. She'd wobbled on how she saw herself, but she was standing steady now.

She'd love for her family to see her like she saw herself, but if that didn't happen, it wouldn't be the end of the world. How she saw herself was all that mattered.

There was a clatter in her chest, as if something had broken. As if she'd cracked something with her words. Her *lie.*

She took a deep breath.

'Come on, Soph,' Zoey said, shifting closer. 'I'm sorry. I didn't mean to upset you.'

'It's okay.' Pure will kept her from giving in to the tears that threatened, proving her words wrong. 'You should do whatever you came home to do, then get back to the hospital.'

She sensed Zoey's hesitation.

'You're not coming with me?'

'No.'

'But you're coming to the hospital later, right?'

Sophia rested her chin on her pillow, not replying.

'Sophia,' Zoey said with a frown, 'I get that things are a bit weird now. But we have to be there for Angie and Mom.'

'Or I can take a moment to clear my head,' Sophia replied carelessly.

'*Soph.*'

'No, Zoey, you don't get to guilt me into doing this. If you and Angie got to leave when we lost Dad, I get to stay here now.'

'You're not staying because you need to process. You're being petty.'

Sophia didn't bother pointing out that this was yet another example of how her sister didn't know her. It would entail admitting to emotions she'd rather deal with herself before sharing them with Zoey.

'I can't… I can't make up an excuse for this,' Zoey said, before turning around and shutting the door behind her.

Sophia immediately lowered to the bed, curling on her side. She didn't let go of the pillow. Only when she heard the front door close did her body relax. She realised then she'd been anticipating another fight with Zoey. Her body had tensed accordingly.

As her mind slowed from the frantic pace it had been operating at during her and Zoey's conversation—argument, she corrected herself deliberately—she tried to comfort herself. This had been her and Zoey's first real argument. They'd had tiffs before, stupid ones, but never something this grave, largely because Sophia took her role as older sister seriously.

She would step away, or give Zoey a moment whenever things got heated. But that meant Zoey rarely knew how Sophia truly felt. Today proved that had been a disservice to both her and Zoey.

But today had also proved that maybe it wasn't her role as a sister that had kept her from being honest. It was fear. Of being compared, of being judged. She hid her feelings and let the resentment of doing so fester until it turned ugly. Until one day, while waiting for her niece to be born, she couldn't take it anymore and ran away.

She knew it was fear because the same thing was happening now with Parker. Her feelings for him scared her. They were new and far too intense for someone she knew less than a day. More importantly, they forced her to consider how she'd be in a relationship. No, that wasn't right, she realised suddenly. She was thinking about how *he* would be in a relationship.

Would he compare her to someone he thought was better? Would that comparison turn into judgement? Would she find herself here again someday, reaffirming who she knew she was, telling herself it was okay?

What would happen when he wanted someone more cheerful around him as his mother struggled with her illness? How would he feel about her honesty if he asked her opinion about how he took care of his mother?

Why would she voluntarily put herself through that? She was already dealing with it with her family, but she had no choice there. She did here. And she wouldn't choose this pain again. Not when it felt like it was tearing her apart now.

It was a long time before she moved. When she did, she put on a dress, did her make-up, fluffed her hair. Then she called for a car.

He'd fallen asleep. When he woke up, he realised he had an hour to get back to the hospital for visiting hours. He took another shower—cold, again, but this time by choice so he could shake off the sleep. After, he heated the pizza he'd ordered but hadn't eaten the night before when he found out about his mother's accident. Sufficiently sated, he drove to the hospital. Sat in the car for longer than he'd admit. Then he made his way to his mother's room.

Both anticipation and dread followed him. He blamed it on the prospect of seeing his father there. Acknowledged it as a lie when he got to his mother's room and saw only her. Awake. Nerves bounced against the walls of his chest.

'Hey,' he said when her eyes fell on him. 'Fancy seeing you here.'

'Didn't you come here for me?'

'Full of yourself, aren't you?' he asked casually, throwing his coat over the chair beside her bed. 'I didn't come here for you. I usually visit this hospital room at this time. You just happen to be in it.'

Penny chuckled, then winced when she tried to sit up. Parker pushed forward, arranging the pillows so she'd be more comfortable. When she eased back, he let out a little sigh.

'How are you feeling?' he asked.

'Sore.'

'Besides that?'

His mother narrowed in on him like only she could. 'What are you actually asking, Parker?'

He took his time, lowering to the chair. 'They told me about the…' His voice faded.

'So much for patient/doctor confidentiality.'

'I've been with you for every appointment, Mom. I would have found out eventually.'

'He shouldn't have assumed.'

'Dad was here when Dr Craven told you.'

Penny sighed. 'That sounds like an accusation.'

'It's an observation,' Parker corrected. He waited a beat. 'So, how do you feel?'

'Fine. I haven't lost my mind yet.'

'Mom.'

'Parker.' With a wheeze, his mother shifted again. 'I need to joke about it. If I don't joke, I'll get upset that I'm going to lose the one thing I could always count on.'

'I know how that feels,' he muttered, looking at his hands.

'Oh, baby,' Penny said after a moment. He heard her shift and looked up in time to see her reach for his hand. Parker moved forward, grasping her fingers.

When had her hand got so frail? Why hadn't he noticed before? What else hadn't he noticed? Maybe if he'd paid attention, he could have—

'No,' Penny said, her voice sharp. Her gaze was sharp on his face, too. 'You don't blame this on yourself. And don't deny that you're doing that either,' Penny added when he opened his mouth. Obediently, he closed it again. 'There's nothing either of us could have done about this.'

'You don't know that.'

'I do.' She squeezed his hand. 'Besides, if you believe that, I'll have to believe that I could have done something to stop this, too. Are you going to let me think that?'

'No, ma'am,' he answered reluctantly.

His mother gave a satisfied nod. 'Good.' Her grip on his hand loosened, and he let go.

'You should rest.'

'I'm not an invalid.'

'You were hit by a car. You need rest.'

'I've been resting all day.'

'Is this how this is going to go?' Parker asked. 'You're going to fight me on every little thing?'

'The doctor said I should try some mental exercises.'

'Did he recommend arguing with your son?'

'No. But I think he knew who his audience was.' Penny grinned at him. He smiled back, though the last thing he felt like was smiling. Then her eyes shifted to behind him and he tensed.

His father.

'Can I help you?' his mother asked.

'Oh, no,' came a familiar voice. It wasn't his father's though. Parker turned. Sophia gave him a chagrined smile. 'Sorry. I didn't mean to interrupt.'

'What are you doing here?' he asked.

'I thought you might…need company.'

The pause in her sentence made him think she'd stopped herself from saying something else. Her gaze shifted to his mother, and he realised why that might have been.

'I don't,' he answered.

'Great. I'll go then.'

'No,' his mother called, 'you won't. You'll introduce yourself, and then apologise for speaking past me.'

'Oh. I'm sorry.' For the first time that day, he saw Sophia thoroughly chastised. 'I'm sorry, Mrs Jones. I don't know where my manners have gone. I'm Sophia, a friend of Parker's.'

There was no hesitation there, though he didn't think he could call Sophia his friend.

'Parker doesn't have friends.'

Sophia laughed. 'I can't imagine why.' She took a step into the room. 'But we just met today, so there's time for him to retain that status.'

Penny's eyes lightened, but she didn't laugh. Parker frowned at his mother. Sophia had made a pretty decent joke. There was no reason for Penny not to laugh.

'How did you two meet?'

'I got into his car this morning.'

'So you're a client, not a friend.'

'I did pay him for that trip,' Sophia agreed. 'But then, I also drove him home, made him a cup of tea before he fell asleep, and cleaned your kitchen. Would that still make me a client?'

Parker's eyes widened, and he looked over at his mother. Her face had split into a wide smile—as wide as she could manage with the bruises anyway—and he relaxed.

'I like you,' Penny told Sophia.

'Thank you, Mrs Jones. I like you, too.'

'Even though I've been giving you a hard time?'

'*Because* you've been giving me a hard time,' Sophia clarified. 'You're protecting your son. I respect that.'

Slowly, his mother looked at him. 'Don't do anything stupid.'

It was an ambiguous warning…to inexperienced ears. But he'd spent years training in his mother's verbal and nonverbal cues. What Penny was really telling him was that he shouldn't screw up whatever was happening between him and Sophia.

Don't do anything stupid had nothing to do with practising safe sex or being financially responsible. It was a *don't mess this up by doing something stupid* warning.

How did he tell his mother he already had?

'I'll leave you two to chat,' Sophia said. She looked at Parker. 'I'll be in the waiting room when you're done.'

'Your niece isn't here yet?'

'They've pulled Angie into emergency surgery. Apparently twelve hours of labour doesn't guarantee your baby will come out the way you want them to.'

'Is she okay?'

'Yes.' Her eyes told him she appreciated the question. Then she looked at his mother. 'It was lovely meeting you, Mrs Jones.'

'I hope I'll see you again, Sophia.'

'You will,' Sophia said confidently, though Parker didn't know where that certainty had come from. 'I'll be sure to visit.'

She nodded at him, and left them alone. When he looked at his mother, she lifted her eyebrows.

'Well, that's given me a second wind. I'm sure I can stay awake long enough for you to tell me who this woman is and why you haven't proposed to her yet?'

'Mom,' he chastised with a frown. 'I met her today.'

'Which gave you an entire day to propose.'

'Since when have you been this eager to get me married?'

'Since today. After meeting her.'

'Mom,' he said again, in the same chastising tone.

'Parker,' she replied with a sigh. 'I just want to make sure that when I'm not here anymore—'

'Don't.'

'It's reality.'

'Not yet.'

'I don't want you to be alone.'

'I'm not alone. I have you.'

'But the me you know will disappear someday.' His mother paused, and Parker looked down in time to see her grip the sheet with her free hand. His heart ached. 'All I'm saying is that it'll give me some peace if I know you have someone. I'd be happy if it were your father, but you've made it clear you don't want him in your life.'

'He wasn't there when it counted.'

'He's here now, when it counts. He came—' She broke off.

'What?' Parker said, though dread had already dropped in his stomach. 'What did you want to say?'

'You need someone—'

'No, Mom. You were specifically talking about Wade. What did you mean?'

'Parker—'

'Be honest.'

There was a long silence before she answered.

'Your father... He wanted to be more involved when you were growing up.' His mother's hand tightened on the sheet. 'I asked him to prove it and he came back.' She shook her head. 'He didn't do enough, and his life was still a mess. I didn't want you to have that instability.'

'He only came back when I was nine.'

'I know.'

'I only saw him on my birthdays.'

'I wanted—I needed him to prove he wanted to be there.'

'You mean he wanted to be around more?'

His mother didn't answer this time. He wasn't sure how to interpret her silence. Was it an implicit yes, his father had wanted to be around? Or was it a no, and she couldn't bear to tell him?

He didn't ask, because he wasn't sure he wanted the clarity. Or no, it was that he already *had* the clarity. His father hadn't pitched up to his twelfth birthday. He'd had an annual commitment to his son, and he hadn't been able to keep even that.

'I tried to protect you, honey,' Penny said softly. 'I wanted what was best for you.'

'Did you decide having him back in my life now was what's best for me?' Parker asked, desperately trying to keep his anger at bay.

'Yes.'

'Why?'

She didn't answer. He took a moment to figure out his thoughts.

'You know,' he said, struggling to keep his tone light, 'ever since you told me you started talking to him the year before he came back, I wondered what you talked about. Did you tell him about the game we used to play with our bills? Almost like Russian roulette, except we'd pay one and hope the gun wouldn't go off with the million others we had?'

'I…we didn't talk about money.'

'I was already working for Marcus by then, so you didn't need to.' The anger grew in his stomach. It was a ball of fire, moving up into his chest, burning his heart. He wasn't sure what would happen if it pushed up to his throat. Still, he sat. 'What changed when I was nineteen, Mom? Why did you start talking to him? Why did he come back into our lives? Really,' he said, hearing the plea. 'Because it wasn't his doing. It was yours.'

She nodded, acknowledging the truth of it. There was

a long pause before she spoke. When the words came, it shocked the insolence from him.

'I thought there was something wrong with me.'

'You suspected this?'

There was a moment when she opened her mouth but didn't speak. Her eyes were tortured, torn, and he saw the truth.

'For how long?'

He knew she wouldn't answer if she could help it. As much as he loved his mother, he could acknowledge that admitting she was wrong wasn't one of her strong points. So he supplied the answer for her.

'It must have been at least seven years then.'

She nodded.

'Did you know it might be this?'

She hesitated. But then it seemed like too much for her, and she nodded again.

'I had an uncle with it. We weren't close,' she clarified, 'and the signs were confusing to me as a child. But when these…these things started to happen, I wondered about the possibility.'

'And you knew that possibility was this?'

'Once I started doing the research, yes.'

His mind raced 'Is that why you were upset with Dr Craven for telling me?'

'It was an official diagnosis,' she said, not meeting his eyes. 'It made things more real. This past year…'

He understood. She'd had suspicions for seven years. He hadn't noticed anything was wrong until this past year, which must have meant she'd known things were getting worse. It proved he hadn't been as perceptive as he'd thought, too, though that seemed selfish to consider now.

He couldn't help it.

'Why wouldn't you tell me any of this? Any of it?' he repeated desperately. 'About Dad, or your suspicions, or…or anything?'

'I wanted to protect you.'

He studied her. Believed she thought it was true. But that was as far as his understanding went. His brain had slowed to the point where he couldn't process anything else. He needed to think, and his brain wouldn't cooperate with his mother looking at him as if he were torturing her somehow.

'Okay, Mom,' he said, moving forward and kissing her head. 'You're tired and you shouldn't be thinking about this right now. I'll be back in the morning. My phone is always on if you need to call.'

'You're angry with me.'

'I'm angry,' he acknowledged with a curt nod. 'I'm not sure if it's at you yet.'

'Liar.'

He walked to the door. 'It doesn't change that I love you.'

'I love you, too,' she said with a broken voice.

It broke his heart, too. He'd never seen his mother like this. He'd never heard her like this either. He wondered if it was his heart that had broken then, or his perception of her. And how that broken perception would change their relationship.

Chapter Fourteen

Sophia was sitting in the waiting room with her family members, but really, she was sitting in the middle of a family feud. Her mother wasn't speaking to her. Neither was Zoey. Although Zoey had informed Sophia—curtly—about Angie's situation when Sophia had arrived.

She'd taken her time before heading to the hospital. She'd grabbed something to eat, let herself recover. Now that she was there, she was glad for it.

Her mother was barely acknowledging her existence. But then, Sophia didn't think that was the result of a feud so much as it was worry. She recognised the expression on her mother's face. It was the same one she'd worn that morning when she'd begged Sophia to come with her to the hospital. Which, Sophia realised, happened to be the same expression Charlene had worn every time her father had come to the hospital.

Her mother was scared.

Sophia stood, ignoring Zoey's eyes on her and settled next to her mother.

'It's going to be okay, Mom,' she said quietly, taking Charlene's clammy hand. Her mother didn't resist or pull away. Sophia considered it a good sign. 'Angie's surgery is routine. The fact that there's surgery at all means they're being proactive.'

'You don't know that.'

'But you do. What was it like with Angie, me, and Zo? Did everything go smoothly?'

There was a second where Sophia thought her mother wouldn't answer.

'Angie's was normal,' her mother started in a small voice. Relief nearly plummeted Sophia. 'Long, like her labour was, but there were no complications.'

'And me?'

'You were more difficult.'

'Then already?' Sophia asked lightly. 'You should have taken that as an omen.'

Charlene's lips spread into a tiny smile, her hand tightened around Sophia's. Emotion drifted up, blocking her throat like a plug.

'The umbilical cord was around your neck. You were in distress. After seven hours of labour, we had to do a C-section.'

'Let's hope that doesn't mean Angie will be having Sophia 2.0,' Sophia added lightly, though the emotion made it hard to joke.

'I'm sure the universe wouldn't be so cruel as to put two Sophias into this family,' Zoey added. When Sophia turned to look at her, Zoey's expression was kind. Her younger sister nodded at her, as if to say she didn't mean it, then nodded to her mother. 'What about me, Mom?'

'Oh, we did a C-section with you straight off the bat.'

'Easy life since then, huh, Zo?' Sophia said. It wasn't teasing, nor was it spite. It was something in between.

The expression on Zoey's face told Sophia her sister knew it.

'It was stressful,' Charlene continued. The content was unsurprising. Their mother found most things stressful. 'But it was also beautiful. Your father—' She stopped, as she usually did when she started to speak about her dead husband. But then she did a quick shake of her head and went on, which surprised Sophia. Usually the stopping was where it…well, stopped. 'He was wonderful. Funny and steady.'

'I think that's probably what Ezra's doing now.'

'No,' her mother replied to Sophia with a smile. 'Ezra is not taking this well.'

'What does that mean?'

'He fainted,' Zoey offered.

'He *fainted*?'

'Apparently.' Zoey smirked. 'Mom said it was before they took Ange into surgery. Something about him seeing her—' her voice dropped '—*you know*—' Zoey had clearly learnt from Sophia's vagina faux pas '—and his face got really pale.'

'Oh, Zoey, you're making it sound more dramatic than it was,' Charlene chastised. 'I think the stress of seeing Angie in labour for so long and then hearing she has to go into surgery got to him.'

'So he fainted?' Sophia asked with a smirk of her own. 'Thank you for sharing that.'

'Are you going to make fun of him?' Charlene asked primly.

Sophia nodded solemnly. 'It's what Dad would have wanted me to do.'

Charlene blinked, then laughed. 'You're right. He

wouldn't have taken into consideration that Ezra hadn't eaten anything today either.'

'Mom,' Sophia said with a frown. 'Why did you tell me that? Now I feel sorry for him.'

'Since when did that stop you?' Zoey muttered.

Sophia gave her a sweet smile. 'You're right. I won't let it keep me from making fun of him.'

Ezra somehow appeared in front of them then. Sophia couldn't imagine how they hadn't seen him, but they all stood as soon as they did. The air got a little thinner as they waited for him to speak.

'She's okay.' He grinned, running a hand through his hair. 'They're both okay. Mom and daughter—' He broke off, his eyes shining with warmth. For some unfathomable reason, Sophia's eyes got warm, too. 'They're both doing fine. Ange is a little groggy from the anaesthesia and I think a little overwhelmed. But they're good. They're…good. Good.'

Sophia was the first one to speak. Apparently the news of the latest addition to the family had paralysed the rest of them.

'We get it, Dad. They're good.' She moved forward, pulling him into a hug. 'Congratulations.'

His arms went around her, holding her tightly. 'Thanks.'

'You did good, too,' Zoey said, taking Sophia's place when Sophia moved back. 'I mean, you did good by sitting there and keeping her company while she did all the work.'

'I know,' he said, wonder in his eyes. He smiled at Charlene, who wrapped him into a hug, whispering something Sophia couldn't hear into his ear. It made his eyes tear up, which got Sophia feeling choked up.

Really. This was getting ridiculous.

'Your sister is amazing,' Ezra said with a shake of his head, trailing his hand through his hair again. 'I don't know… I can't… I mean…'

'Don't hurt yourself,' Sophia advised with a smile. 'Can we see them?'

'Um, I don't know.' He looked around, though his expression was confused, as though he wasn't sure what he was looking for. 'They've been pretty strict about only letting people in when it's visiting hours.'

'They'll let Mom in though, right?' Zoey asked.

Ezra blinked a few times. Then his eyes refocused. 'Yes. I'll fight them if they don't.'

He gestured for Charlene to move ahead of him. As she did, she looked back.

'I can find my own way home.'

'Nonsense,' Zoey said with a wave of a hand. 'I'll wait.'

'Thank you,' Charlene said, eyes shining with gratitude. Both Sophia and Zoey waited for their mother and brother-in-law to disappear through the doors, then they looked at one another.

'We're aunts,' Zoey said after an awkward silence.

'That we are.'

A few more awkward seconds passed.

'It seems wrong for us to start our journeys as aunts while being in a fight.'

Zoey was looking down. Sophia suspected she was trying hard not to shuffle her feet.

'It does seem wrong, doesn't it?' Sophia said slowly.

She ran her tongue along her teeth. Considered. Sighed. 'I needed a moment back at the house. I'm sorry for… you know.'

'Yeah,' Zoey said after a beat. 'I do.' Another beat. 'I'm sorry for not seeing how good you are with us. You distracted Mom from worrying about Angie earlier. And all the things you did—*do*—for me…' She trailed off, still avoiding Sophia's gaze. 'I guess I… I didn't see you. And I *was* looking through Angie filters.' Colour tainted her cheeks. 'I'm sorry.'

Sophia studied her sister. 'Thank you.' When something on Zoey's face relaxed, Sophia softened. 'It's not your fault, Zo. I did it to myself, too.'

'You did.'

Sophia chuckled. 'I guess we should start looking at people's actions and intentions. And realise they don't come in one-size-fits-all packages.'

'And maybe also realise that the people who know and love us can't know what our intentions are if we don't let them in.'

Zoey's words were soft—so why did they ring in her ears? Why did they echo in her heart?

'Fair enough,' she said eventually. Blew out a breath. 'Learn from my mistakes then, Zo. If you feel something, show it. Embrace. Let the people you love see it. And don't compare yourself to me or Angie,' she added for good measure. 'Don't think you have to change because you see some things that are different in us.'

Zoey's eyes flickered. 'You're so preachy, Soph.'

Sophia frowned, her instincts tingling. Had Zoey been doing it, too? Had she been comparing and finding herself lacking? She opened her mouth to ask, but Zoey spoke before she could.

'You have a visitor.'

Sophia turned, saw Parker standing at the edge of the waiting room. Something about his expression sent a wave of anxiety, then protectiveness, through her. It was a strange feeling, but not unfamiliar. She usually felt it for her family though, not people she'd only known for a day.

She nodded at him, then turned back to Zoey.

'Are you okay?'

'Yeah, of course.' Zoey waved a hand. 'I'm fine.'

'Zo.'

'It's okay, Soph.' Zoey kissed her on the cheek. 'We're okay, too, if that matters.'

'It always matters.' She pulled at one of Zoey's twists. 'Are you going to be okay with Mom?'

'Just go, Sophia.' Zoey rolled her eyes now. 'Stop using us as an excuse to avoid the hottie.'

Sophia pulled her face, but gave Zoey's twist one more tug before walking to Parker. As she reached him, Zoey called out, 'See if you can get a picture of his front this time.'

She gritted her teeth. 'Thanks, Zo.'

'You're welcome,' came the cheery reply.

He didn't think he was in the mood to smile. But that was before Sophia's sister confirmed what he'd suspected and Sophia had been denying for the entire day.

'I'm happy to pose for you,' he said as they walked out the hospital. 'Front profile, too.'

'Funny guy,' Sophia said darkly, which only made his smile deepen.

'I'd prefer you take the photo with my knowledge. As you already know, I believe in consent, and—'

'I wasn't taking your photo for social media, Parker. You're not a thirst trap,' she scoffed.

'You looked thirsty earlier. Or was I mistaken?'

She blushed. And scowled. Scowled harder when the blush deepened.

'Is this going to be something you bring up casually in conversation now?'

'Only when it's us.'

'Good thing we probably won't see each other again,' she muttered. Her eyes widened as she looked at him. 'I'm sorry. I didn't mean to—'

'Don't worry,' he said with a half-smile, though panic ran free in his chest. 'I got it.'

She exhaled a little. 'This is complicated.'

'It is.'

'I knew it was a bad idea to like you.'

'I…can't disagree.'

'Then again, you're a pretty good kisser.'

Her ability to bounce back was remarkable.

'Thank you. You're not too bad yourself.'

'I know. I had a lot of practice.'

With that, she got into the car, leaving him staring. He shook his head when he wanted to smile again, then thought what the hell and smiled anyway. He got into the car.

'Where to?'

'You came to find me.'

'Technically, you came to find me first.'

There was a pause. 'Is your mom okay?'

'Fine.'

She clucked her tongue. 'I've asked variations of that question a lot in the last thirty minutes. You're the second person who's lied to me about it.'

He switched the car on, pulled out of the parking spot. They were on the road before long, though he hadn't yet answered her not-quite question. He drove to the Waterfront, because it was the closest place he could think of that would still be open this time of night.

'She knew,' he said without realising it. Automatically, his hands tightened, one on the steering wheel, the other on the gearbox. He brought them both to the wheel, forcibly relaxing them. 'She knew that she was getting sick and she didn't tell me.'

'Why not?'

'She said she wanted to protect me.'

'From what?'

'I don't know.'

'Okay.' She reached out, put a hand on his thigh. Carefully, he lowered one of his hands and threaded their fingers together. 'That's okay.'

He wanted to say thank you, because somehow, she'd known that was exactly what he needed to hear.

'What else?' she said after a long pause.

He lifted his hand, put on his indicator, turned. Seconds later their hands were twined again.

'My father…might have wanted to be in my life.'

There was a surprised silence. Then an impactful, 'Oh.'

'Yeah. Oh.'

'She kept that from you?'

'Yeah.'

'Well,' she said slowly, 'she must have done it to protect you, too.'

'That's what she says.' He frowned. 'How did you know?'

'I assumed. If she was protecting you from her illness, she must have been protecting you from your father.'

'You make it sound simple.'

'It might sound simple, but I know it's not.'

'You understand?'

'Yes.'

'Did your father hide his illness from you, too?'

He asked it without thinking. Her hand stiffened in his. He didn't have to look at her to know her entire body had stiffened, too. If he wasn't driving, he would have closed his eyes to marinate in his stupidity.

'I'm sorry. I didn't mean to bring that up.'

'It's okay,' she said, though she released a shaky breath. 'It's been up today anyway.' She paused. 'He didn't hide it, but that's only because he wasn't like your mother. He didn't particularly care about protecting us from things, I don't think. Or he did, but not from the kind of stuff your mother protected you from. I don't know. I'm not making any sense.'

'No,' he agreed with a squeeze of his hand.

They'd almost reached their destination when she spoke again.

'You have the kind of mom who pretended like everything was okay so that you wouldn't have to worry. Right?' she asked, shifting toward him as if she'd only then realised she didn't know his mother.

'I don't know if I'd describe her that way,' Parker said slowly. 'I think it's more accurate to say she's the kind of mother who, even though you knew things weren't okay, would always make you feel like they were going to be.'

'That's pretty incredible,' she said after a moment.

He angled his head in agreement, but didn't verbalise it. His mother *was* incredible. But he didn't feel like saying it out loud. Not when he was still processing her protective measures and his feelings about it.

'My parents weren't like that,' she continued. 'My mom still isn't. Though I think she's trying,' Sophia said, thoughtfully. She wriggled her shoulders. 'Anyway, my point is that my parents were open about things. They expected us to carry our weight, so we had a lot of responsibility, a lot of which probably shouldn't have been ours.'

'You're telling me this didn't just happen when your dad got sick?'

'Oh, hell no,' she said with a snort. 'I told you Angie looked after us pretty much our entire lives. I helped when I could, and we both kind of took care of Zoey. Which I guess makes no real sense since she's not that much younger than us.'

'Sounds...'

He didn't finish the sentence. He wasn't sure how to.

'I mean, my dad was there,' Sophia said, as if he hadn't spoken. 'Angie wasn't entirely responsible for us. But it was bad enough that *we* could feel that *she* felt that responsibility.'

'And your mom?'

'She's not like your mother.' She paused. 'She's a very dependent kind of person. Not that there's anything wrong with that. It's just… I mean, it's not always the kind of approach you'd like your mother to take, you know?'

'Yeah, I get that.'

'Dad spent a lot of time taking care of Mom, which was fine, because they genuinely loved one another. I guess that meant they were co-dependent, though that seems too easy a term to describe it.' She waited until he pulled into a parking space before she said, 'Talking to you about this makes me realise how messed-up my family is.'

'So let's not talk about it,' he said, getting out the car. He held out his hand; she took it. Like a real couple, they made their way from the parking lot to the Waterfront mall entrance.

'Okay. If we're not talking about my weird family and your mom's secrets, maybe you can explain why you brought us here?'

'Because it's eight at night and it was the closest place I thought would be open.'

'How romantic,' she said, fluttering her eyes at him.

He laughed. 'Do you want romantic? You don't seem like the—'

'Stop.'

'Why?'

'Do you remember what happened the last time you made a broad statement to me? About my name,' she clarified with a quirked brow when he shook his head. 'I thought you'd learnt your lesson.'

'Oh. Oh,' he said again. 'Right. I'm sorry.'

'You've only known me a day. I forgive you.'

'How magnanimous of you.'

'Don't choke on that big word.'

Her expression made him think she was seconds away from sticking out her tongue. Fortunately, she saved them both from that.

'But to answer your question,' she said with a roll of her eyes instead. 'I appreciate thoughtfulness. Though, to be fair, that is the entire point of romance. Or it should be.'

'You mean the point isn't to bone?'

'Great,' she muttered. 'We're back to you being annoying.'

'I thought you liked me that way.'

'Up to a point. You're reaching it,' she told him.

He grinned. 'I like you, too.'

He caught the smile before she managed to hide it, and it sent a flush of pleasure through him. He didn't question it, or how she was succeeding in distracting him. Instead, he thought about how it made him want to give her romance.

He didn't need that desire to tell him something had shifted. It had already happened when he'd realised his resistance to relationships was because he was worried he'd be left. Realising it hadn't significantly changed things, but it clarified them, at least where Sophia was concerned. He was more comfortable with her because he didn't have to worry about her leaving—he already knew she would be.

Except… He *was* worried about her leaving. Not because he didn't trust her, or think she'd be like his father, but because he wanted her to stay. But wanting that was asking for the exact thing he'd steered away from relationships because of: disappointment.

It was more complicated than he'd anticipated. With everything his brain was going through when it came to his parents as well, he decided to give it a break. To not try and question his every desire. If he wanted to give Sophia romance—if he wanted to show her he could be thoughtful—he would. And if that meant her last memories of him would be romantic, that would be an added bonus.

He changed their direction, headed to the Cape Wheel.

'You want romance?' he asked, joining the short line. 'You get romance.'

Chapter Fifteen

He was a cheesy, annoying fool, but man, did he know how to make her heart beat faster.

She could have blamed it on the height. On the fact that they were in what was essentially a Ferris wheel except bigger, and enclosed in glass. They were also standing, which made the height thing more plausible since she could almost see herself leaning too far forward and toppling the entire thing.

She *might* have had a small fear of heights, which she hadn't told him about. Strangely, she hadn't even felt it on Table Mountain. Perhaps because then, she was in emotional turmoil. Or perhaps it was because she'd been deep in lust, kissing a man before asking him to show her what his tongue could do.

Heat flushed up her neck, but she refused to feel ashamed for claiming that piece of her sexuality. Sure, she had got cold feet before he could show her, but she was proud of her seduction techniques.

And *that* thought proved she would much rather think about something embarrassing than face the turning in the pit of her belly.

'I'm disappointed,' he said softly. 'I thought you'd find this romantic.'

'It is,' she answered. 'Of course it is.'

'Tell that to your face.'

'Only seconds ago,' she said, ignoring him, 'I thought about how annoying and cheesy you are—'

'That's not helping.'

'—but that you were romantic,' she continued over his interruption. She took a step closer to him, waiting to see if the glass trap they were in would tilt. It didn't, so she rested her hands on his chest. 'I really like that you're doing this for me.'

He looked down at her. For a moment, she felt like they'd been engulfed by a heat wave. It was ridiculous; the air had turned cool outside, typical Cape Town weather unpredictability, and the wind had picked up. Not enough for them to turn off the Cape Wheel, obviously, because she was still there, in the glass box. She took a deep breath.

'Okay,' he said. 'I'm confused. Your mouth and your body are telling me one thing, but your expressions are telling me another.'

'I'm scared.'

'Of what?'

'Heights.'

'Didn't we go to the top of Table Mountain together?'

'Yes, but that was different.'

'How?'

'You distracted me.'

'So you're saying I need to distract you now?'

'No,' she said quickly, shaking her head for emphasis. 'I don't want this thing to move and cause us to topple over.'

'So you're not afraid of heights, you're afraid of falling from heights?'

'They're the same thing.'

'Not strictly,' he disagreed. 'I think you felt better about Table Mountain because we were never close to the edge. The cable car is much bigger, too. Steadier than this. And you don't really see big, steady things detach from their mechanisms and fall down in movies, do you?'

'Parker.'

'Just the other day I watched a movie where a girl was thrown to her death by falling out—'

'Stop talking.'

'You know what to ask me.'

'You're *bribing* me?'

'You know what to ask me,' he said again, a curtain of desire falling over his face.

'You're infuriating.'

'You know what to—'

She cut him off with a kiss. She had to shut him up, and she'd be damned if she asked him for anything when that was what he wanted her to do. If she needed a distraction, she would provide it for herself, and not expect a man to do it.

That was feminism, right?

It must be. How else could she feel this powerful when he immediately groaned against her mouth and pulled her body against his? The distraction was working, she thought, because she didn't care that the impact he'd done it with might cause the wheel to break somehow. She only cared about his mouth that had got to know hers *so* well in the last day.

She hadn't been exaggerating or playing to his ego when she'd told him he was a good kisser. He knew when to give in to the passion, and when to pull back. His kiss was a combination of gentle and sinful, punishing and pleasurable. She feared falling in a completely different way now.

Then he drew back, his expression kidnapped by desire and hunger.

'Why did you stop?' she whispered, her voice apparently a victim of the kidnapping, too.

'We're at the top.'

He spun her around gently, reminding her of when they'd been like this in her bedroom. Her breath was caught by the memory, her body primed by the kiss. When he wrapped his arms around her waist and stood behind her, she leaned against him. She felt steadier, no longer terrified of falling. Perhaps because his arms were around her and he felt steady. Or maybe because she knew he'd protect her if she fell.

You're in trouble.

'Look at this,' he whispered into her ear before she could react to her mind's betrayal. 'Look at how beautiful it is.'

And it was beautiful.

Lights from the city sparkled up at them, the busyness of one of the most popular tourist attractions in Cape Town quiet beneath them. It was dark, but she could still see the shadow of Table Mountain. Though it couldn't compare to being on top of it, seeing it like this was an experience in itself. Below them was the inky darkness of water. Docked ships rocked gently in the bounce of it, lights along the edge of the marina guiding those close by.

The paths along the water were busy, full of lovers looking out at the water, whispering promises to one another. Restaurants at the edge of the water were busy, too, though the clientele was different there. Wealthier, because restaurants at the edge of the water cost money, and a select few could afford it.

'This almost makes the fear worth it.'

He chuckled. He was still behind her, his mouth still close to her ear, and the sound sent a shiver through her body. The vibration set her nerves on fire.

'I'm glad.' He paused. 'I'm prefacing what I say next because I want you to know that I know it's cheesy.'

She smiled. 'Okay.'

'It's not a line though.'

'Okay.'

'You have to promise not to make fun of me.'

'You already know I can't do that,' she said, her smile widening.

'I guess you'll never know what I wanted to say then.'

She rolled her eyes. 'You're much too dramatic to be wasting your talents on journalism, Parker. Perhaps consider soap opera writing, or screenplays. Angie writes romance novels. Maybe you should try that.'

He didn't reply, and despite herself, she chuckled.

'Fine, I promise.'

'As beautiful as this is,' he said immediately. 'I still think you're better to look at.'

She wanted to roll her eyes. To turn around and tell

him he was being cheesy and that she would absolutely
be making fun of him for it. But he sounded so sincere
that instead of all that, she sighed. A breathy, lusty sigh
that she'd seen done in movies and had always scoffed
at. She wasn't even mad at herself for it.

'You're dangerous, Parker Jones.'

'Do you like danger?'

Just like that, the air changed. Snapped to attention,
as if suspecting on some level that a different kind of
seduction had commenced. Not of her heart, but of her
body.

'It depends on how dangerous you are,' she said
slowly. The wheel had started its descent, but it was
impossibly slow. She hadn't been happy about that on
the way up. She felt differently now. 'Are you a vam-
pire? Am I a victim?'

'With that imagination, maybe you should be the one
writing screenplays.'

Even as he teased her, his mouth found her neck. He
kissed her in the sensitive hollow just before her collarbone began, then traced a pattern with his lips and
tongue to beneath her ear.

Her breathing had gone shallow, the rapid movements of her chest forcing her nipples to rub against
the material of her dress. It was one of those awkward
designs that didn't allow for a bra. So, she'd thrown on
a jacket and called it a day. Now, she wondered if she'd
been fooling herself. Maybe she'd known all along she
wanted Parker to have easier access to her breasts.

As if he heard her thoughts, his hands lifted from
her waist to just beneath her breasts, stilled there. He
spread his fingers, his thumb grazing the swell of them.

'Now you're just being a tease.'

'Ask for it then. Or do you want me to ask?' His right thumb moved up, stopping just below her nipple. 'Can I touch you here, Soph?'

'Yes.' The word shuddered from her lips as lustily as her breath had earlier. 'Please,' she added for good measure, because in the second since she'd said yes he hadn't done anything and she needed him to do something.

'Since you asked so nicely…'

His thumb brushed over her nipple. Her breath rushed out her lungs. Then his left hand grazed her other nipple and the air rushed right back in with one quick inhale.

'I wanted to do this this afternoon,' he said, his fingers still moving. 'More.'

She moaned, then gripped his wrists before turning to face him. 'How are you doing this?'

'What?'

'Making touches and kisses more erotic than anything I've ever experienced before.'

He smiled at her, and it occurred to her that she might be a victim. Something inside her had put its hands up and surrendered at that satisfied smile, after all.

He reminded her of the men on the covers of the romance novels Angie had hidden under her bed when they'd been younger. Fierce, predatory. Charming in their preying nature.

'Because I want you,' he said.

'I want you, too,' she whispered. Helplessly.

Slowly, she placed a hand around his waist. With the other, she reached between them, to the hardness she felt pressed against her. His intake of air had *her* smiling now. She hoped it was as predatory as his smile had been.

When his eyes met hers, she stopped smiling. Because he was looking at her with a need she'd never seen anyone show her before. Her hand stilled, then moved up, around his neck, and she pressed up to kiss him.

It wasn't like any of the others. Her throat was thick and her eyes felt strange, but her mouth moved against his and she thought of nothing but him. Her body, her heart yearned for him. She didn't think she could stop them. His tongue in her mouth sent wave after wave of pleasure through her. His hand had gone under her dress and had one butt cheek in it. He squeezed, pressing her against him as she rocked herself against his hardness.

'Sophia,' he said. He didn't move any other part of his body except for his head, and rested his forehead against hers. 'We're almost on the ground.'

She nodded, swallowed, and didn't say anything because she was afraid her voice would betray her. He moved his hand, pulled down her dress, but still held her. She rested her head on his chest, and closed her eyes, hoping she wouldn't give in to the urge to cry.

Then they were on the ground, in the cool air of the night, and Parker was pulling her toward the marina.

She followed him. She was in too deep to resist. Then again, she didn't *want* to resist. She wanted to follow him. Even though she was sure following him would be walking off a cliff and plummeting to her death. Truth be told, she already felt like she was dangling over the edge.

It was quieter here, less busy, probably because it was

dark and the only thing they could see was the ocean crashing against the edge of the bridge. She clung to the sound of it, then to him when he stopped and put an arm around her.

'I can hear you worrying.'

'I'm not,' she said automatically.

'Your brain's pretty loud, Soph,' he said, leaning a hip against the railing and bringing her with him.

'You're not worried?' She searched his face. There was only the moonlight to illuminate his features, but it was enough. 'Why aren't you more worried?'

'I don't know if *worried* is the word I'd use,' Parker said carefully.

'What would you use?'

'I don't know. I'm not trying to give it a name. It's easier that way, I guess. I'm…enjoying it.'

'You're enjoying this? This…this desperation?' She tried to move, but his arm tightened. She didn't try again. 'Why aren't you giving me space?'

'Because you're going to start spiralling if I do,' he told her, his tone serious. 'First, you'll pace. Then, you'll run to the mall's entrance and get into the first taxi you see. I know, because that's what you did this morning.'

'I was upset.'

'You're upset now.' He kissed her forehead. It felt like he'd punctured her; all her resistance gushed out. 'It's going to be okay.'

'You didn't think so when we left the hospital.'

'That wasn't about this.'

She let the silence sit for a moment. 'It's too complicated.'

'My life?' he asked lightly. 'I agree.'

She rolled her eyes, sprawled her hands over his chest. Then frowned.

'You know what the worst part of this is?' she said, looking at her fingers.

'Tell me.'

'I didn't even get to see you naked.'

He laughed, the sound vibrating through her hands, rattling her own body. Her nerves were still alive from what they'd done in that glass container—and in the garden that morning; waiting for the bus; on Table Mountain; her bedroom. His laughter made her feel as though she were on a high, and Sophia wondered what would happen when she crashed back down when all this ended.

'Technically you did see me naked. Almost.'

'Are you talking about when you came out of the shower?' she asked. He nodded. 'That doesn't count.'

'Did you want me…completely naked?'

She smiled. 'Is the answer to that ever no?' She didn't wait for his confirmation. 'But no, it doesn't count because I didn't get to touch you.'

She lowered her hand so it covered his abs. The muscles contracted beneath her fingers. She was sure the smile that it evoked on her face was as satisfied as…a woman who had seductive power over a man she really, really liked.

Nerves rolled in her stomach. She thought her own muscles might tremble because of it.

'Do you want to go back to my place?'

'Why would I want that?' She opened the top button of his shirt. 'I can touch you right here.'

To his credit, he didn't look as shocked as she intended for him to.

'Not sure I want to get arrested for public indecency tonight.'

'It would make for a hell of a story.'

'True. Except I have responsibilities.'

'Hmm.' She popped open another button, then stopped there, pressing a kiss to the exposed skin. 'You're right.'

She kissed his collarbone, his neck, nuzzling there before trailing gentle kisses along his jaw until she reached his mouth. The kiss she pressed there was gentle. A sigh left her lips when he responded in kind.

Then the panic was back, the funny feeling in her throat, the prickling in her eyes. When they broke apart, his eyes swept over her face. She pulled away, and he let her go this time. Folding her arms, she leaned against the railing, looking out over the ocean.

It was something spectacular. The air was salty and crisp, nothing like the humid air of earlier that day. She couldn't tell if that was because they were standing above the ocean, or if the weather had changed that drastically. It didn't matter. The temperature suited the scene. The waves that were crashing against the wall that kept them from getting wet. The moon in the distance, the stars above them. He'd wanted to give her romance; he succeeded. They even had privacy, which for a second made her consider persuading him into showing her some skin again.

She almost laughed at the thought. It was unlike her to be so...wanton. She settled for that description instead of the crasser one her mind offered. It mitigated the discomfort fluttering in her chest. If she could swallow the description of the way she was acting, perhaps the fact that she was acting like it at all would be less alarming.

And was it really that new, this wantonness? She was sexually attracted to men. That wasn't a surprise nor a discovery. Yet *this* sexual attraction was surprising. It did feel like a discovery. She didn't know if she was discovering a part of herself that had always been there, or if Parker had sparked it in her.

It occurred to her that she never allowed herself to explore her sexual desires. That attraction she'd claimed as unsurprising moments ago had never been a motivating factor for her. If she unpacked it, she supposed she could blame the one time that she had used it as motivation. It had got her a boyfriend…who then disappointed her when her father got sick.

And then her life had been about her father's sickness. After, it had been about his death. Five years later, she was still distracted by things outside herself. Her family, for the most part. She hadn't had the energy to add men into the equation as well. And considering the energy she'd expelled on her family and Parker today— in these last minutes alone—perhaps Past Sophia had been onto something.

'You're worrying again.'

'No, I'm not,' she denied. She pulled her jacket tighter around her. He immediately wanted to take her away, into the mall where it would be warmer. But he didn't think she'd take kindly to his impulses. He settled for the lesser of the evils.

'Would you like my jacket?'

She looked over her shoulder at him. His heart stopped, stared at her, then realised it wasn't beating anymore and made up for it by pumping furiously. Parker didn't even care. A heart attack was an appropriate reaction to how beautiful she was. Even with her brow furrowed in concentration, those wonderfully full lips set in a line, she was breath-taking.

He supposed he could blame the backdrop of a dark ocean and the moonlight. The stars, perhaps, since they twinkled above her as if they'd chosen her for some special mission. He didn't blame it on that. Because it was all her. Not because she had features that were pleasing to the eye, or that her short hair highlighted those features sharply. It was that those features could become animated in a second. They usually settled somewhere on the annoyance spectrum, which, he thought, might incur a similar expression on his own face. But that was part of the appeal of her, only heaven knew why. This woman with her harmless name and her pleasing features that could fire up annoyance and desire in him within a single breath.

He was right when he'd told her *worried* wasn't the right word. He was *changing*. The excuses he'd used to enjoy the moment before going on that Ferris wheel were fading quickly, leaving behind the alarming truth: he wanted to change. To believe that something more was possible with Sophia. That didn't worry him; it terrified him.

'I appreciate your gentlemanly offer, but I'm fine. The cold reminds me not to get too comfortable.'

'The worry does, too, huh?'

'I wasn't worrying right now,' she said, though she didn't deny what he said. 'I was thinking about how I haven't felt this hot for…anyone, in the last six, maybe seven years.'

'You've felt this way before?'

She turned to face him more fully. 'You haven't?'

'No.'

'Maybe everything feels more intense because of the stuff with your family.'

'Did things get more intense because of the stuff with your family?' he asked, irritated that she was trying to invalidate his feelings. 'Or was that the reason you haven't felt this way in the last six, maybe seven years?'

'Touché,' she replied after a moment. 'Maybe I didn't find the right person to awaken the need to work through grief with sex.'

'That isn't a thing,' he denied, though there was a part of him that thought she might be right. It would be an easy explanation for why hearing her talk about the right person made him yearn. It would explain his other feelings for her, too. But he knew that wasn't it. They were simply more excuses. His stomach twisted.

'You don't know that. Though it wasn't for me, obviously. Nor my sisters.' Her head tilted. 'Maybe it isn't a thing then.'

'Even when you don't make sense I want to take you back to my place. Maybe it is a thing,' he muttered to himself.

She smiled. It was somehow hungry *and* satisfied. He had no idea how she managed it. He only knew his body responded to it.

And then it changed. The expression on her face, the feeling in his body. She lowered her eyes, turned away from him completely. It felt like a warning: she was putting distance between them.

He took a step forward, physically breaching some of the distance. Wanting some of the cold that had gone down his spine to disappear.

She angled back to him. 'You're using me, and this, as an excuse not to face what happened at the hospital with your mother.'

The statement came out of left field. So far out of it that he had to take a moment to figure out how to reply.

'A one-day distraction,' he said softly. 'Isn't that what we agreed to today? Both of us,' he clarified, when she opened her mouth on what would no doubt be denial.

He didn't say it because he thought she was right. He did so to figure out whether she still felt the same way in light of everything that had changed. Because at some point during the day, their time together had gone from wanting to distract one another from their lives to…something else. Something more meaningful. Something that had little to do with their families.

'Except distraction isn't going to work for much longer,' she told him. 'Hell, it didn't completely work for me today. It gave me more to worry about though.' She bit her lip, then turned to face him completely again, resting her back against the railing. 'I struggle. Struggled.' She shook her head. 'No, struggle. Realising things doesn't make them go away.' She sounded as though she was talking to herself. She exhaled. 'Sorry. My point is that today with you made me realise things

I had no intention of realising. I think I could have happily lived my life without knowing them, in fact. Or not happily, but—'

She broke off with another shake of her head.

'What are you talking about?'

'You asked me if I compared myself to my sister earlier. It was the first time I allowed myself to realise that I did. Because I did, I let Zoey and my mom do it, too. I didn't ever think about how crap that made me feel until today. I mean, I knew it made me feel crap, but I didn't realise it was because of that until today.' She huffed out a breath. 'That makes no sense, does it? I'm sorry. I'm still trying to figure it out.'

'Why did you compare yourself?' he asked gently, understanding what it was like to have a mind that spun.

'Because my parents did.'

'And it made you want to be like Angie.'

'No,' she denied immediately. 'It made me think that being like Sophia was…' She trailed off with a frown.

'What?' he asked, desperate to know what she'd just realised.

'It made me think I wasn't good enough.' Her eyes met his. The openness there stole his breath. She was letting him see it. He felt honoured. 'I've been so defensive about being who I am because I didn't think I had to be like Angie to be good enough. But I think I was… I don't know. I think I *did* think I had to be like her to be good enough. Which messed up our relationship, and the relationship I had with everyone in my family. I was annoyed they didn't think I was good enough either, but really it was me who thought it.' She brought her hands to her hair. 'I made my head hurt.'

He didn't go to her like he wanted to. 'That can happen.'

She grunted. 'This is unfair. I wanted *you* to have some kind of realisation, not me.'

Except he had. Only it had to do with her, and not what was going on in his life. And it had happened long before this moment, with all the changes and the shifting: he didn't only really like her; he was falling in love with her.

He wasn't even surprised by it. Things had been tightening and expanding throughout their day together. His thoughts on relationships had been challenged. There were significant feelings, emotional and physical. Sophia had claimed a stake in both those spheres, and he was scared, but not put off by it. He wasn't sure how that was possible. They'd spent a day together. Barely that. And most of it had been riling each other up; taking each other down.

'The least you could do is have a realisation of your own,' she said darkly. 'Something like, "Hey, I'm pissed at myself for being pissed at my mom when she's sick".'

'I didn't need to have a realisation for that. I already knew it.'

'How about, "I'm actually pissed that I'm going to lose her someday".'

'Again, not news.'

She studied him, her eyes sharp. Seeing. And he stopped thinking about the two of them, of his feelings for her.

'"I'm pissed because I don't know how to turn to people for help and losing my mother might force me to."'

'What?'

'"I'm scared that when I lose my mother, I won't have anyone else."'

Her words were blunt, but her expression was gentle. As if he were a wounded wild animal she had to be firm with, while still having compassion for. His heart thudded slowly when the metaphor and her words resonated with him, sending pulses of pain into his chest. Some of it shot up, into his skull. A light pounding filled his head.

She was right. And he needed to hear it. But it felt… wrong.

'Sophia—'

'"What happens to me when the only person I love is gone?"'

'Stop it,' he bit out. 'Stop.'

'I'm right,' she said, her expression going even softer. For some reason, it made him angrier. And made the pain, the *grief*, worse.

'I said, stop,' he growled.

'You know I'm right.'

'You didn't have to say it.'

'You know that's a lie, too. You know you needed someone to say it. If it wasn't me, it would have been your mother, and you shouldn't be angry with her now.'

'It's rich that you're accusing me of not being able to ask for help when you can't either.'

'At least I know it.'

'I'm not only talking physical help here. I'm talking emotional. Like this stuff that you realised and kept to yourself. If you opened up to someone, *anyone*, before this, you wouldn't be in your mid-twenties figuring it out.'

Her eyes flashed with hurt, but her tone was calm. 'I'm going to let that one slide because figuring stuff out is hard.'

'You don't think your fight with Zoey today could have been prevented if you'd been honest with her?'

'About what?'

'That you resent her. You resent her for having to take care of her. Same with your mother. Your father. And your issues with Angie are because she didn't resent it. She did it perfectly and never complained.'

He was lashing out. As he said the words—words he knew he couldn't take back—he knew it. But he kept talking. It helped him ignore the new wave of terror her accusations had caused in him. About his mother, about losing her, about asking for help. But also his fear that if anything happened between him and Sophia, she would come to resent him, too. She'd have to help take care of his mother, she'd eventually start taking care of him, and she'd resent him for it.

'You don't know what you're talking about.'

'That hasn't stopped you from making claims about my life.'

'Oh, Parker, you're such a child sometimes,' she said, exasperated. 'I'm trying to help you. You're trying to hurt me.'

'Is it working?' he asked sharply, hating himself as he did.

'Yes,' she replied easily. 'It is. Or the accusations are. I don't know. I'm going to add it to the things I'll spend the rest of my life trying to figure out. What's one more anyway?'

'Sophia—'

'No, stop it. Stop talking. You're making me mad.'

'Ditto.'

'Yeah, but I'm mad because you're doing exactly what I told you you're doing and you can't even see it.'

'Let's leave this, okay? I'm not in the mood to be forced into realisations.'

'You're never going to be in the mood. Maybe that's why your mother didn't tell you things.'

'Why do you keep pushing?' he said through gritted teeth.

'Because I want you to hate me,' she exclaimed. 'I want you to be so angry at me that you don't have energy to be angry at your mom. You shouldn't waste the time you have left with her. While she's lucid and able to make confessions.'

It struck him. And he went cold. Just…cold.

'I can hate you and still be angry at my mom,' he said quietly. 'I *am* angry at my mom. And your experience with grief doesn't mean I don't get to have mine. Just because you wish you could do things differently with your father now that he's dead doesn't mean I have to listen to you.'

A long, drawn-out silence followed his words, giving him plenty of time to feel the shame that doused him.

'Soph—'

'You're right,' she interrupted, silencing him with a hand. 'You don't have to listen to me. But I'm not telling you things because I wish I'd done them differently. My father and I were different people. I was resentful right up until the very end because of what he allowed me and Angie to go through. I was resentful today, when I thought about how he's the reason Zoey thinks

I should be nicer. That *I* worried I should be nicer. If he was alive, I would have told him that as soon as I realised it consciously. And he would have brushed it off like he did everything else I told him. He loved me, but he didn't listen to me. I was his child, and he was the parent, which made him perpetually right and me, perpetually wrong. That wouldn't have changed if I'd done things differently. It probably would have made things worse.'

He stared at her. Whatever she saw on his face made her say, 'That's what you don't get, Parker. My dad being dead doesn't change our relationship. I know who he was; he knew who I was. We were content with those limitations. If we'd wanted to change things, we would have.' There was a moment of silence before she continued. 'My feelings about him and who he was as a father won't change because he's not here. We're still living the effects of his choices.'

'You're choosing to live the effects of his choices,' he interrupted when she took a breath. 'You sound very calm and certain about what you feel about him, but you forget he's not here anymore. You can do whatever the hell you want to now, and you still choose to follow the path he set out for you.'

She didn't reply immediately.

'If I am, it's because my sister and mother can't walk that path alone.'

'Or you're telling yourself that because you're used to the way things are and you don't want them to change.'

'No,' she said with a shake of her head. 'I want things to change. I'd love for them to change.'

'Things changed when Angie left, didn't they? Did you love it then?'

'She walked away—'

'Because she chose not to follow the path your father set out for her. You can't keep blaming her for that.'

She exhaled. 'No, I can't.'

'So you admit that you're choosing this?'

'I don't know. Maybe.' She shrugged. Her gaze found his. Sharpened. 'Is this really all so you can avoid talking about your own issues?'

He rolled his eyes. 'It's getting old now, Sophia.'

'You're right,' she said after a moment. 'Admittedly, I got distracted and went the roundabout way through this… Look, I have two things to say to you, and then I'm done. One, maybe you're so obsessed with my relationship with my dead father because you're unhappy with your relationship with your father. If he died tomorrow, would you want to go back and change things?' She barrelled on, not waiting for his answer. 'Two. Your relationship with your mother is so much better than anything I've ever shared with my father. You're going to regret wasting the time you have with her being angry. Get over yourself, and talk it through with her. Or push it aside and pretend it didn't happen. But make the most of your time with your mother, Parker. You won't get these moments again.'

Chapter Sixteen

The conversation had veered so far off course that Sophia was certain they would crash. The crash would come with more carnage than his questions. His astute observations. He'd hurt her, and she was still grappling with the fact that he'd wanted to hurt her. So she walked away, before she could add one more thing to what she'd said to Parker.

This is why we would never work out.

Yes, a crash was imminent.

She walked to the entrance of the mall where taxis waited, then pushed past them, down the long road that led out of the Waterfront. It wasn't meant for pedestrians. There was no place to walk. She stayed on the edge of the road, pressing to the side of it, trying to stay out the way of cars. The road eventually curved to the opposite end of the mall to where she and Parker had been. She thought she'd stop there, take one of the taxis, but still, she walked. Then she heard laughter.

The sound juxtaposed everything she felt inside. It was light and happy when she felt heavy and dark. And it meant preoccupation with something outside her and not the turmoil in her head. She walked toward it as if she were a moth and the laughter a flame that would heat the ice in her chest.

She stopped in front of a comedy club, the light from the door gleaming in a dark alleyway. The laughter sounded again, and she was so desperate for the joy of it that she bought the exorbitant ticket at the door. But she mistimed it. As she walked in, the comedian had begun to look for people to bring onto the stage. She turned on her heel.

'Ma'am? Hey, miss. With the red dress and denim jacket.'

She made it to the door but was blocked by a large man. He didn't move when she hissed at him. The comedian called again. With a clench of her jaw, she turned back to the stage.

'Are you running away?'

'Yes,' she said. The crowd chuckled.

'Why? We're perfectly nice people here, aren't we?' The comedian, a scrawny guy with an afro, gestured to the crowd. Obeying, they cheered.

'You want to bring me up on stage because you want to be nice to me?' she asked.

'Sure.'

She only looked at him. He gave a mock shudder.

'Things are getting chilly in here.'

Oh, great. He wasn't a good comedian either.

'Fine,' she said. She wanted to be preoccupied, didn't she? 'Let's get this over with.'

She made her way to the stage amongst cheers, which she imagined came from a bloodthirsty crowd sensing a possible confrontation. She would not give them what they wanted. Certainly not in a segment of a comedy show she despised. Why did comedians think roasting the people in their audience was funny?

Because their audience finds it funny, she heard Zoey's voice say in her head. It was a memory more than a hallucination. This wasn't the first time Sophia had asked the question. The audience's current reaction seemed to prove Zoey's answer, too.

Sophia nearly grunted out loud; she settled for swearing at them in her head.

'What's your name?' the comedian asked once she reached the stage.

'Sophia.'

'Nice to meet you, Sophia. I'm Loyiso. They already know this, but I thought I'd introduce myself to you since you just got here.'

'Thank you,' she said, taking his hand. 'If you didn't say that, I probably wouldn't have known who you are.'

That got a laugh out of the crowd, and Loyiso's eyes went sharp. She wondered if it was a sign that he was one of those people who could dish it out but couldn't take it. Or perhaps he simply recognised a sparring partner. Either way, she thought she might have misjudged his abilities.

'Okay,' he said after a moment, offering her a smile. 'Obviously you aren't going to take this lying down. Fortunately, I like that in a woman.'

'Oh, sex jokes,' she said blandly. 'Very unique. Well done.'

Loyiso tilted his head. 'I don't usually get this much of a response from my volunteers.'

'I'm betting it's the same with the women you have sex with.'

Again, there was laughter from the crowd. Loyiso's smile turned genuine. For the first time, she thought he might not be an asshole. Just a man doing his job. His abilities were still up in the air considering she was getting more laughs than he was, but she respected that he was trying.

'Speaking of which, are you busy later?'

Okay, she deserved that, she thought, her lips twitching.

'No, I take that back,' he said. 'I should first ask whether you're here with anyone before I proposition you.'

'You could *not* proposition me,' she told him. 'But since I don't think that'll happen, I'm going to say yes, I am.'

'You walked in alone, didn't you?'

'Aren't you meant to be making jokes?'

'Usually, I rely on my quick wit and sharp tongue. I'm betting you can say the same?'

'Are you flirting with me or roasting me?'

'The former,' he said, his eyes going serious. 'I like you.'

The room went wild, the tone changing from a comedy routine to something different. Sophia looked at the front of the audience, the only people she could see because of the lights. Their expressions looked a lot like Zoey's did when she was watching one of those reality shows she liked. Before the man chose the woman, or vice versa. It was that moment of anticipation, of escape. She questioned her mental state when it almost tempted her to give in.

But as she thought it, Parker's face flashed in her

mind. A tightening at the base of her throat joined the image shortly after. It took her a moment to recognise the feeling as loyalty. Which definitely made her question her sanity because she had no reason to be loyal to Parker.

They'd known one another for a day. He'd told her he wanted to hurt her so he wouldn't have to think about his problems. Her own mind was still full of the realisations their day together and her conversations with her family had evoked. Her heart was confused by its feelings for him.

'Oh, no,' Loyiso said, talking to the crowd now. 'I already know how this is going to go down. Maybe I shouldn't have admitted that in front of a crowd of people.'

'It's fine,' she said through numb lips. She didn't want to embarrass him. 'I mean, I'm sure there are plenty of other women who'll feel sorry enough—I mean, who are attracted enough—to go out with you.'

'Ouch,' he said, wincing. 'I should have stuck to jokes about religion and politics. Safer.'

'Much,' she agreed, smiling.

He didn't think he'd ever seen someone go toe to toe with a comedian before. He wasn't surprised Sophia was the reason for the first time he did. She was his first for a lot of things. And in the space of twenty-four hours—less than.

No wonder he was pushing her away. Her power over him was potent.

That didn't mean he wanted other men to hit on her. He watched the exchange between Sophia and the comedian with sharp irritation building in his chest. When the man said he liked her, that irritation cut through him. He had to consciously stop himself from marching to the stage and punching the guy. He did so by imagining how Sophia would have reacted if he had.

'What are you—a dog?' she said in his head. *'Marking your territory? And since when are women territory, anyway? Do better, Parker.'*

He shook his head, hoping her voice would fade. It was too sharp. Too familiar already. If he didn't curb it now, force it to fade, he'd hear it for the rest of his life. What good would that do? What good would come of it pointing out when he was doing something stupid? Or when he was being an idiot? How would it help if her voice called him out for avoiding his feelings? For being a jerk to his mother?

Now, it was telling him he was pushing Sophia away because she was right. And because she scared him. Those feelings, those shifts in his views; they scared him. Told him he wanted her in his life, and the last time he'd wanted someone in his life, he'd got his twelve-year-old heart broken. He was on the edge of having his twenty-six-year-old heart broken with his mother, too. He couldn't afford to add Sophia to that. Even if he wanted to.

Still, he waited for her to finish. The comedian's set ended at the same time, and they walked off the stage together. Parker's fists closed as he watched them huddle close, the man's lips near her ear. She shook her head, smiled, and took a step back. Then with a nod, she turned away, walking to the door. She stopped when she saw him, the remnants of the smile she'd given that man disappearing.

'What are you doing here?' she asked.

'I'm your ride home.'

'Did you follow me?'

'Did you think I'd let you walk alone at night?'

She rolled her eyes. 'We've come full circle then.'

'Let me take you back to the hospital and then we can say that.'

'Home,' she said after a moment. 'Zoey messaged an hour ago to say she and Mom were home, so take me home.'

'Of course.'

With a sigh, she followed him out the club. They took a more conventional route to the parking lot, going through the mall instead of around it. All the time, Sophia didn't speak. He was acutely aware of how tense she was, perhaps because he'd caused it. He opened his mouth to apologise, but he didn't know what else to say besides 'I'm sorry.' He was still figuring out the rest, and if she prodded, he would snap at her. Again. So he left the silence.

It stayed throughout their drive home, until he reached the corner of her road.

'Stop,' she said.

He checked for cars behind him—nothing—and obediently pulled to the side of the road, putting his hazards on.

'What's wrong?'

'Nothing's wrong,' she said, turning to him. She unclicked her safety belt and turned to him. 'Well, not nothing, but I'm not asking you to stop because I think something's wrong.'

'I don't understand.'

She poked her tongue into the inside of her cheek. Sighed. 'This is probably the last time we'll see each other.'

Panic poured into him, hot and melting, like lava.

'What do you mean? Of course we'll see each other again.'

She gave him a look. 'Fine then. This is the last time I *want* to see you.'

'What?'

'This day has run its course,' she said softly. 'It's been a really good day. Up until the last hour, anyway. Then again, the last hour might still have been necessary.' She paused. Sighed again. 'Point is, it's over now.'

'You sound so sure.'

'I am sure. You are, too,' she said, 'or you wouldn't be trying to hurt me.'

He let out a breath. 'I'm sorry, Soph. I shouldn't have said those things. My feelings for you—'

'No,' she interrupted. 'Don't say it. Nothing good can from it if you're already pushing me away. Plus, if you don't say anything, it'll make things easier for the both of us.'

'This is easy?' he scoffed as his fear was eclipsed by pain.

It was familiar. The same pain he'd felt when his father had left him. The same pain he was dreading his mother's illness would bring. He hated that Sophia had been clumped in with the darker things in his life. She was light, and she wasn't leaving because she was being selfish, like his father. She wasn't leaving because she didn't have a choice, like his mother. She was doing this deliberately, for his benefit.

'See?' she said quietly. 'You know this is easier. Our lives…they wouldn't allow this, *us*, to go past today. That's why I was freaking out about liking you. Why you were trying to enjoy the moment.'

And now she was trying to make him think it was for her benefit, too, but he wouldn't fall for it.

'You're only saying that be—'

'Parker,' she said sharply. 'Don't fight me on this. Please.' Her voice broke on the plea. 'We can't have this.'

But I want it. I want you.

He couldn't say it. What if she was right? What if everything that had happened—that *was* happening—with his family was supposed to keep them apart? What if it was protecting them from more heartbreak when they both had plenty enough to deal with already?

'It's better this way.'

'Sure,' he said bitterly.

She looked over, her eyes pleading with him to understand. And he did. Which was why he was so bitter.

'What you're going through isn't going to get easier.' Her voice was gentle. 'You're lashing out, and until you've processed things, you'll keep doing that. At me, if I'm around. One, because I know what it's like and two…' She hesitated. 'You'll get tired of hearing the truth from me. And I won't lie to make you feel better. I won't change because I want you to like me and not hurt me. This is me. Saying goodbye now—' She broke off with a shaky breath. 'It'll prevent the future pain.'

He clenched his jaw. Forcibly relaxed it. His mind wasn't as easy to calm, though. His thoughts were scrambling to find reasons to convince her to stay. They were also fighting against the fears of what would happen if she was right, and he kept hurting her because he was hurt. Even the prospect pained him. He took a deep breath.

'I have two things to say, too,' he said slowly. 'One, I really am sorry. You didn't deserve what I did. I was lashing out at you, but I promise, it'll never happen again. Even if that's because we never see each other after tonight,' he forced himself to say. 'But even if we do, I wouldn't—' He broke off. 'Can you forgive me?'

'Yes,' she said quickly. Quietly. He wondered if it was because she thought they'd never see one another again.

'Two.' He inhaled deeply. 'I don't want you to change. I never have, even when you were annoying the hell out of me. Even—' his voice softened '—when you were forcing me to face the truth. I... I adore you, Sophia. You're caring and quick-witted and too damn smart for your own good.' He brushed at the hair falling over her forehead. 'You're also annoying, sarcastic, and, I'm pretty sure, a witch—' he paused so he could memorise that smile '—and I wouldn't change a single thing about you.'

'You're just saying that,' she whispered.

'No,' he disagreed. 'Though that might be because I haven't met Angie yet.' He laughed when she swatted his arm, caught her hand, and brought it to his lips. 'I think you're scared that I do, Soph. I see who you are and I don't want you to change. I don't expect you to, and I won't ever compare you to anyone either. Hell, I'll probably be comparing the women I meet after tonight to you. You'll be the standard.'

My standard.

Her eyes flew to his. There was a strange combination of emotions there. Pleasure at his words. Surprise, too. He couldn't read the rest, and he desperately wanted to know what they were. He kept himself from asking.

'I think that's the thing I find most annoying about you,' she said softly.

'What?'

'Your charm. You piss me off and in the same breath make me swoon.' She looked up, blinking rapidly. His heart fluttered in much the same way. 'There's no future for this, and yet I still want there to be.'

'Me, too,' he admitted, although he wanted to disagree.

There could be a future. Just not one either of them was ready for.

She looked at him again, her expression serious—comically so. The little furrow in her brow was adorable. The part between her lips enticing. He wanted to lean forward and kiss her. Distract them both from what was happening. Give them one last memory.

She put a hand on his knee. 'We should say goodbye.'

He leaned forward. 'Okay. Let's say goodbye.'

She hadn't meant for their goodbye to be this way, but when Parker edged toward her, something desperate cheered inside her. Her fingers traced his face, its tender expression reminding her of that afternoon in her bedroom. She inched forward to meet him halfway, and sighed into his mouth when her lips felt like they'd found their home.

She refused to think about that and fell into the kiss.

Let the movement of their lips say goodbye, let the duelling of their tongues tell him she'd miss him. She cupped his face, before lowering her hands and resting them on his neck. She could feel the unsteady drum of his pulse under her fingers, took satisfaction from its fierce tempo. Her fingers slipped lower, to the skin that was still exposed from earlier, when she'd unbuttoned his shirt.

She left the kiss to press her lips there, looking up at him in inquiry as her hand hovered over the buttons. Without breaking eye contact, he nodded. She undid the buttons further, revealing smooth brown skin. No, that was a lie. There was nothing smooth about it. Too many ripples, too many curves, too many lines and dents.

She frowned, tracing the intricate pattern of his chest, his abs.

'Put your chair back,' she commanded. He obeyed without a word. She did the same with hers, leaning over the gearbox to get a better look.

'You know,' he said slowly, his voice a deep rumble in the confines of the car. 'The last time I got examined this thoroughly, it was for a doctor's appointment.'

'I can pretend to be a doctor if you like.' Her eyes flickered up from her inspection. 'Tell me what aches.'

He groaned, reached out, and pulled her so that she was sprawled over him. It was not elegant, but it was surprisingly satisfactory. Her breasts pressed against his chest, her mouth was level with his, and they kissed again. Hungry. Feeding their appetites.

She gave her hands free rein over his body, arching into him as his hands explored her own. He touched everywhere, trailing lazily over places, gripping oth-

ers more fiercely. He couldn't seem to decide what to
do with her thighs. He stroked the thick flesh, squeezed
it, ran his fingers over it. Then his hand found her butt
and stayed there, before moving to the sensitive area
between her thighs.

'This seems a bit over the top for a goodbye,' she
said as she struggled to breathe.

He smiled. 'I don't think there's over the top with
this.'

'Glutton.'

'For you,' he said, nipping at her neck. 'Very much.'

She adjusted herself, trying to find a comfortable
spot. There was none. He offered no assistance, simply
continuing to caress the soft flesh of her inner thigh. He
must have been purposefully teasing her, because he
moved no further up. Each stroke made the ache only
centimetres—*centimetres*—away ache more. She was
very tempted to take his hand and move it to where
she needed it, but she felt like she'd be losing if she
did. Instead, she snuggled closer, putting her hand on
his open chest.

'Do you know we could just as easily be arrested for
public indecency here as at the Waterfront?'

'The chances are slimmer here,' he replied. 'Besides,
this is…tamer than what you wanted to do at the Waterfront.'

'How do you know?'

'Something about your eyes.'

She brought her lips above his, barely touching, but
close enough that he could feel her breath. 'What are
they telling you now?'

He studied her. She allowed him to. Mostly because

she wanted to see his expression as her hand moved down, over his chest, his abs, settling above the bulge straining against his jeans.

Surprise. Anticipation. Desire.

'You're warning me.'

'No,' she said with a quick shake of her head. 'Asking permission.'

'Granted,' he said without a beat. He brought one hand up to cup her face. 'You're going to make things more complicated, aren't you?'

She smiled. Sank into the moment. They wouldn't have any others, and she'd be damned if she didn't take advantage of what they did have. If she didn't give her body, her heart, this.

The smile widened with satisfaction.

'Not complicated,' she said. 'Harder.'

The smile killed him.

Sure, she was currently opening the front of his jeans, but it was that smile that gripped him. It was a feral smile; or not entirely a smile at all. Just a show of teeth that told him exactly who was in charge. It turned him on more than a hand in his pants could.

And then she put her hand down his pants and he realised that wasn't true at all.

Her eyes had caught the expression from her smile; her gaze never left his. As she gripped him, she shifted closer, so that their lips were centimetres apart. Her hand tightened slightly; he groaned. Then she began to move, and his lips parted, his breath rushing out. He tried to inhale, but pleasure took over, pressure built, and he let go of any attempts at something as menial as breathing. Besides, if he died, at least he would die happy. There were worse ways to go.

He put his hand on the back of her head, drawing her closer so he could kiss her. He wanted her over him, so he could offer her some of the pleasure she was giving him. Unfortunately, that was nearly impossible with the small space they had to manoeuvre in. He settled for her lips, and hoped she still thought him a good enough kisser to make up for it.

Her grip tightened; lightly, steadily, sending wave after wave of pleasure through him. Her mouth closed over his, their tongues tangled, his free hand finding her breast. He pulled down the strap of her dress, silently thanking her for not wearing a bra, and ran a thumb over her nipple. She groaned. It vibrated through him. He tore his mouth away from hers to wet his thumb, then went back to teasing her nipple. She gasped when he made contact, then groaned again. Deeper, with such ecstasy that he hardened even more from the mere sound of it.

Then she pulled away from him, shifted her head to the side, and sneezed.

There was a beat. He opened his mouth to speak, but then she cupped her hands together and sneezed into them. A third sneeze quickly followed, then came a long, pointed silence as she lowered her hands to her lap and looked at him.

'Did you just…'

'Yep.'

There was another silence. Her eyes swept over him, lying on the driver's side, almost flat on his back. His shirt and jeans were open, his erection still in clear view. When she cupped her hands in front of her face again, he thought it might be for another sneeze. But the sound was too loud, too consistent for a sneeze. No, she was *laughing*.

'Really?' he asked dryly. 'You think this is funny?'

'Don't you?' The words came between peals of laughter. 'No, I'm sorry, you wouldn't. This is terrible. The worst timing ever. I'm sorry.'

The laughter took away some of the impact of her apology.

He supposed he could see the humour in it. After a few moments, he felt the humour of it. If not for the fact that what had happened had been utterly ridiculous—the sneeze, and what had happened before—then because of her laughter. It was loud and lyrical. Passionate, joyous, free. He hadn't heard her laugh like that that day. Oh, she'd laughed, but not like this. He wondered what else he hadn't seen of her. What else he would miss by saying goodbye.

But she was right. There was no tomorrow for them. He had to work through his stuff before he could be with her. She had to work through hers.

That didn't seem to matter in the present though. When he was looking at the most beautiful woman he'd ever had the pleasure of getting to know. Her spirit was infectious, as was her ability to annoy and be annoyed.

He would miss her. Damn it, he would miss her.

He reached out, brushed a curl over her forehead. 'That was one hell of a goodbye, Sophia Roux.'

She angled her head and pressed a kiss to his palm. 'I wanted you to remember me.'

'No chance of me not.'

The edges of her mouth lifted, though it wasn't a smile. Somewhere on the spectrum of it, but it wasn't a smile. He would miss even that, he realised, trying to commit it to memory.

'I should get home.'

He nodded, sat up. Then he remembered his state of undress. He made quick work of his shirt and jeans, then righted his seat and turned the key in the ignition. He was dimly aware of her righting her own clothing and seat, putting on her safety belt though her house was metres away. When he pulled into the driveway, he looked over.

She was staring straight ahead.

'This is it,' he said, for lack of anything else.

'This is…it.' She nodded. Still didn't look at him.

'Thank you, for today,' he said softly.

'Thank you,' she replied.

More silence. Finally, she turned her head. Her eyes gleamed, but she said, 'Goodbye, Parker. I hope everything works out with your mom.'

'I hope everything works out with your sisters.'

She opened the car door and walked away. She didn't look back.

Chapter Seventeen

Sophia felt like a different person when she woke up. It must have been because she'd had a decent night's sleep. Decent was relative, since she'd taken hours to actually fall asleep. She'd had to open the window, let the cool night air in before she didn't feel like her skin was too tight. The fresh air did nothing for her heart that still ached, her head following suit shortly after. But she'd eventually fallen asleep, and according to the clock on her phone, had slept for six hours.

Pure exhaustion, she thought, since she hadn't got nearly enough sleep the night before. But six hours had made her feel like a human being, and still put the clock at six in the morning. Visiting hours at the hospital were only that afternoon, but after thirty minutes of deliberation, Sophia thought screw it. Things might have changed, but they hadn't changed that much. Arbitrary rules weren't going to keep her from speaking with Angie. Something deep inside her told her speaking with Angie was pivotal. Which proved that some things *had* changed.

She messaged Angie.

Are you up?

It was a long five minutes before she got a reply.

I just had a baby. What do you think?

Congratulations!

A bit late, but I'll take it.

Did you even have your phone on you yesterday?

No :-)

Sophia chuckled, then sent the next message.

Can I come see you?

Visiting hours are only at one.

I know. She chewed her lip. Please.
There was no pause between that and Angie's reply.

I'll get Ezra to sneak you in.

Sophia smiled.

'Sophia wants to visit?' Ezra asked, frowning. 'She actually said that?'
    'Honestly, Ezra, you act as if my sister and I have
no relationship.'
    Angie cast her eyes over the glass box that stood next

to her. Technically it was a crib, but she refused to call it that when it looked so clinical. Her heart filled when she saw the little girl lying there. Her baby moved, and Angie let out a sigh of relief. Now she wouldn't have to poke the kid to make sure she was still alive. Angie had done that far too many times that day. It was barely seven in the morning.

'*Relationship* is a generous term for what you and Sophia share, don't you think?'

She agreed, but she would never let her husband know. She might be a mother now, but she was still a wife. Wives kept their husbands on their toes. Even when they were exhausted and tingling in areas that shouldn't be tingling, wives did their jobs. At least, that was the kind of wife she was. She would never tire of giving her husband a hard time.

'Sophia asked to see me. It doesn't really matter what the nature of our relationship—' she said the word slowly '—is, we're family.'

'You mean, you're worried about her.'

Angie sighed. 'I am. She would have never asked to see me if she didn't need something.'

'Maybe she wants to see her niece.'

'She could come during visiting hours to see Caledon.'

Ezra frowned. 'Did you just call our daughter Caledon?'

Angie wrinkled her nose. 'I was testing it out. It's not working, is it?'

'No,' Ezra said with a chuckle. He leaned over and kissed her. 'I appreciate the sentiment though.'

'I could have called her after the motel she was con-

ceived in and you would have appreciated the sentiment. You're overly grateful to me right now. Which
you should be. And you will be—forever—after this.'

'She was not conceived in a motel.'

'Sure she was. That seedy one in Caledon?' She widened her eyes. 'Shoot, that wasn't you?'

Ezra gave her a look. 'You're chirpy for someone
who spent an entire day being uncomfortable.'

'They've got good drugs here.' In all honesty though,
Angie was waiting for the moment she crashed. She
was tired. So much so that she was wired. 'Besides, it
was worth it.' She looked over at her daughter again.
Nothing could have prepared her for the love she felt.
She thought she read enough romance novel epilogues
to know that, but clearly not. 'She's got your mouth.'

'Her mouth is too tiny to tell,' he protested, but he
leaned over and looked anyway. 'She's got your eyes.'

'Oh, no, don't tell her that,' Angie said. 'Babies' eyes
change. I need them to change into yours.' She lifted
a hand and cupped his face. 'It was part of the allure
with you.'

'I'd rather my daughter not have allure.' He kissed
the top of her hands, threading their fingers together.

'Would you have minded if it weren't a daughter?'

'Still checking my biases two years and one baby in?'
She shrugged. 'It was part of our vows.'

Ezra grinned. 'We'll rewatch the wedding video and
find out.'

'I can't wait.'

He looked back at the baby. When his eyes met hers
again, they were warm, glistening with emotion. And
tears.

'I can't believe you did this.'

'Me neither,' Angie said, emotion clogging her own throat. 'It feels like the other day that we were in that café. Now we're married. We're *parents*.'

'You made my dreams come true.'

'Oh, stop that,' Angie said, feeling the wetness at her eyes. She reached for a tissue and pressed it to the tears. 'Stupid hormones.'

'Blaming them again?' he teased softly.

'They *are* to blame. Otherwise I would have never cried at seeing you do the skin-to-skin thing with her.'

'Right. That's not an emotional experience at all.'

'See, you understand.' Another tear slipped onto her cheek. 'I'm just really overwhelmed by all of this. I love you and her and these hormones are *the worst*.'

Ezra laughed, pressed a kiss to her forehead. 'We love you, too.' He leaned his forehead against hers. 'We're grateful to you for being so brave and getting her here.'

'What other choice did I have?'

'None. But we'll pretend.' He smiled. 'Now, are you sure you want to see Sophia?'

The phone sounded as he asked the question. Angie sighed. 'Sneak her in.'

'You look terrible,' Sophia said when Ezra came to find her in the waiting room.

He gave her a look. 'We just had a baby.'

'The baby didn't come out of you, did it?' she asked, then grinned. 'You're exhausted. You should get some sleep.'

'I will. As soon as Angie does.'

'She hasn't slept?'

He shook his head. 'I think she's worried she might wake up and the baby will be gone.'

'She knows this isn't a television show, right?'

He shrugged. 'She's your sister.'

Sophia took a deep breath when nerves rippled in her stomach. Angie *was* her sister. And she needed to talk with her.

It was the first time in her life that she felt such a deep compulsion to do so. Even after their father's diagnosis, they'd dealt with it pretty clinically. Angie had asked her if she was okay, she'd said yes, and that was that. It was easy to do that with Angie. She would never push, unless she thought she had to. In that case, she hadn't thought so.

As often as Sophia had judged Angie, she couldn't fault her sister for knowing who she was. For knowing who Zoey and their mom were, too. Which told her that she must have known their family needed her when she left. Her reasons for leaving seemed all the more important to learn.

She followed Ezra through the passageway, the smell of disinfectant and sterility adding to the nausea already in her stomach. She felt more nervous now than she had telling Parker all those personal things the night before. Which…alarmed her. Was part of the reason she was freaking out.

No one stopped them, not even when they reached the curtained-off corner of the room Angie was in. Four of the five other hospital beds were empty, though the signs above them told Sophia they would be filled soon. The fifth bed was directly opposite to where Angie lay.

It was occupied by a woman who looked about to pop. Her hair was tied in a bun at the top of her head, and she was patiently doing a crossword puzzle while a nurse fiddled with her drip.

'Don't make eye contact,' Ezra told her under his breath. 'If you pretend not to see them, they pretend not to see you.'

'The patients, or the nurses?'

'Both.'

He waited for her to step inside the curtain, then pulled it closed. He didn't come in again.

Sophia shifted her weight between her feet. 'Hey.'

'Hey,' Angie replied. She was sitting up against the pillows. A small bundle of human was in her arms, making a suckling noise at her breast. Sophia watched in fascination, then in horror when she realised the baby was suckling on Angie's nipple. That *must* have hurt.

'Um, congratulations?' She lifted a gift bag she'd swiped from Zoey's bedroom that morning. 'I got this for you and her.'

'Thanks. Could you put it over there?' Angie gestured to the bedside table. 'My hands are kind of full right now.'

'Yeah.' Sophia moved closer, slowly lowering into the visitor's chair as she put the gift bag on the table. 'This is weird for you, right? Please tell me it's weird for you.'

'You mean the fact that my body is making food for this tiny human being that my body also made? Or the fact that it's coming out of my nipples?'

Sophia could feel her face twisting. 'Both.'

'Oh, yeah.'

Sophia lifted her gaze to Angie. Her sister's eyes twinkled at her. In humour, yes, but also from an emotion Sophia hadn't seen on her before. On anyone before, she thought. It made her heart full even though she had no idea what it was.

'Congratulations,' Sophia said again. This time, more sincerely. 'You're a mom.' She hesitated. Pushed through. 'You're going to be amazing.'

Angie's expression changed, and she began to blink rapidly. Sophia thought she heard Angie curse, then say, 'Not again'. She hid her amusement.

Angie cleared her throat. 'Thanks.' There was a beat. 'Now, tell me why you're here.'

'Can't a girl just visit her sister after she gave birth?'

'Usually that girl would do anything she could to avoid visiting said sister,' Angie replied dryly. 'So no. Spill.'

'I don't avoid you—' She broke off on a sigh. 'Okay, I want to be honest with you, because tip-toeing is annoying me and I'm tired of things being the way they are between us.'

Angie's head reared slightly, but she gave a curt nod.

'Are you sure?' Sophia asked, though she wasn't sure herself. 'I know you're emotional and stuff because of the baby.'

'I'll try and contain myself.'

Angie's voice was dry again, a little sharp, too. Sophia almost smiled. If she'd thought giving birth would change Angie, she'd be dissuaded of that notion now.

'I...compared myself to you,' Sophia started after inhaling deeply. The best way to do it was to jump right in. 'I did it because Mom and Dad did it all the time.

It was clear who they preferred. No,' she cut Angie off when her sister opened her mouth, 'I'm not saying that to make you try to defend them, or to make myself feel worse. It's a fact. They compared us, and they preferred you.'

She curled her fingers into fists to keep from fiddling.

'I was upset with you because of it. For a long time. But I realised that I was holding myself to your standard, too. When you left... I was angry. I knew there was no way I could live up to who you were. I knew that Mom and Zo knew it, and that they'd spend the entire time thinking about how they wished it was you.'

She stopped then. She had to catch her breath. She had to catch her emotions, which were running wild in her chest, finally free. But if they stayed wild, they would run into trouble. *She* would run into trouble, and she didn't want trouble. Not for this conversation. She only wanted honesty. And answers.

'I had no idea you felt that way,' Angie said into the silence.

'Why did you think I was upset you'd left?'

'I left you alone to deal with the after-effects of Dad's death.'

'I guess that was part of it,' Sophia said after considering. 'But it was mostly because I thought I wasn't what they needed.'

'What do you mean?'

'I told you I couldn't be you.'

'And what does that mean?'

Sophia huffed out air. 'Kind. Patient. Cajoling.' The wave of resentment was less intense now, which she chose to see as progress. 'When Dad didn't want to go to treatment, you'd sit with him quietly, letting him be a jerk, and eventually, he went. When you weren't around, I told him he could either go to treatment or let Mom see him wilt away.' She winced now, the words harsh to her own ears.

'*That's* how you got him to go?'

'Yeah. What did you think?'

'I don't know. He was so mellow after treatment when you took him. I didn't expect that.'

Mellow? That wasn't the word she'd use to describe how her father had reacted to her demands. But he'd got up and gone to the doctor. And after, they wouldn't acknowledge it at all, but he'd stop acting like a self-indulgent jerk. At least for the rest of the day. Was that his way of showing he accepted her?

Her question had no answer, not now. Then again, she probably wouldn't have had the answer ever, even if her father had still been alive. She would never have asked; he would never have told her. And if she had asked, he wouldn't have answered. It would have shown too much of his mind, his thinking. It would have made him feel too vulnerable.

How that could make her miss him, she had no idea. But it did. Probably because she recognised some of that in herself. And if she could miss a stubborn old man with a fear of vulnerability, it must have meant she'd accepted him as he was. So maybe he *had* accepted her.

'You were nice to Mom and Zo, too,' Sophia said, trying to distract herself from the emotion welling up in her chest.

'So were you.'

'Was I?' she asked doubtfully. 'No one describes me as nice.'

It isn't a suitable description for people. People are... more complicated.

'Yeah, well... Nice is overrated,' Angie said, drawing her out of the memory of Parker's words. 'I wasn't being nice when I left. I was running away from being nice because I knew what would happen if I stayed.'

The baby made a sound. Angie gently pushed down on her breast, making her nipple pop out of the baby's mouth. Sophia moved back before realising she had. Angie cast her an amused look.

'Breastfeeding isn't contagious.'

'It's not the breastfeeding I'm worried about—although again, it's so weird.' She forced herself not to shudder as she thought about a baby's mouth clamping on her own breast. *No, nope, nopity no, no.* 'It's this entire thing.' She couldn't stop the shudder now.

'You don't want to be a mother?'

'Definitely not.' Angie gave her a strange look. Sophia tried to mitigate how enthusiastically she'd replied. 'I mean, I'm really happy about being an aunt. But the thing about being able to give the baby back... That sounds more like my jam.'

'How did I not know this?'

'How would it come up?'

'I don't know. Maybe in the last nine months that I've been pregnant?'

'Why would I tell you I don't want to be a mother when you were about to become one?' Sophia asked. 'That would be a bit inappropriate, wouldn't it?'

Angie studied Sophia, then looked back down at

the baby and lifted her before gently patting her on the back.

'I'm burping her,' Angie informed Sophia, 'because I'm determined to pretend like I know what I'm doing even though the nurse was in here before you came because the baby didn't want to latch.'

Sophia's lips curved. 'Okay.'

Angie nodded at her again. 'You can talk. What were you saying?'

'You were saying. About why you left.'

'Oh, yes.' She went quiet for a moment. 'When Dad died, I knew Mom wouldn't be able to cope well. She'd look for someone else to depend on, and…' She sighed. 'I didn't want it to be me. I didn't think I could handle it.'

Sophia tried to hide her surprise.

'All that niceness and patience took its toll on me,' Angie said softly. 'I was tired of looking after everyone. Losing Dad made…everything worse. I wasn't in a good space, and I had to leave or I'd move into an even worse space.'

A small burp came from the vicinity of Angie's shoulder. Angie's eyes widened in delight.

'Baby, you burped. What a good job!' Angie said, before looking at Sophia. 'Do you want to hold her?'

'Oh. Um. Okay,' Sophia said, though she was sceptical about being given so much responsibility.

She heeded Angie's instructions as to how to hold the baby though. Then she was doing it, and it felt… warm. Not the baby itself, though the bundle she held was warm, but in her chest. She felt warm in her chest. It spread out, unfurling and slithering over to her heart as she bobbed her niece up and down. She was so tiny, her features smooshed and unattractive in that way newborn babies had. Sophia could see neither Ezra nor Angie in the baby, but she could see some of her Dad in the discontented expression on the baby's face.

Despite the smooshiness and the unattractiveness—and the fact that she'd just compared the baby to her father—Sophia thought she was pretty darn cute. The warmth curled out more, turning into a fierce feeling of protectiveness Sophia had only ever felt with Zoey.

'Feeling a tiny bit broody now?'

Sophia laughed. 'Not at all.'

'You really don't want kids, huh?'

'Why is that so hard to believe?'

'It's not... Is it because you had to take care of Zo and Mom? Has it put you off wanting to take care of people?'

'What? No, of course not.' Sophia shook her head for extra emphasis, though the words stuck for some reason. 'No, I don't want kids because none of this is appealing to me.' Sophia looked at Angie. She shook her head. 'It's not that hard to understand, Ange.'

'I know. I... I gave birth a couple of hours ago, okay?' Angie said with a little exhale. 'My brain's still trying to catch up.'

'Which is why we've been having three different conversations at once?'

'Conversations are two-way streets. I'm the only one of us who has given birth.'

Sophia laughed again. 'I'll give you that, though it made no sense.' She paused. 'I also won't tell Ezra you tried to figure out why I didn't want children when you give him crap about women's agency and choices all the time.'

Angie winced. 'You're right. I'm being terribly backwards. It's probably because…' She trailed off with a sly look.

'Because you gave birth.' Sophia rolled her eyes. 'Yeah, yeah, we get it.'

'I was going to say because this is the first real conversation we've had in… Years,' Angie said.

'Yeah.' Sophia took a breath. 'Things got complicated, didn't they?'

'Understatement.'

Sophia studied Angie. 'How did you manage to make it look easy when you felt that way?'

'I put you and Zo first. I tried to protect you against what Dad did to me.' Angie sighed. 'It didn't work if you feel the way you do.'

Sophia softened. It was completely unexpected. Probably as unexpected as the fact that Angie had tried to protect them. But now that Angie mentioned it, Sophia could see her sister's attempts.

She'd always thought Angie had been an over-achiever or a brown-nose when it came to doing things for their parents. But no, she was simply trying to keep Sophia and Zoey from having to do the same—and to suffer the consequences for it.

Sophia would have to forgive Zoey for not seeing her as she'd wanted to be seen. She'd done the same thing with Angie, and it had happened so damn easily.

'You did a good job, Ange,' Sophia said fiercely. Another unexpected moment. She didn't care. 'You saved us from a lot.'

'But not enough.'

'Who says?'

Angie looked at the baby in Sophia's arms. Sophia did the same. The little girl was struggling to keep her eyes open. Sophia handed her back to Angie.

'Would you believe me if I told you there's nothing wrong with you?'

'Yes,' Sophia said. 'I think that, too.'

Angie chuckled. 'I thought you said you were comparing yourself to me?'

'Are you implying that everything with you is right?'

'Hell, no.' Angie's eyes narrowed, sharpened. 'So, you didn't come here for help. You came here for confirmation.'

Sophia shook her head. 'I came here to apologise. It wasn't because of you that I felt the way I did, but I treated you like it was.'

'It's okay,' Angie said, shaking her head. 'I was mad at you plenty of times, too. I didn't like that I felt forced to take care of you guys. That wasn't your fault, but I let it affect our relationship.'

'It's okay,' Sophia said, too. 'Zo got upset with me yesterday. She called me mean.'

'Is that why you're here? To figure out whether I think you're mean?'

'Do you?'

She didn't reply for a long time. So long, in fact, that Sophia wished she had the baby in her arms so she'd have something to do with her hands. She desperately wanted to fidget, but she resisted. Out of principle, more than anything else.

'I don't think you're mean,' Angie said slowly. 'I

think you're straightforward and blunt, but most of the time, I think that comes because you care.' Sophia's heart did a little leap. 'You weren't telling Dad to get his act together because you wanted to be mean. You wanted him to go to treatment, so he could get better. You got Zo to do her homework within minutes of getting home after it took me hours to, and Mom...' Angie trailed off. 'You somehow got Mom to try and be independent after Dad's death.'

'That wasn't me.'

'It could only be you,' Angie said gently. 'I dreaded coming home because I thought things would be falling apart.'

'I told you they weren't.'

'I thought you were...embellishing the truth. You were angry at me,' Angie said at Sophia's questioning look. 'Your two-sentence emails didn't make me think otherwise.' Sophia grimaced, but Angie shook her head. 'My point is that I thought I'd come home and find everything as bad as it was when I left. Maybe worse. It was neither. You'd got Mom to face a future without Dad. And you got Zo out of her downward spiral.'

'That *really* wasn't me,' Sophia interjected. 'She went missing for three months and came back the way she is now.'

'She...went missing,' Angie repeated slowly, her expression an interesting mixture of shock and confusion.

Sophia winced. 'Yeah. Sorry. She was sending us all emails and messages. I spoke to her once a day. She just wouldn't tell me where she was, only that she was safe.'

Now Angie was gaping at her.

'I didn't want to tell you because there was nothing you could do about it. She called Mom, too, every second day—you know how that is—and told her she was safe, too.'

Angie came out of her stupor with a shake of her head. 'Where did she go?'

'I don't know.'

'What did she say when she came back?'

'Nothing. She refused to speak about it. Then life kind of went back to our new normal.'

Angie took a deep breath, tightening her hold on the baby. 'This is…disturbing news.'

'Yay for honesty?' Sophia offered with a grimace.

'You know what? I'm going to finish what I was saying and pretend like that didn't happen. No, wait.' She frowned. 'I'll probably come back to it when I can wrap my brain around it. There's a *lot* happening right now.'

Sophia didn't comment. There was a lot happening.

'What I was going to say, is that you get things done. Maybe it doesn't look like how I used to do it. Maybe Mom and Zo won't see it that way. But there's nothing wrong with the way you show you care. Just because you're speaking in a different language doesn't mean someone won't understand you. Even if that someone isn't your family.'

She immediately thought of Parker. Realised how much having someone who spoke her language scared her. Having someone see her? Hear her? It had freaked her out. Encouraged her to accept it when he'd pushed her away… Hell, maybe it had encouraged her to push him away, too.

She'd gone on the defensive. Accepted the hurtful things he said to her instead of pushing back like her instincts had told her to. She'd found herself wondering if he should be with her. Wondering when he'd get tired of who she was.

It was a habit, she saw now. Doubting herself. She got defensive about it and pretended that she didn't care what people thought about her. But she did. She cared about what the people she loved thought about her.

But the last twenty-four hours had shown her that her habit had been formed largely because of her own perceptions. She allowed herself to believe that who she was—how she was—wouldn't be accepted. Appreciated. It had been so ingrained in her that certain characteristics were better that she let it influence her life, her relationships. Pure stubbornness was the only reason she hadn't conformed to what the world told her she should be. So when a man had come along who accepted her as she was, it had jolted her.

Not that that changed anything. Parker still had his family issues. And things would change for her now that she'd had these realisations. She should focus on that. On working through how even the anticipation of an imaginary relationship with Parker had fear spiralling down from her mind to her heart. On how she still had to trample down the *what if he wants me to change* thoughts.

But then she was speaking.

'Ange,' she said slowly, 'didn't you say you fell in love with Ezra after one day?'

Angie blinked at the change in subject, but she nodded. Then shook her head. 'It wasn't the entire falling so much as a…topple?'

'You *toppled* in love with him?'

Angie ran a hand over the baby's head. 'I like that. Yes. Yes, I think I did.'

'He…' She hesitated. 'Did he speak your language?'

Angie's gaze sharpened. 'He understood me, yes.'

'And you knew that after a day?'

'What's going on, Soph?'

Sophia blinked.

'What?' Angie asked. 'You don't want to tell me?'

'No, it's just that… I can't remember the last time you called me Soph.'

Angie's expression softened. She pulled one hand out from under the baby and brushed it over Sophia's hair.

'Me neither.'

They shared a smile, and it felt like a weight had been lifted off her shoulders. Then Angie said, 'Come on, tell me about your one-day topple. I need inspiration for my next novel.'

Chapter Eighteen

Parker slept like a baby. And by that, he meant terribly. He woke up every few hours, and at times, felt like crying himself. Except there would be no one to offer him comfort. He was alone, because he pushed everyone away.

He grunted at the thought, ignoring the alarm he'd set—in vain, as it turned out—for hours later. It was barely five in the morning, but he couldn't keep trying to fall asleep, get frustrated when he couldn't, then be pissed at being frustrated. He put on his jogging gear and went for a run, pushing himself to that line where exhaustion almost became throwing up. Broaching the line did make him retch, though nothing came out. He couldn't remember when he last ate anything. His dizziness when he got back from his run proved it.

His mood did not improve when he found his father's car in the driveway.

Taking a deep breath, he rapped on the window. His mother had given Wade a key, but he wouldn't dare use it when Penny wasn't around. Parker still couldn't figure out the dynamics of his parents' relationship, which pissed him off even more. He wanted to go to the gym

and let out his frustrations on something more construc-
tive than his father.

Gritting his teeth, he took a step back as his father
climbed out of the car. He was slightly shorter than
Parker. Ironically, when he'd shot up as a teenager,
Parker had always wondered whether he was the same
height as his father. In his memories, Wade had been
tall and steady. He'd looked up to the man both literally and figuratively. That had changed quickly enough.

'Hey, kid.'

'Dad.' Sweat dripped from his forehead. He made
a vain attempt at wiping it with his forearm, but it was
just as sweaty. He needed a shower. 'Are you here to
talk to me?'

'Yeah. Why else would I be here?'

'Who the hell knows?' he muttered. Cleared his
throat. Told himself to get a grip. 'Can it wait until
after I have a shower? Or something to eat?'

'Yeah. Of course.' His father hesitated. For a moment, Parker thought he might turn and get back into
the car. He sighed.

'You can wait inside.'

They didn't talk as they made their way to the
front door. Parker unlocked it then went straight to the
shower, spending much too long there, even he could
admit. But the water was much nicer than having to
deal with his father, so he took his time. Hoped his
body would cool down from the post-run heatwave,
too. When he was ready, almost forty minutes later, he
went to the kitchen.

His father gave him a knowing look when he entered,
but there was no malice in it. It made Parker want to

make him wait longer. He clenched his jaw, then made himself a cup of coffee and put toast into the toaster.

'What are you doing here?' Parker asked eventually.

'I hoped we could talk.'

'So talk.'

'I don't want to fight with you.'

'I'm not in the mood for fighting,' Parker lied. His father gave him another knowing look. Parker bit down on his tongue.

'I wanted to talk about your mother.'

Parker bit down harder. If he wasn't careful, he'd break the skin. He transferred his aggression to his coffee mug, holding it much tighter than it required—and burnt himself in the process.

'She's going to need some assistance—'

'I know,' Parker interrupted. 'I'll get someone to help her. Maybe a live-in nurse.'

'I was thinking the same thing. I'd like to contribute to the costs.'

Parker studied his father. Since he wasn't biting his tongue anymore, he asked, 'Why? Why do you want to help Mom so badly…now?'

He deliberately waited between those last two words, hoping his father would get his implication. Based on the sigh Wade heaved, he did.

'What?' Parker asked, bitterness controlling his tongue. 'This is too hard for you, too? Answering a simple question?'

His father didn't flinch. 'I was trying to figure out how to put a lifetime's worth of explanations into one sentence. It *is* hard.'

Shame coated Parker's tongue, preventing him from

speaking. From saying anything the reckless bitterness wanted him to say.

'Penny told me you know,' Wade started. 'About everything.'

'You mean how you two were friends and have since rekindled your friendship?'

'Yes.'

Parker watched his father. Saw the struggle there. Felt it reflected in himself. His father obviously wanted to say more, but he was waiting for Parker to give him the go-ahead. And Parker was deliberating about whether he should. That would be making things easy for Wade. The man who made a lot of Parker's life difficult.

And yet... He was curious. And he thought that maybe knowing would help him to finally let go of the anger. He suspected that anger was part of what had led to his lack of a future with Sophia. Of what was keeping him from properly processing his mother's illness, too.

After a few minutes, Parker gave in. 'I guess you have something to add to what Mom told me.'

'Yes,' Wade said gratefully, but took a while to get started. 'Your mother... Penny was always sharp. Smart, perceptive. The dumbest thing she ever did was sleep with me. And that wasn't a decision as much as a consequence of a dry spell and alcohol. For the both of us,' Wade clarified.

Parker didn't need that information about his parents, but he didn't interrupt. He was afraid of what he'd say if he did.

'When we found out she was pregnant, we thought we'd do the right thing. That was the way of things during that time, and we were friends and we liked one another… We thought it wouldn't be the worst decision we could make.'

'But it was,' Parker said flatly.

Wade nodded. 'We weren't good in a relationship. Marriage… It takes commitment. A kid takes more. The pressure of it… It got to me. I wasn't a good man, Parker.' The words were said carefully. 'I did nothing but sit around, bark at your mother, ignore you. I got mad because I felt trapped. I got madder when the bills started to pile up and your mom asked me to help.'

'If you're hoping this story will redeem you, you're doing it wrong.'

'I'm being honest,' Wade corrected. 'You deserve the truth. It's long past the time, and with your mom sick, she needs us to be on the same page. Even if that page is a reluctant truce. You'll have to make that decision.'

Something about it made him nod in agreement. He wasn't sure if it was because everything his father was saying was true, or because of the sincerity in Wade's voice when he expressed concern for Penny's health. Parker reined in the sharp responses on his tongue. Waited.

'One day I got a little too drunk and a little too mean, and your mother asked me to go. She needed space. Told me I needed space, too.'

His stomach turned. 'You never came back.'

'No.' Wade didn't meet Parker's gaze. 'I was angry enough that she dare ask me to leave that I took all I thought I needed and drove to my mother's place in George.'

'Drunk?'

'I'd half-sobered by then.'

'A four-hour drive when you were half-sober.' He didn't give his father the chance to reply to the snarky comment. 'Did you say goodbye to me?'

Wade looked over. Parker saw his answer in the regret. He took a moment to process it—wasn't sure why this, out of all of it, upset him—then nodded.

'What happened next?'

'My mother kicked me out.' Wade lips curved into a faint smile. 'She told me to go back to my wife and child.'

'She sounds…badass.'

'She was. She adored you,' Wade said quietly. 'But a heart attack took her shortly after she kicked me out.' Pain flickered in his eyes. 'It was part of why I cleaned up my act. I…disappointed her with how I acted. I wanted to make it up to her since I couldn't while she was still alive.'

There was a long silence after those words.

Parker hadn't known any of his grandparents, and hearing about one of them sounded like a fairy tale. It intrigued him that his grandmother had been strict with his father. But if he was honest, Wade's entire story intrigued him. It gave him layers Parker hadn't seen before. It was a lot harder to blame someone for being a villain when their origin story seemed to prime them for the role.

'Not immediately,' his father continued suddenly. 'I first drank myself into a stupor, bounced between friends' couches. I went from feeling like a failure as a husband and father to feeling guilty from running from those failures.'

'It would have been easier facing it.'

'No,' his father disagreed. 'I needed to feel it so I could get my act together. I first stopped getting drunk. It was about a month after I left. I called your mother—'

'She didn't know where you were all that time?' he asked, disbelief coating his words.

'My mother called her.' But Wade had the decency to look ashamed. 'Penny had her connections, too. She knew where I was.' He paused. 'But you're right. I should have done it myself. When I *did* call her, she told me not to bother coming home. She'd rather raise you herself than have me mess you up. She was right, but it put me into another spiral. When I crawled out of that one, she told me she wanted a divorce. I gave it to her. I was tired of myself at that point. I couldn't blame her for being tired of me, too.'

Parker took a moment to process. 'Okay—then what?'

'Then I decided I'd show her.' His eyes became amused. 'I got a job with a friend of a friend doing electrical work. Very timid stuff at first, but I learnt quickly, saved up for my qualification. Started my own business, brought it back to Cape Town.'

'That's when you came around?'

'Yes,' Wade said. 'I was better. I thought I could be a decent father.'

'What happened?' Parker asked when he didn't continue.

'Your mother gave me another chance. And I let you down.'

'Why?' he asked, knowing his father was referring to that birthday they were supposed to go to Table Mountain. He was asking why for that twelve-year-old boy who was still somewhere inside him, waiting for an answer. He cleared his throat at the emotion that realisation brought. 'Why didn't you come?'

'I got scared.'

'Of what?'

'Everything,' he admitted. 'Being a father mostly, when I'd already screwed up so much. When I first started coming around, you were nine,' Wade told him, his voice a plea. 'I messed around for *nine* years. I called on your birthday, but that was it.'

'You sent cards,' Parker said mutedly.

'I sent you cards,' Wade repeated, though his voice was full of scorn. 'Most of that time, you couldn't even read.'

There was a beat. 'You did okay for those first three birthdays after you came back.'

'Yeah, but they were…harder than I expected them to be.' Wade let out a shaky breath. 'I kept waiting to disappoint you. I knew it would happen eventually. That day…taking you out…' He shook his head. 'It was a lot of pressure.' There was a pause. 'I know it's inexcusable. I saw you once a year. How could I possibly feel pressured by that?'

'I looked forward to them,' Parker said, compelled by that twelve-year-old boy again. Or no—by *this* version of himself, too. By the part of him that wanted to let go of the anger. To forgive. He'd hidden that desire, ignored it, but it was there. 'The cards, I mean. I liked the pictures.'

Wade's lips cracked into a smile. 'Yeah?'

Parker let his own lips smile. 'Yeah.'

A strange moment followed, where they smiled at

one another. Things felt almost cordial, as if his father hadn't admitted to being overwhelmed by his parental duties. Stranger was that Parker didn't feel that pressing desire to escape a connection with his father. He could almost hear his mother's approval.

Bound by loyalty, he said, 'Mom struggled, you know. We both did.'

'I know.' The smile disappeared. 'She wouldn't take my money unless it came with more emotional commitment. Told me she wanted to be able to look you in the eye someday.'

His eyebrows rose as emotion rolled around in his chest. They'd struggled financially, and they might not have had to if his mother had accepted his father's money.

But then he remembered how disappointed he'd been on that birthday his father hadn't pitched up. How after, he'd wondered if his father's absence had something to do with him. If his father *had* been around and had not been invested, he would have blamed himself for that, too. He would have wondered what more he could have done to make his father like him. Love him.

His mother had never made him feel that way. She made him feel loved; made *them* feel like a family. They might have struggled with money, but if they'd been in danger of starving, Parker knew she would have reached out to his father. Besides, the financial damage would have ended at some point. The emotional damage? That wouldn't have been so easy. His mother had known it.

So she *was* protecting him. The stubbornness and protectiveness had merely mixed, and come out in a way that was classically Penny Jones. He almost smiled.

'Look, Parker… Your mother was protecting you from who I was. She gave you an example you deserved, and she raised you right.' He paused. 'I know this might not mean much, but I'm proud of you, son. Of who you are, of how you've taken care of your mother.'

Parker tried to swallow down the emotion in his throat so he could give a snarky comeback, but it didn't work. He settled for a curt nod.

'The last six years I've been helping out because I wanted to make up for the twenty years I didn't. Both for your mom and for you. She was easier.' Wade's cheek lifted. 'Maybe because she knew me before I acted like a jackass. And after.' Seconds passed. 'Or maybe she knew how things were going for her and she needed the help.'

'She did know,' Parker said with an exhale of air. 'She told me she did.'

Wade studied him. 'Well, then, you might want to ask yourself why she'd do that if for twenty years before, she refused my help.'

'She said she was protecting me.'

'From the knowledge, maybe,' Wade said, considering. 'I think she might have been protecting herself from that, too.' He shrugged. 'But I think she was accepting my help because she knew she needed it. She's going to need more of it in the future, Parker. You don't have to offer it alone.'

It was a long time before Parker replied. When he did, he met his father's eyes.

'How should we help her?'

Chapter Nineteen

'I won't get in that car without her.'

'Dad, you have to.'

'No.'

'Dad.' The woman's tone went about an octave higher. 'We're going home. You need to get into the car so that we can go home. What about that don't you understand?'

The older man—Sophia judged him to be about eighty, though what the hell did she know about aging people?—slammed a hand on the hood of the car.

'I told you I won't go without her.'

'You don't even know her,' his daughter snarled. Apparently, the patience she'd displayed for the last ten minutes had snapped. 'She's a strange woman you flirted with in your hospital room.'

Oh. Sophia hadn't seen that one coming. She'd for sure thought the old man had been talking about something innocuous like a hat he'd given female properties to. As she considered it, she realised she had a very poor perception of who and what older people were and did.

'Liza is not some woman. We're going out on a date.'

'Nonsense, Dad. You've known her for all the length of your recovery from the gallstone surgery.'

'We bonded.'

'Dad,' the woman said, blowing out a breath. She ran a hand through her green hair, which was a bold choice, but suited her round face. 'Please don't do this. You know I hate saying no to you.'

'So don't say no, sweetheart.' The man smiled winningly. Sophia smiled herself. Whatever he lacked in romantic relationships, he had his relationship with his daughter down pat. 'You want me to be happy, don't you?'

'Yes. I'd also like you to be happy with Mom.'

Sophia's eyebrows might have become one with her hair at that, she wasn't sure. She leaned forward on the bench, resting her forearms on her thighs. She'd chosen to sit in the small garden right next to the parking lot after she'd spoken to Angie. Going home had no appeal, and she wanted some time to think about how different her life would be from now on. She might not have known how things would change, but she was certain they would. Because she had.

'Don't you agree, young lady?'

Sophia jolted when she saw the man and woman look at her. She had no idea they'd even known she was there. She'd been fairly stealthy in her— Oh, who was she kidding? She leaned forward when she heard the old man was married. The only thing missing was her popcorn.

'What should I be agreeing with?' she asked.

The garden was tiny, really a small square of grass that had been added to the lot with a bench she supposed was designed to make a hospital visit less intimidating. She could easily have this conversation with them from her seat. Which was exactly what she chose to do.

'Men aren't meant to be monogamous.'

'Excuse him,' his daughter said before Sophia could reply. 'He's got a lot more daring with age. And the fact that my mother tends to ignore him.'

'Just because we're old doesn't mean we shouldn't still be having sex.'

'Dad,' the daughter moaned.

'You're a grown woman, Courtney. You should know by now that I enjoy sex,' the man said philosophically. 'Your mother used to, too. We used to go at it like rabbits, once upon a time.' The man's eyes sparkled. He winked at Sophia; he was riling his daughter up. Sophia hid her smile. 'Now that she's got that hip replacement she thinks she shouldn't be giving it up anymore. But I still have needs.'

'*Please* stop talking.'

'Do you mind, dear?' the man asked Sophia instead of replying to his daughter's plea.

'Not at all. In fact, I agree one hundred per cent. If you have an itch, it should be scratched.'

'Exactly.' The man beamed. 'See, darling?'

'Thanks for that,' the daughter told Sophia without heat. She directed her attention to her father. 'I never thought I'd pick you up after an operation and have to worry about infidelity, not infection.'

Just like that, Sophia saw what the man was doing. He gave Sophia another wink, then turned around and shouted, 'Liza, I'll be back for you.' He got into the car.

His daughter sighed. 'I guess this is what they mean

when they say you begin to parent your parents,' the woman said apologetically.

'I'm not so sure about that,' Sophia replied slowly. 'You were scared for him, weren't you?'

The woman blinked. 'I was concerned. He's eighty-three. Routine operations aren't that simple anymore.'

'I get it,' Sophia told her. 'I think he does, too.' The woman's brow furrowed. Sophia gentled her voice. 'I'm sure he teases you all the time?' she asked. The woman nodded. 'So things have gone back to normal then? Like they were before the operation?'

'I… I suppose so.'

'Nothing to worry about then.'

The woman blinked again, and realisation dawned on her face. It came in the form of a sheen of tears, one of them dropping down her cheek before she hastily brushed it away.

'Thanks,' she said.

Sophia raised a hand. 'I did nothing.'

The woman nodded, gave an awkward wave before getting into the car and driving off. Sophia stared after them for a long time, wondering how things would have been if their father had still been around. He'd be closer to seventy than eighty, and he likely wouldn't ever joke about cheating on their mother. But she liked to think he'd tease them. If not her, since she hadn't really been receptive to his teasing, then Zoey.

Daniel and Zoey had shared a sense of humour. And Zo could lighten up any room when she tried. Sophia had probably infected her with scorn over the years, which might explain why she'd lost some of the bubbliness since their dad's death. Or maybe it had nothing to do with Sophia, and was just a result of grief.

Sophia had learnt a lot about the emotion since her father's death. She'd learnt that people grieved in different ways. That often they grieved for the destruction of what that death had left behind as much as they did the actual loss. Sophia could see that in Angie's actions after their father's death. Saw the consequences, the cost of being as compassionate as Angie was in how her sister had grieved. Angie was soft, absorbent. If she'd stayed, she would have taken on Zoey and their mom's grief—maybe even Sophia's—and ignored her own.

Respect surged inside Sophia. For the fact that Angie had recognised what would have happened, and that she'd done something about it.

Sophia didn't blame her so much anymore, though she was sure the resentment would flare again with the right trigger. But she could see that blaming her sister was a part of her own grieving process. Just like running away, dimming her light, had been part of Zoey's. And being unbearably sad but still waking up, getting up was part of her mother's.

Blaming Angie had given Sophia a clear outside enemy, allowing her to ignore the stuff going on inside. The comparison and the resentment. Of Angie, of her father and the situation his actions had left them in. But it had also led her here, to this moment where she could see she'd been grieving. And comparing. Where she could realise that maybe it had been a good thing she'd been the one to take care of Zo and their mother. She hadn't taken their emotions onto herself. She'd pushed

her family forward, through their grief. And if she believed Angie, they were okay because of it.

Some unknown part of her floated down, like a
feather from a bird in the sky, to the floor. And settled. Finally.

'Soph.'

Another part of her flew out of the nest in panic.

She opened her eyes, only realising then that she'd
closed them. Parker stood in front of her. He looked
drool-worthy, though he only had on blue jeans and a
black T-shirt. His expression was careful, as if she had
him half-naked in his car. Or perhaps because she had.

Are your reasons valid? Or are they simply excuses?
Angie's words echoed in her ears. *Because if you re-
ally want more than a day with him, you'll find a way.
Trust me.*

She did trust Angie. Which was partly why her sister's advice had paralysed her. Was there a chance for
her and Parker? A real chance, without excuses blocking their way?

'Are you okay?' he asked, taking a tentative step
forward.

'Fine.' She wrenched the word out her mouth. 'I'm
fine,' she repeated, when her initial answer sounded as
if it had been wrenched.

'Why are you sitting outside here then?'

'I was visiting my sister and my niece.'

'Yeah? Everything's still okay?' His face split into a
grin that made him even more unbearably handsome.
'Congratulations.'

'I said this before, but I apparently have to say it

again: you don't have to congratulate me. I did nothing. I wasn't even here during her labour.'

'But there's a new member of your family, right?' he asked calmly, unfazed by her sass. 'And you're an aunt when you hadn't been before. I happen to think that's worthy of a congratulations.'

She rolled her eyes, but she was smiling. 'Thank you.' She paused. 'She's quite ugly.'

Parker gaped, then chuckled. 'I don't think you're supposed to say that.'

'She's a newborn baby. She's been living in a sack of liquid for the last nine months. Did you think she'd be pretty?'

'You're family. She should be pretty to you.'

'I'm her aunt, not her mother. I'll always tell her the truth.'

Parker studied her. 'You're in love with her.'

'Madly. Enough that I'll tell anyone I don't know she's beautiful and punch them if they dare contradict me.'

He laughed. 'Seeing you in this role is…something.'

'Wait until the kid's eighteen and I'm driving her to the nearest family planning centre.'

'Eighteen?'

'If she wants to go earlier, she'll have to ask Zoey. I'm all for delaying sexual activity since it rarely comes without emotional activity.'

'Is that what happened yesterday?'

Oh, she'd walked right into that one.

'Sure,' she said carefully. 'I have emotions about yesterday.'

He walked over, took a seat beside her. The bench

was tiny, so of course, they touched. Only their legs, his knee bumping against hers. But it lit a match and had fire lighting over her body. Her breath felt as if she had been left in a room with that fire burning. No oxygen. No chance of escape.

Forcing herself to calm down, she looked out at the view from the hospital lot. There wasn't much to see. The hospital was on the outskirts of the city, closer to a residential area than the main town. But the lot was on top of the building, giving them a clear view of what was in front of them.

A car dealership on the far right, a grocery store next to it. Directly in front of them was an empty field with a large 'For Sale' sign. Sophia couldn't help but think if they wanted the property sold, they should have done some work on the upkeep of it. Grass rose high above the ground, interspersed by weeds. An occasional flower peeked out, too, and the early morning sunlight shone in a streak across the green.

On second thought, perhaps the property owners knew exactly what they were doing.

'What kind of emotions?' Parker asked into the silence.

'You're about three minutes too late on that question being natural,' she said, amused.

Her body had seemingly recovered enough from the onslaught of desire to allow her to tease him. Then Parker shifted, pressing his leg against hers in the process. The fire was immediately stoked again. It was as if her body were telling her, *Try again.*

'I was trying to build up my nerve to ask.'

'Why?'

'I don't know.' He leaned forward, linking his hands together. She wondered what he'd do if she reached out and gripped them in hers instead. 'Maybe those emotions are negative.'

'Some of them are,' she answered softly. 'I feel like a fool for falling for a man who's emotionally unavailable to me.'

He sucked in air, the silence that followed allowing her to hear every mangled decibel of it. It made her heart feel mangled, too, and she hated the vulnerability of it. He was the only man she felt comfortable enough with to be vulnerable. The only man who made her feel vulnerable, too.

It gave him so much power. She could only imagine the damage he could do with it. And with her words, she'd handed that power to him on a platter. Because of Angie's encouragement to go after what she wanted. To let herself feel if she wanted to feel. To stop making excuses.

She almost growled.

She must have made some kind of sound because Parker looked over and angled toward her.

'I'm sorry,' he said. 'I didn't mean to do that.'

'It's fine,' she said with a calm she didn't feel. Or perhaps with a coldness? She definitely felt cold. 'You were proving my point.'

'You might be right.' He didn't meet her gaze. 'You are right,' he corrected. 'I'm used to protecting myself.' The way he frowned almost made her think he'd just discovered it. 'There was a lot of that happening with me and my mom growing up. We protected each other, and we protected ourselves.'

'It sounds like you've figured some stuff out.'

'I wouldn't say figured it out,' he said dryly. 'But I'm heading toward it. I see more of it now.' He paused. 'Yesterday…was overwhelming. I ran from the feelings of everything because… Well, because I was overwhelmed. So, maybe not emotionally unavailable. Emotionally overloaded.'

She got it. She wasn't entirely convinced by his distinction, but she got that there was a lot happening for him. It had been similar with her. Less hectic, but similar. She'd had to get it out to think it through.

'It's okay not to know how you feel about everything,' she said. 'You should talk to someone who can help you sort some of it out.'

'You sound sure about that.'

'I am sure about it.' She hesitated before telling him the rest. 'Angie and I talked. A real talk, for the first time in years.' She gave him a sly look. 'Because of you.'

'Me? How? Why?'

'Well, I wanted to prove you wrong about me choosing to be in my situation with my family.' Which she hadn't been able to do. 'I also wanted to confirm there wasn't anything wrong with me.'

'I told you there wasn't last night.'

Her lips curved. 'Yes, that's why I said "confirm".' She let out a breath. 'Thing is, you helped me see *I* thought there was something wrong with me. I was defensive about who I was and stubborn in it, but deep down, I compared myself because that's what I'd been taught to do.' She gripped the material of her jersey. 'It's what I was choosing to believe.'

He reached over, covered her hand with his. After a brief hesitation, she turned her hand around, threading their fingers together. Refusing to feel hopeful because of it.

'I'm sorry.'

'Don't be. I've figured out more things in the last day than I have in years. It'll change things.'

'How?'

She snorted. 'It's been less than twenty-four hours. I have no idea.'

He laughed, tightening his grip on her hand. 'Yet you're sure you have feelings for me.'

She gave a deep sigh. 'Yes.' Released another puff of air. 'You're infuriating, but you're kind. You care about strangers, and you protect them even when they don't need—' she looked at him, rolled her eyes '—when they don't *think* they need it. You care about your family. You're willing to sacrifice anything for your mother. You're worried about losing her because you love her. You prioritise her.' She paused. 'And then there's the undeniable attraction. How even your leg touching me makes me want to jump you.' She let out a puff of air. 'Of course I have feelings for you, Parker. I don't know whether they'll stay or for how long, but they're there. And they…they don't want to be ignored.'

He didn't speak for a long time, his hand still clasping hers.

'I spoke with my dad this morning,' he finally said.

'How do you feel about that?'

'Messed up. I have to work through the years of judgement I have about what he did. Who he is.'

'That's good. It's progress.'

'Yeah.'

'Now you have to speak to your mom.'

'No,' he said. 'I get why she did what she did. I don't blame her for it. She's the same mom who took me up Table Mountain when my dad didn't show up on my birthday, and who worked two jobs to get me through university.' He paused. 'She's human, too. She makes mistakes. But I... I don't want to waste my time with her.'

She squeezed his hand, unreasonably proud of him for coming to that conclusion.

'It's nice of you to let her know so quickly.'

'I think she already knows,' he said quietly.

'Then why are you here?'

'For you.'

'For... What?'

'To tell you that I'm emotionally available. To you. If you're ready to be emotionally available to me, too, I mean.'

She stared blankly at him, then grabbed at the most innocuous part of what he'd said.

'You're here for me?'

'Yes.' The hesitation he'd spoken with earlier was gone.

'How did you know I was here?'

'Zoey.'

Sophia opened her mouth. Nothing came out.

'Why are you here?'

'I told you—'

'No, I mean what brought you here? What's different between last night and now?'

'For one, I have my clothes on properly and I can

think,' he said, teasingly. 'For another, I had an honest conversation with my father and the first thing I wanted to do after was talk to you about it.' He took her other hand. 'I wanted to hear your annoying take on how my father doing what he did was part of his journey to becoming who he is now or whatever crap you'd tell me because you're annoyingly philosophical at times.'

She gaped at him.

'I wanted to see your incredibly unique lips part and hear you gasp when I tell you that I let him talk, and didn't brush him off or push him away. I welcomed his help.' His thumb brushed over her lips, which were, to his credit, parted. 'I like that you're unapologetically yourself. You don't care about being nice but being honest. But you're not mean. And when you are, it's intentional, not careless.' His lips curved. 'Hell, I kind of like that.'

'What are you saying?' she finally managed to ask.

'I have feelings for you, too, Soph. I don't know if they'll stay or for how long, but they want me to pay attention to them.'

She stared at him. Then, when her brain started working again, words tumbled out her mouth.

'Are you sure you like honest? Because you might not like it when I—'

'Yesterday was a good illustration of what to expect, I think,' he interrupted. 'I know I didn't do well in response. I… I can't promise I won't struggle with it when I don't want to hear it. But I *can* promise I won't lash out again. I don't want to hurt you ever again.'

'Not deliberately,' she said, fear encouraging her.

'But one day you'll realise that you want someone nice or kind or sweet or whatever, but you'll only have me.'

He lifted a hand, gripped her chin gently. 'I know what I'm signing up for, Sophia.' There was a pause before he continued. 'I see you. Not who I want you to be, or who I think you should be. I see *you*. And I want *you*.'

He smiled. It was fond and endearing and went right to her heart.

'It won't be easy. Life won't be easy for me. For us, if you want to be with me.' He hesitated. 'You might have to go through what you went through with your father again. You'll help take care of my mother, and you might even…take care of me.' His grip tightened, before he dropped his hand. 'I'll understand if you don't want to sign up for that.'

'I do,' she said hastily, not bothering to feel embarrassed by it either.

'Think about it, Soph. You've already been through a sick parent. You took care of your dad and then your sister and mom. You don't have to do it again.'

She considered it for all of a few seconds.

'Part of what I've accepted about myself is that I take care of people. It's who I am.' She shrugged. 'And I think being through what I've been through makes me the perfect support system.'

His face visibly loosened in relief. Her heart filled.

'In fact, I'm exactly who you need at your side,' she continued, teasing him because her heart demanded it. 'I'm a boss with encouraging people to get their act together. I carried my whole family through their grief. Helping you will be easy.'

He shook his head, but she saw the smile. 'I was

going to ask you if you were sure about being with me. Give you one last opportunity to run. Now I'm wondering whether I should run.'

'Too late,' she said. 'You already admitted to having feelings for me.'

He heaved a sigh, his eyes twinkling. 'You're right, I do.' He leaned forward and placed his lips next to her ear. 'I have to warn you though,' he whispered. 'Some of those feelings *are* physical…'

Epilogue

Six months later

'A fundraiser for dementia research,' Sophia said, tilting her head where she sat on the couch. 'That's not a bad idea, sport.'

'Thanks,' Parker told her dryly before turning to his mother. 'What do you think, Mom?'

His mother gave him an even look, but Parker could read her like a book. She was touched by the suggestion, though she wanted to tell him not to go through the effort for her sake. But she couldn't tell him that because he'd positioned the event as a contribution to a local non-profit that helped research the illness. She wouldn't dare complain about that. Which was why he'd done it.

And she knew it.

'I think it's a lovely idea, Parker,' she replied mildly. 'It sounds like a lot of work.'

'I've been in touch with the non-profit. What?' he said at his mother's surprised look. 'I was writing a story about them. That's how I got the idea. Anyway,' he continued, 'they've agreed to help coordinate the event. They're even reaching out to sponsors. Everything is still tentative, of course, and if we do it, it'll have to be at the end of the year or early next year. I wanted to run the idea by you first.'

'But you've already been in touch with the non—' Sophia stopped talking when he shot her a look. She smiled innocently. 'Such a lovely idea, Parker,' she finished, her smile widening.

The doorbell rang, interrupting what he was about to say. Sophia got up, brushing a hand across his back as she disappeared into the hallway to answer the door. It was still surreal to him that she was there. That they could touch as easily as she'd just done—although that was never a problem with them—and that she felt comfortable enough to open the door at his house.

As it turned out, their feelings hadn't only stayed in the last six months, but had grown. They'd said 'I love you' weeks after that conversation in the hospital garden, and had been around one another almost every day since. He could never tire of her— No, he thought. That was a lie. She still annoyed him more than anyone else did. It exhausted him at times. But even when she annoyed him, he still wanted her around...

So he could annoy her in return, as the universe intended.

'It's Evie,' Sophia announced, entering the living room again.

She went to the couch and retrieved her handbag. She had to bend over to get it, and the skirt she wore rose up a little. It wasn't quite the view he hoped for considering it was autumn and she wore tights under her navy skirt. But he could still see the shape of those spectacular legs, and not for the first time, he wished they could opt out of their plans to do something more interesting.

She quirked a brow at him when she turned around and caught him staring. He grinned, winked, then turned around and said hello to his mom's evening companion.

It had taken some time to get his mom used to the idea of having a companion. She'd acquiesced when Parker had used her own words against her. Penny wanted him to have a life outside of her disease—and outside of her mistakes, she'd told him, when they'd finally spoken about his dad—and that meant relationships. He needed his free time to build said relationships. Unashamedly, he told his mother he couldn't do that if he wasn't spending time outside the house because he was worried about her.

Penny had grumbled about her independence, before his father, who had been in the room since he was offering to pay for the companion, compared it to live-in help or assisted living facilities. She'd relented. He hadn't liked strong-arming her, but she was still processing her diagnosis. And since she'd walked in front of a damn car, he wasn't taking any chances.

'I'll see you tomorrow, Mom,' he said, putting on his jacket and brushing a kiss on her cheek.

'Planning on staying out?' his mother asked, eyes sharp.

'I have a shift after dinner,' Parker said.

'I wouldn't have him anyway, Mrs Jones,' Sophia said. 'I'd kick him out before I disappointed you.'

'That's my girl,' Penny said with an amused—but

knowing—smile. 'If you don't kick him out, be safe, okay?'

'Mom,' Parker groaned, at the same time Sophia said, 'Absolutely.' Evie chuckled behind his mother in the kitchen.

The air was cool outside when they finally left, the leaves going orange and red, warnings of the coming winter. He opened the car door for Sophia, and she popped a kiss on his nose before getting in. His heart leapt in a way it probably shouldn't have for a grown man who'd been with his girlfriend for six months. Then again, there were no 'shouldn't haves' with his and Sophia's relationship. If there were, they wouldn't have agreed to date after a day of *mostly* liking each other's behaviour.

Since he didn't see any chance of them slowing down, he didn't care about what they should have done. This had worked out pretty well for them.

'Do you ever think about six months ago?' Sophia asked as he pulled onto the road. 'We wouldn't have been here, doing this, if we hadn't bumped into each other at the hospital.'

'How do you know that?'

Sophia made a sound of disbelief. 'We wouldn't have met then. And I certainly wouldn't be dragging my boy toy to my oldest sister's place for dinner.'

'Boy toy?' he repeated, amused.

'I would have stormed out of the hospital,' she continued, ignoring him, 'and sat angrily somewhere before going back to the hospital and sitting angrily there.'

'So I changed your life?'

'*I* changed my life,' she corrected, giving him the side-eye. 'But you helped give me the courage to.'

'And now we're visiting your married sister and I'm taking you to your very own apartment after.'

'Only if you're safe,' she said slyly. He laughed.

When they got to Angie and Ezra's place, Sophia took the bottle of wine they'd bought from the back seat and got out. It had started to rain, but neither of them had brought a raincoat or umbrella. They hustled to Angie's front door. He caught Sophia's hand before she could ring the doorbell.

'What?' she asked. Water misted over her hair, her cheeks rosy from the cold. She was pursing her lips, though he couldn't tell if that was from the weather, too, or because she disapproved of him letting them get wet.

'I do think about six months ago,' he said softly, coming closer. 'And I have no qualms about admitting you changed my life.'

Her eyes went soft, but she shook her head. 'It's not a competition.'

'Ah, but it is. And I'd much rather you admit your defeat now than have to coerce it from you.'

'You're such a—'

He cut her off with a kiss. It was hot, spurred by the wave of emotions that overwhelmed him when he thought about how lucky he was to have her.

'I love you,' he whispered when he pulled back.

'I love you more,' she said with a smile, eyes gleaming. 'I think that means I've won the most important prize.'

'Please don't say—'

'Your heart,' she finished with a grin.

'I can't believe I want to spend my life with some-one as corny as you.'

Her eyebrows rose. 'You want to spend your life with me?'

'Just until these feelings go away.' He nipped at her lips again, not caring that he'd admitted his feelings when he hadn't meant to. 'It might take a lifetime. I want you to be prepared.'

'Yes, sir,' she drawled. 'I'm ready and willing.'

She sealed her corny words with a kiss.

* * * * *

Reviews are an invaluable tool when it comes to spreading the word about great reads. Please consider leaving an honest review for this or any of Carina Press's other titles that you've read on your favorite retailer or review site.

Look for Zoey's story, the last book in the One Day to Forever series, coming from Therese Beharrie and Carina Press in 2020.

To find out about other books by Therese Beharrie or to be alerted to new releases and other updates, sign up for her newsletter at theresebeharrie.com/newsletter.

Acknowledgements

My sincerest thanks to the Carina Press team. Writing for two publishers has been a learning experience, including learning about my own limitations. Once I communicated that to the team, they immediately did everything in their power to accommodate me. I was never once made to feel bad or awkward about what I needed, and I'm well aware of how special that is. Angela, Stephanie and Kerri, thank you.

I haven't included John, my editor, in this, because they deserve their own paragraph. A wise friend of mine once told me there are few things you can control in publishing. Writing the books you want to write is one of them. The other is, when you can, to choose to have people in your corner who are genuinely enthusiastic about you and your books. I've found that in John, and I have never taken that for granted. I am lucky that that enthusiasm comes with a sensitivity and expertise I constantly learn from, and that I'm a better writer and person for it.

I have an incredible writing support system, and again, I will never take them for granted. I'm particularly grateful to those who listen to my endless fears during anxiety attacks, and patiently wade through the terror with me. Jenni Fletcher, Olivia Dade, Collette Kelly, I can't thank you enough. To Kate Clayborn, Talia Hibbert, and Dorothy Ewels, who are always there when I need to talk: you are so important to me, and so valued. A special thank-you to every blogger who has supported me and my work: I see you. Please know how much your contribution means to me and the rest of Romancelandia.

And to my husband. I don't know how to thank you for your support. I appreciate every word of encouragement, and every hug when I'm an emotional mess. I know it isn't easy, but you never waver, and I can't tell you how much that means to me. I spend my days writing romance novels because you inspire me; and with the rest of my time, I'll make sure you know how much love you inspire in me, too.

About the Author

Being an author has always been Therese's dream. But it was only when the corporate world loomed during her final year at university that she realised how soon she wanted that dream to become a reality. So she got serious about her writing, and now writes books she wants to see in the world featuring people who look like her for a living. When she's not writing, she's spending time with her husband and dogs in Cape Town, South Africa. You can find her on Twitter at www.twitter.com/ThereseBeharrie and Facebook at www.facebook.com/theresebeharrie or catch up on her newsletter at www.theresebeharrie.com/newsletter or her website at www.theresebeharrie.com, where she keeps a writing blog.

*Now available from Carina Press
and Therese Beharrie*

*Of all the weddings in all the world, Angie Roux
had to be mistaken for a bridesmaid in this one.*

*Read on for an excerpt from
A Wedding One Christmas,
the first book in Therese Beharrie's
One Day to Forever series*

Chapter One

If the universe wanted Angie Roux to get home for Christmas, it had a hell of a way of showing it.

In the four hours she'd spent driving that day, Angie had been caught in stop-and-go roadworks four times; had been stopped by a traffic officer twice; had to change a flat tire, and now this.

People.

A crowd of them, standing outside the brick chapel next to the café she'd stopped at. She'd never actually seen the chapel in use before, though she wasn't surprised she'd encountered it now, considering the universe's current treatment of her. She just hoped the 'if you talk to me, I'm going to punch you in the face' expression she'd perfected at a young age would deter—

'How did you get outside so quickly?' a tall woman asked, walking toward her.

Angie looked behind her, and then, when she saw no one else, looked back at the woman. For good measure—her 'talk to me at your own peril' expression rarely didn't work—she asked, 'Are you talking to me?'

'Of course I am.' The woman frowned. 'You should still be inside. They're signing the register.'

'Okay,' Angie replied slowly. 'What should I be doing inside?'

'Waiting for them,' the woman answered with an impatient sigh. 'Have you never attended a wedding before? Aren't you thirty-two? Thirty-five? This can't possibly be...' She trailed off when Angie took a step back. Then another.

'Where are you going?'

Angie didn't answer. Instead, she turned around and began to walk back to her car. Her strides were slow, as if that would somehow mitigate that she'd left someone midconversation. Even if said person was trying to insult her.

The insult hadn't landed though. Angie had never thought looking older was an insult. In fact, she considered it a compliment. She carried herself maturely, which came with a certain amount of authority. Authority that had helped her growing up as the oldest of three girls.

She was more insulted by herself and how slow she'd been on the uptake. The people outside of the chapel were celebrating a wedding. Which seemed pretty clear to her now, when it was too late. When she'd already walked into a *wedding*.

She shuddered, her steps quickening.

'You've done enough to me today,' she muttered to the universe. 'Please, not this.'

As if in answer or punishment, a car turned into the gravel car park. Her feet stopped at her dilemma: because she'd taken the quickest route to her rental car, she was walking in the middle of the car park. She'd have to move to avoid being run over. Except she had nowhere to go.

There were empty parking spaces on either side of

her, but that would risk being trapped or having to manoeuvre around the car—no, *cars*, she saw, taking in the line that had begun to form behind that first car—which would likely involve talking to people. Going forward wasn't an option at the moment and back meant...

She shuddered again.

But then she was hooted at—multiple times—and that first car edged forward, forcing her back. Resisting the temptation to show the driver an impolite hand gesture, Angie gritted her teeth and turned around.

She tried to walk stealthily toward the crowd, so the woman who'd spoken to her earlier wouldn't see her. Angie kept an eye on the woman, but she paid no attention to Angie. Relief soothed some of the apprehension in Angie's chest. She might be able to make it to the café she'd come to without attracting any more—

'Hey.' A young woman with pink highlights stopped her. 'Are you trying to get back into the chapel?'

Why did everyone think she wanted to get in the damn chapel?

'No.'

'Oh,' the woman said disappointedly. Seconds later she brightened. 'You're arranging something cool for them for when they come out, aren't you? Please tell me it's a flash mob!'

'It's not a flash mob,' Angie responded immediately. Apparently managing the woman's expectations was more important than getting herself out of her current predicament. 'I am trying to arrange something for them, but I have to get past you to do that.'

'You're too late,' the woman said, panic in her eyes. 'They're here.' Her expression turned sympathetic. 'I'm sure they'll forgive you though. You can go through here.'

The woman stepped back, creating a path for Angie before nudging Angie forward. The man she bumped into glanced back with a frown, then his eyes lowered over Angie and he nodded, shifting so Angie could move forward. The couple in front of him did the same, as did the people in front of them, until finally, Angie found herself with an unobscured view of the wedding party as they made their way out of the chapel.

Seeing the bridesmaids clarified why Angie was in this situation. There wasn't—as Angie had begun to fear—a sign on her forehead identifying weddings as one of her least favourite activities, challenging people to change her mind. She was simply wearing an almost identical dress as the bridesmaids.

Hers was shorter, with a deeper neckline, but she could understand why no one had noticed those differences. Hell, she was wearing the dress and it had taken *her* a moment to.

It was unfortunate, and reinforced the voice in her head that told her she was too dressed up for a road trip. But the dress helped her feel confident, which was something she'd desperately needed to keep the unravelling at bay.

It was there even now, taunting her. Telling her she should have listened to the rational part of her that warned her against stopping at the café. Claiming that being mistaken as a bridesmaid at a wedding was punishment for not listening.

She took a breath to compose herself, to push the unravelling away, and told herself she'd expected this. She'd known the trip back to Cape Town would be hard. When she'd seen the green board with its white lettering indicating the turn-off to Caledon—when she'd put on her indicator and turned— she'd known it would be a challenge, too.

It had been three years since she'd been in Cape Town, after all. Three years since she'd seen her mother, her sisters. Three years since her father—

She stopped the train of thought. Tried to focus on something else. Like the fact that it had been even longer than three years since she'd been to Caledon. The last time had been with her family. Her whole family; not the incomplete unit it had become.

Fortunately, she didn't have time to dwell on that when the bride and groom appeared. The guests began throwing rose petals at the newlyweds, and it reminded her of the picture that sat on her mother's bedside table. It was of her parents on their wedding day. They stood at the top of the steps outside the church, looking at each other lovingly, happily, petals raining over their heads. The last time Angie had seen them together, the love had still been there, but the happiness had been missing...

You're unravelling.

She swallowed and moved to the basket that had the rose petals in it, grabbing a handful and joining in on the excitement. Though it felt cringey, she clapped. When the photographer announced they'd be taking group photos, she tried to slip away...

And was foiled. Again.

'You should stand right in front, young lady,' an old man told her, shifting and blocking her way.

His entire head was white, sharply contrasting his dark brown skin, his face lightly lined with deeper creases around his eyes. He seemed like the type of person she might have liked had he not just stopped her from escaping.

She almost growled, but instead managed a polite, 'I'm not a part of this wedding.'

'Of course you are. And you're beautiful.'

'I'm sorry—*what*?'

'You're beautiful,' he repeated. 'You don't have to be afraid of being in front of the photographers.'

'Wow, thanks,' she deadpanned, adding his face to her rapidly growing list of people who didn't have any boundaries with strangers.

'Could you let me past?' she asked, keeping to her strategy of pretence. 'I'm going to go around the crowd so I can get to the front quicker.'

'Good idea,' he said approvingly, moving so she could walk past him.

She could feel his eyes on her, so she walked slowly around the edge of the crowd. When she passed enough people, she hid at the side of the chapel, where she fully intended on staying until she was out of this nightmare. It was pathetic, but she was willing to be pathetic for the sake of self-care.

As if to test that willingness, a couple began walking her way. She slunk deeper into the shadows, but they kept moving forward. When the woman pulled out a packet of cigarettes—seriously, they were going to smoke right next to a *chapel*?—Angie stepped back again.

She wasn't obscured, and the couple was almost near her, but there was nowhere to go. Her back was against the wall—or against the shrubs, as it were. She panicked for about a second, then decided she'd had enough of the damn wedding.

Swallowing her pride, she ducked through the shrubs.

It rattled. Or rustled. Or made whatever sound a shrub made when someone went through it. She groaned and almost pleaded with the powers that be to make sure no one saw her duck through a shrub to escape a wedding. But with her current luck, that would all but ensure someone would follow her through to ask why she wasn't in the photos.

Fortunately, the shrub hadn't been a large one, and she made it through relatively unscathed. Her hair needed some convincing to disentangle from the branches, but rather that than the dress. It had been expensive. And it was gorgeous. She'd bought it to soften her mother up when they eventually reunited. Instead, she'd worn it for a five-hour road trip.

Maybe she already was unravelling.

When the thought had her heart thumping against her chest, she swallowed and took a steadying breath. She could do this. She could make it to the café and wait the wedding out. She *could*.

She straightened and tried to formulate a plan. She was currently on the edge of a large field that was a hub of busyness. People milled around, carrying boxes or guiding cars into what seemed to be designated spots. Some of the cars were sedans, others trucks, and their spots seemed to depend on that distinction.

Her eyes lifted before she could confirm it, settling on the road she'd taken to enter the town, visible from where she stood. It was a reminder that she'd consciously made the decision to come to this place. Despite the memories it had of her life before she'd left South Africa—or perhaps, because of the memories—she'd decided to stop there.

Almost instantly the lid of the container she kept those memories in popped open and she remembered.

The family trips to the Eastern Cape. How she and her sisters, Sophia and Zoey, would nag until their father stopped barely an hour outside of Cape Town. How he'd always made it seem like some huge concession, stopping at the small town where he and Angie's mother had once lived. In reality, Daniel Roux had been happy to spend time at the casino that had become a major tourist attraction for Caledon. Angie and her sisters would play games in the arcade, before they'd all take the obligatory drive through town so her parents could reminisce. The detour would end in a meal at the café that was just a few metres away from where Angie currently was.

Her heart broke a little, and she closed her eyes, forcing air into her lungs. She hadn't thought about any of this in years. Had actively avoided it. And for the life of her, she couldn't figure out why she'd decided to come here now when she knew it would force her to face those memories.

Unless it didn't, she thought, opening her eyes again. She needed to distract herself. Or, at the very least, figure out how she could put herself back together again before she unravelled completely.

She walked along the edge of the field, staying close to the shrubs—since she was so comfortable with them now—in case she had to hide again. To avoid the wedding, or in case someone on the field noticed her and tried to get her to participate in the activities. She wasn't in the mood for that either.

A few metres later, she found a well-looked-after pathway. She supposed it was the usual way people got from the property that held the café to this field, though she had no idea why they'd want to. How many people needed to seek refuge from a wedding?

And on a related note—what were the chances that, if she took this pathway to the café, she'd need to seek refuge again?

Realising she didn't have much of a choice, she took the steps down to the pathway, consoling herself with the idea of hiding in the shrubs that lined it if she needed to. Which was so ridiculous she almost laughed. Knew her sister Zoey would, too, when she told—

She stopped the thought midway. She couldn't keep doing this. She'd already exceeded her quota of memories and nostalgia for the day. Sticking to that quota was pivotal to her mental health. She'd learnt that very early on in the life she'd built for herself after she'd left Cape Town.

She shook her head and walked into the open air again, immediately bumping into the old man she ran from earlier.

Seriously—what did I do to you? she asked the universe silently, before fixing a smile onto her face. 'Fancy seeing you here,' she said in a falsely bright voice.

'Where did you just come from?' he asked without preamble. 'Are you alone?'

'I just—' *Oh, what the hell?* 'No. My boyfriend's still back there.' She smoothed her dress down and offered him a chagrined smile. 'I'm sorry. Weddings are just so romantic, and with the group pictures being taken, we thought we'd take a moment to ourselves. Very quickly,' she assured him, ducking her head as if embarrassed. 'I'm sure we weren't missed.'

'I'm not sure that's true,' the man said with a frown. 'You're a bridesmaid. Part of the group.'

'Yes, well… The family pictures are being taken,' she said, mentally crossing her fingers as if somehow, that would keep her from tripping over the elaborate tale she was weaving. 'I'm sure you can understand.' *And leave me alone.*

There was a pause, then the man smiled. 'Well, if the family pictures are being taken, I'm sure you aren't missed.'

'Me, too. I should probably run back though. Before they realise I've gone.'

Before you start asking about why my boyfriend hasn't come out of the shrubs yet, too.

She nodded her goodbye and walked in the direction of the café, hoping he wouldn't notice she wasn't heading back to where they'd first met. But at this point, she didn't care. She was counting on not having to see him again. Except when she looked over her shoulder, he was still following her.

She couldn't say anything about it. Perhaps the wedding celebrations had moved. Perhaps the photos were being taken elsewhere. Or perhaps he was checking that she was heading back to do her duties. He must have thought her a terrible bridesmaid. She didn't blame him.

The café was only a few steps away, and she didn't dare check if he was still behind her. Instead, she stopped walking and dug around in her handbag for her lipstick. She held it up triumphantly when she found it, before making as if she were heading to the bathroom in the café.

Her eyes widened as she entered and took in all the

people there. People who were dressed smartly. Who were milling around as if waiting for something. Who were—

Damn it, who were wedding guests.

She didn't peek out the door to check for the old man as she'd intended to before snagging a table for herself. She looked, but none seemed to be free, and she was starting to draw attention to herself by not moving from the doorway. The last thing she needed was attention, especially not from wedding guests.

Wielding her lipstick in front of her as if some kind of shield, she moved farther into the café, her eyes sweeping over the room until it rested on a booth in the corner. There was only one man sitting there, papers strewn all over the table.

Not a wedding guest then.

Before she was fully aware of it, she was walking toward him.

And then she was sliding into the booth opposite him.

'Please,' she said, her voice surprisingly hoarse. 'Please pretend like I'm here with you.'

* * * * *

Don't miss
A Wedding One Christmas
by Therese Beharrie

Available now wherever
Carina Press ebooks are sold.
www.CarinaPress.com